COUNTENANCE OF WAR

A HISTORICAL NOVEL OF SCOTLAND

J R TOMLIN

ALBANNACH PUBLISHING

MAP OF MEDIEVAL SCOTLAND

[Image: CastleMap7Feb13 (3).jpg]

His hair was black, so I heard say.
  His limbs were finely made and long,
  His bones were large, his shoulders strong,
  His body was well-knit and slim,
  And so say those who set eyes on him,
  When happy, charming was he,
  And gentle and sweet in company,
  But those with him in battle saw
  Another countenance he wore!
  - *The Brus*, John Barbour, 1375

CHAPTER 1

*J*ames, erstwhile Lord of Douglas, pushed aside a thick branch, heavy with leaves, to peer up the long slope. Draped in wisps of mist, Douglas Castle made a hulking shape against the golden coin of the early morning sun. His castle, though an English banner and army sat within, was no great fortress, yet it was a strong place with a massive stone keep surrounded by a square of curtain walls fifteen-feet high and flanking towers at each corner. Taking it by storm was outwith his strength.

In the quiet, a lark trilled. It soared, reached a peak, and plummeted toward earth. James waved away midges buzzing about his neck. In the dense woods behind him, another lark answered.

He stepped to the edge of the forest, under a gnarled limb of a giant oak, and turned in a circle to look over the field. The ground was broken and rolling before him, toward the castle road soft and muddy from the spring rains, and stony beyond the road. Yellow-bloomed, thorny gorse bushes gave a spicy scent. A few trees dotted the hill near the castle, but past the forest's edge, most had been cleared to permit a watch for approaching enemies.

Cattle lowed, deep and protesting in the distance. They cleared the rise, and a man bent over his horse's withers to smack the lead cow, urging it to a faster pace. The herd was a mass of shaggy red hides and wide, swinging horns. At the rear, two men waved their arms, shouting.

A horn blew within the castle. Shouts drifted on the sweet morning air.

The herd thundered past the castle. The rumbling mass gained the rocky road. James's heart pounded in his chest in time to the hoofbeats. Under his steel helm, sweat dripped down his brow.

The castle gate thudded open. Horsemen trailed over the drawbridge. They'd be cursing the Scots who dared take back the animals the English had stolen. Squinting, James counted twenty in all, armor glinting where it caught the rays of the sun.

The English had swallowed the bait.

James dashed back into the cover of the trees, grabbed his reins, and swung into the saddle. He jerked his horse into a turn to edge further into the dense forest. Dew-damp leaves slapped his face as he rode. He brushed them aside. It was dark amongst the trees, but he made out the shapes of his men. "Wat! They're moving." He swung his small kite shield from his back and flexed his shoulder as he set his hand into the leather straps. Thanks be to Saint Bride, it had been his shield arm that had been injured at the Battle of Loudon Hill.

A horse snorted. Metal rattled as one of his three-score of men on small, rough-coated horses pulled his sword free.

Wat said, "Steady, men. Let the thieving English pass us."

James's heart thumped hard against his breastbone as he bent to pat an archer's shoulder. Beyond the man, fifteen more clothed in the green of Ettrick foresters stood, well screened by the heavy oak from the oncoming cattle and their pursuers. "Nock and hold," James said. "Easy now."

The rumble of cattle hooves, though still distant, grew closer.

"Hoi! Move you!" a voice shouted.

The rumble grew louder. Shouts came from further behind. James nudged his horse into the dense, leafy branches and shoved them aside. The cattle, at a dead run urged on by shouts of the waving riders, surged past.

James pulled his sword. "Hold," he said softly.

The riders from the castle had strung out in a line. A bareheaded knight, blond hair streaming, galloped on a heavy bay in front. James grinned. *Thirwell.*

"A Douglas," James shouted and swung his sword down— halting and pointing it at his enemy. He dug his spurs into the horse's flank. His mount surged forward. "A Douglas!" James burst through the branches, his men beside him.

Arrows sighed over his head. The morning erupted with the screams of men and horses. "Ambush!" the knight shouted.

Another flight of arrows arched up from behind James, from where his few archers stood. The English fought their horses into a turn, shouting. Another flight of arrows fell, and two more men slumped from their horses and went down.

"Scotland and King Robert!" James shouted as he reached them. A man swung at him. James hacked and caught him full in the chest, shearing leather and bone and muscle. James wrenched his sword free as the man fell.

He stood in his stirrups, looking for the knight. He glimpsed Wat's horse, gutted by an unhorsed Englishman, and a swarm of their men hard behind him. Wat vaulted free as his horse died under him. He rose, untouched, laying about him with his sword. He caught an Englishman full in the chest as the fool came at him in a full run. A dozen others slashed wildly to fight their way free.

James shouted, "A Douglas! A Douglas! Don't let them escape."

The knight's horse reared and slashed, lashing out with iron-shod hooves. It shattered a man's head in with a kick. The knight wheeled and raced for the castle.

James put his spurs to his horse's flanks and charged, cutting him off. Their horses slammed together. James's light steed went back on its hocks. His quarry met him, sword raised, and swiped a blow at James's face. James slammed it aside.

The knight was tall and burly, wearing a mail hauberk, but his head was bare. Blond hair thrashed around his face as he dodged James's blow. "Douglas!" he screamed. "You're mine."

James hacked at his head and shoulders. The man grunted, swinging at him and sweat dripping down his face. "Devil take you," the knight panted, chopping savagely at James.

James barely got his shield up in time, and pain exploded in his half-healed shoulder from the slamming impact. The man bellowed as he raised his sword high for a blow that would have split James's head like a melon. James buried his sword in the knight's belly.

"He'll take you instead," James told him.

As James jerked his sword free, Wat shouted, "After them, lads."

A handful of horsemen galloped toward the castle, a good three horse's length ahead of Wat on an English mount. The rest of his men tailed behind. "Hell mend them," James said through gritted teeth. No one remained but a dozen bloody corpses. Pain shot through his shoulder when he moved his arm, but he whipped his horse's flank. Bending over its neck, he galloped toward the splashing mud of the pursuit.

Shouts drifted from the walls of Douglas Castle. "Ride!" The fleeing horsemen thundered over the drawbridge. Metal grated, iron upon iron. The castle portcullis slammed down.

James pulled up and stood in his stirrups, glowering at the castle gate. A crossbow bolt thudded into the ground a yard ahead. Hooves threw up splashes of mud as his mount circled their snorting, rearing horses. He waved his sword over his head and shouted, "Retire! Pull back."

One of his men shouted a curse up at the men peering through the embattlement. A crossbow twanged. James heard Wat's bellow of, "You heard him. Back," as he harried the men into order. James ground his teeth and glared at his castle as he flexed his aching shoulder. He'd not planned the ambush aright. If they'd been a little faster...

"Back," he shouted again and waited as his men scattered past him, then turned his horse's head and cantered after them. His jaw ached from the clench of his teeth as he paced his horse at the base of the rise. Two of the towers still showed black stains from when he had burned the castle to try to keep it out of the hands of the curst English. He'd have to do better.

Wat rode toward him. When he pulled his stocky, short-legged garron up beside James, he scratched at his stubbled chin. "Too bad we didn't get it, but that was Thirwell you took down back there. I'm sure of it."

"You have the right of that. I've rid my castle of one inter-loper." James twitched a grin. "Once you're finished here, lead the men back to camp. I'm going to make my way to Will's and see if he has gathered more news."

Harness creaked, and weapons clattered as James's men gathered around the two of them. James cast a glance over all of them looking for injuries. "All here? How many did we lose? Who was it that Thirwell rode down?"

"Gavine," one of the men said from the back of the throng.

James clamped his lips tight. Gavine had followed him from that first fight at the kirk. He circled his horse as he looked them over. Thom leant over his horse's withers, blood dripping from a slash to his head. James motioned to Richert Kintour, the fiery-haired youth had a good hand with tending wounds.

"Retrieve Gavine's body, Wat. I'll leave none of our people to English mercies." He spat on the ground. "Not even our dead. I think they won't be in a hurry to bother us, but don't tarry. Strip the English of armor and weapons. And you see that any coin on them is evenly divided."

"What about your share?" Wat asked.

James thrust his chin toward the tower topped by a yellow Clifford banner, scattered with starlings, flapping in the morning breeze. "I missed my prize this time. But I'll claim the next."

CHAPTER 2

*J*ames looped the reins of his horse on the branch of a sapling beech tree and knelt, peering through the black of night. At the top of the hill, the black hulk of Castle Douglas cut off the scatter of stars. Watch fires made a smudge of light at the tops of the towers.

Frogs in the Douglas Water issued their musical challenges. A quarter moon hovered above the horizon, and a tall pine creaked in a breeze that carried a green scent up from the river. The air was soft on his face, but his hauberk dragged on his shoulder, and every muscle ached as though he were an old man. With a grim chuckle, he reminded himself never to suffer another wound as he had at the battle at Loudon Hill.

He straightened, untied his bag from behind his saddle, and walked past the line of trees. The freehold he approached made a black hump in the lesser darkness. In a pen, goats and sheep bleated and bumped. James pressed his back against the wall next to the door and rapped hard. He waited. In the distance, an owl hooted. He rapped again.

The door opened a crack, and Will peered at him, a flickering shadow in the faint glow of firelight. He stood back, and James slid inside and dropped his bag.

"Prowling under the Sassenachs' noses..." Will shoved the door closed and let the bar thud into place.

Alycie appeared in the doorway to her sleeping room, slender and supple, her honey-colored braid hanging over her shoulder, rubbing her arms. She frowned at him. "It's too much risk for you to come here." She shook her head before she dashed across the room. Sliding her arms around his waist, she pressed her face into his shoulder. He kissed the top of her head and breathed in the grassy scent of her hair.

"It's too much risk," she said again, her voice muffled against him.

James snorted. "Breathing's a risk." He raised an eyebrow at Will. "You know there was a skirmish today?"

Alycie sighed and released him. She smiled a little and stooped in front of the hearth in the center of the room, added a small faggot of wood, and poked at it.

"Aye, they were all over the village looking for weapons, to see who might have aided you. Mad as hornets, too." Will stroked his short blond beard and grinned. "We were all innocent lambs still suckling at the teat."

"Anyone hurt?"

"They roughed up Liam's lad a mite."

"Broke his arm," Alycie said. "It could have been worse. Nothing that won't heal."

James unbuckled his sword belt and sucked in a breath at the fire that lanced through his shoulder.

Alycie, still frowning, took his sword belt from his hands. She stood, searching his eyes for a moment. "You're all right?"

"Only tired."

She ducked her chin with a look that made James smile.

"The shoulder pains a bit, hen. That's all.."

Hanging his belt from a peg, she shook her head. "You tear it open, I'll make you think it pains, Jamie Douglas."

Will grinned. "The Sassenach are nothing as fierce as a Scotswoman, my lord."

"I'll not argue with that." James pulled the hauberk over his head with a grunt as Alycie busied herself at the hearth. "Any news, Will? Today was nothing more than an annoyance to them. I need something better." He tossed the armor aside. It would need cleaning before morning, but that could wait.

"My cousin in Bothwell Castle sent word that a supply train should be arriving in the next few weeks." He frowned. "I swear that with Lanark fair in two weeks that the English will either buy or steal what they need, but I've not heard anything definite."

Alycie pushed a steaming mug into James's hand. "Willow bark tea. It will ease the aches. Not that you deserve it. Now take off your shirt and sit you down." She pointed to the floor in front of her stool. "I'll rub salve on your shoulder."

Will snickered. "At her feet, you ken."

Alycie gave her brother a severe look and sniffed. "If he doesn't want to feel better, he can stand."

James flapped his way out of the sweaty linen shirt and sank cross-legged onto the floor. "At your feet suits me well." He sipped at the mug and made a face. "By the Holy Rude, this is nasty pap." He looked hopefully at Will. "A dram of uisge beatha would liven it up."

"Shame to spoil the uisge beatha though." Will took the cup and strolled across the room.

James leant back against Alycie's slender legs as she smoothed a grassy-scented salve onto his shoulder. Her fingers began to work it into the muscles. He gritted his teeth against a grunt as she worked a sore muscle, but the pain was a good one. "Did she learn how many guards? What size the supply train will be?"

"Large, she thought. And no one is moving without plenty of guards with that demon the Black Douglas about."

James snorted a laugh.

Will came back with two cups and handed James one that wafted a sharp, smoky scent. "It's still early. Roads still aren't much more than bogs."

"We need definite word of what they're about. It's been a long winter and with me abed half the time with this cursed wound." Will had dumped out the tea, and the uisge beatha scalded and soothed at the same time as it went down. "Since I'm well again, I'll..."

Alycie sniffed, but he wasn't sure if it was from the smell of the drink or the idea of him abed. She rubbed some of the salve into the red scar that ran the length of his shoulder and ran her hands up and down the muscles of his shoulders as though erasing the knots and kinks. "Abed half the time, you have not been. How do you expect it to heal when you won't let it be?" Her fingers began gently to work at the tight spots.

He reached up and took her hand to rub his thumb over her soft fingers and kissed the inside of her wrist. Her hand smelled of the grassy salve as he wound their fingers together. "There's no time for letting it be. You know that."

"I know." She rested her cheek on top of his head for a moment.

Will pulled up a stool and sat down. "You'll what, my lord?"

"Robert Keith is by way of being a cousin of sorts." James sipped the liquor and sighed as the warmth curled in his belly. "He's with the English in Carlisle."

Will gave a non-committal grunt.

"If I were thinking of making peace with Edward of Caernarfon, it is him that I'd have negotiate for me."

Alycie's hands stilled on his shoulders. "Jamie," she said in a breathless protest.

"If..." Will gulped down the last of his uisge beatha and reached for James's cup.

James breathed out a small laugh. "It will get me inside Carlisle for the news that we need. I need to write the Keith a letter. Will, find me a quill so I can trim myself a pen. I have a piece of parchment I've carried in case I needed to write to the King." He grinned and tilted his head to look up at Alycie. She began to work along the back of his neck and lightly stroked it from hairline to shoulder. He shivered.

Even one night at peace was more than he could spare, James thought, frowning. But, Saint Bride, it was hard with Alycie soft and grass scented so close, and he felt so weary. How could he feel bone-weary and yet still be in his twentieth year? He shook the thought out of his head. "If the supplies aren't expected for a few weeks, I have more than enough time for a visit to a cousin in Carlisle."

Will took a slow sip of his drink. "They'll be looking over their shoulder for you. They mutter about the devil of a 'Black Douglas' enough."

"All the better. I keep them looking over their shoulders for me, and they have no time for looking for the King in the north." James chewed his lip as he considered. "I haven't forgotten the supplies going to Bothwell. There is a bend in the Clyde, not that far below the bluff where Bothwell stands. It's almost within sight of the castle. They'll think themselves safe so close, but the trees are thick on both sides of the road."

"Men." Alycie squeezed his hand and pulled her fingers loose to rub his shoulder again. "Can you think of something other than fighting for even a night?"

"Soon." James laughed up at her. "Perhaps for a night."

11

Will tossed back his drink and thumped his cup down. "I'll find a quill for you," Will said.

James dumped the contents of his bag onto the table: his razor, a piece of soap and ivory comb, a small round metal sheet for baking bannocks over a fire, a cup, and a small bag of oats. At the bottom was a creased and stained parchment he'd saved. Trimming the quill was short work. He chewed his lip as he bent over the letter and made it brief and to the point. Would his cousin meet with him in secret to talk about negotiating his entering the English King's peace?

"We need someone who'll arouse no suspicion to carry it," James said.

"Iain Smythe was able to make a few helms and gauntlets in secret for you. Perhaps he could take some to Carlisle to sell. I'll talk to him."

James nodded thoughtfully. More often he disguised himself as a horse trader to cover his spying, but Carlisle was too far for that to work. "We need the armor but need news even more."

Will started for the door.

James nodded, grateful for his discretion as ever. "Thank you, Will."

Alycie was smiling when the door closed behind her brother. "Did you miss me?" she teased and wrinkled her nose.

"Every minute," James admitted.

She stood up and reached down to tug him to his feet. He pulled her close, and her head nestled into the hollow of his shoulder. She was sweet to hold close.

"You'll miss me all the time whilst you're off to Carlisle," she said as she led him to her little room. "And then Bothwell with only hairy men for company in the cold spring rain."

"You don't know how much." He would have loved to take her with him, but as much as she was at risk with an English garrison so near at Douglas Castle, it was nothing to the danger of his camp as they struck and ran as they harried the Sassenach. An occasional night visit was the most he dared. He would do anything he could to keep her safe. "I'll come as often as I can," he promised. "The curst English don't know that I do, and your brother will see that you're safe. I visit as often as I'm able."

Alycie softly closed the door to her little room behind them. Through the narrow slats of the shutters, James could make out a flickering watch light at the top of one of the towers of Douglas Castle, but he was distracted by another sight. Bending, Alycie took her kirtle by the hem and drew it over her head. She tossed it aside. Her shift followed. "I don't like to think of you sleeping cold and lonely," she said as she stood close, golden and lovely in the faint light, one hand flat against his chest. "Will it help when you think of me? How long..."

"Whist," he commanded. Her lips tasted of apple as he licked his way into her mouth. Her small firm breasts pressed into him as she wrapped her arms around him.

"Jamie," she whispered when he broke off the kiss. "My sweet Lord of Douglas." James pulled her back into his arms.

CHAPTER 3

a gnarled grandfather oak shaded the dirt road. James paused beneath it to wipe the sweat from his brow. It had been a long walk from where he'd left his horse with two of his men. Above the serrated tips of the spars of docked ships, a cloud slid past the noonday sun. He scanned the high yellow walls of the town of Chester. Just as when he'd passed through the town in Bishop Lamberton's service, guards armed with crossbows marched atop the wide walls, and pikemen stood in the shadows of the gate at the end of the wide stone bridge. A wain piled with barrels rattled past him waved through by the guards.

He squared his shoulders, blanked his face and strode toward them. His footsteps thudded on the stone, and below the waves swished against the riverbank.

One of the guards lowered his pike to bar the way. "Your name and business," he said in a bored tone.

"Iain of Lanark. I'm in the service of Sir Robert Keith. He's expecting me."

The man's mouth twisted in a sneer, but he lifted his

weapon and jerked his head to motion toward the way into the town. "The Scots *lords* are lodged in the castle."

James nodded and stepped around the man. The sun gilded the castle atop a hill beyond the slate roofs of the town. Oaks and beeches dotted the way, and a church bell rang peacefully, calling the midday Angelus. Down the street, a crowd hooted and jeered at a scarecrow of man in rags, hair in tangles down to his shoulders, shouting curses and shaking his fists at the sky. James wended his way past two soldiers in mail, holding each other up as they staggered into an open door. A crude sign hung over the door, and the smell of stale ale gusted out. A baker's boy, laden arms around a heavy basket, shouted, "Hot eel pies!" and a merchant in a leather apron swept a doorstep. A gang of urchins dashed past into an alley chasing a dog, blood dripping down its sides. No one gave James a second look.

A trickle of sweat ran down his back. He sucked spit into his mouth to moisten his tongue and trudged up to a guard in the deep shadows of the tunnel that led into the castle. "I'm looking for Sir Robert Keith."

"Keith. One of the damned Scots. He rooms at the top of the Half-Moon Tower." The guard turned on his heel and marched into the bailey yard. He pointed.

"My thanks."

The man grunted and strode back to his post. Across the bailey, a farrier clanged away as he bent over a horse's hoof. A group of boys huffed and puffed and hit at each other in their heavy padding under the watchful eye of a gray-haired master-at-arms. A wain piled high with barrels was being unloaded, the men grunting and grumbling as they worked in the heat. It was a short walk to the arched entrance to the tower, and James took the narrow stairs up to an age-darkened door.

He rapped and a lad opened the door. "Sir Robert sent me a message. Tell him his cousin is here."

"Let him enter, Amery," a deep voice said from across the chamber.

Amery stepped back with a courteous half-bow and held the door open for James. Robert Keith was sharp-featured with rust-colored hair, simply dressed in a brown tunic and high leather boots. "Welcome, cousin." But his glance was wary.

A woman sat at a table with a lass who peered at him with a look of alarm.

"Robert." James smiled. "It's been a very long time."

"Amery, go to the kitchens and bring bread, some of that white cheese and apples, and some good dark ale to wash it down." The lad bowed and left. "My lady wife, Barbara, and our daughter, Elayne." The two looked the part, both dressed in a blue that matched their eyes and blonde hair neatly tamed into braids.

"Well met," James said as he seated himself. Interesting that Keith carefully omitted mention of his name. Perhaps he had little trust in his wife, but which side did she fall on? "England agrees with you well, I'm glad to see."

James wondered what it would be like to have a wife and daughter and decided he would rather not find out. There was too much suffering if you lost them.

Elayne spoke up. "It does. London was so exciting. The Queen is beautiful. And the gowns she wears—"

"London isn't our home," Keith snapped. "There is no point in pining for it. When things are more settled, we'll return home to Scotland."

"I hardly even remember Scotland," the lass said, her lips trembling. She was a pretty lass, who sounded thoroughly spoiled. "London is warmer, and there are fine lords and no fighting and—"

"Quiet. You don't know what you are blathering about."
Robert de Keith snorted. "No fighting..."

The woman arose. "Sirs, my daughter and I will leave you
to your business. Come." She smiled faintly at her daughter.
"We'll gather thyme from the herb garden to sweeten the air."

Amery bowed past her as he came in with the tray. Once
the lad had poured them ale, his master sent him away again
to polish their horses' tack in the stable. Keith went to the
door and stood in it for a moment. After closing it firmly, he
turned and said, "They say you burned Douglas Castle."

James shrugged. "And Clifford rebuilt it."

"You'd really make your peace with Edward? You're
serious?"

"I'm here, aren't I? But it's not that simple. When
Lamberton tried to convince old Longshanks to accept my
fealty, he nearly got thrown in a dungeon. So, the question is,
will his son be of a different mind?"

"He is. Hard to think of two men more different in their
ways. He's released Bishop Lamberton, you know."

James's heart thudded. "You jest."

"Not at all. He's still under guard and pledged not to leave
England." Keith's smile twisted with wry amusement. "The
old king hated him, and that's enough for the son."

James blanked his expression, although his heart raced.
News indeed well worth the trip and the risk. "Old Longshanks hated me even as a lad. So, you think that would
mean something?"

Keith nodded thoughtfully. "It might. Lamberton is in
Durham, and I've heard he's well enough. Edward is fond of
him, it would seem."

"So, the English King would take me into his peace..."
James smiled into his cup as he took a drink of the ale. "In
spite of everything."

"It would pull a sharp thorn from their side. And that

17

would please him. With what he is and what his nobles think of him." Keith pulled a grimace. "They wouldn't mind so much who he rutted with if he didn't rub their faces in it. He's the King and they'd ignore it. Stupid. Stupid man. If he'd rid himself of Gaveston and be quiet in what he does... men would abide it. But if he's to keep that peacock at his side, he'll be forced to invade to take their mind off the other."

James thought over the 'their' but let the phrase go. The Keith didn't seem all that attached to his friends in England, but he wasn't here to bring Keith into his own King's peace. He studied the man's bland face. Traitors made his hand itch for a sword, but how could you kill every man who'd sold their soul for a day's safety? "So, you think he'll lead an invasion himself?"

Keith grunted. "He'll have to. They're calling him a coward and worse. Not that he is. Or I think not. Just strange."

James thought he'd better renew his pretense. Something more worthwhile might slip. "How are matters between him and Clifford? If I make my peace with him, I'll want my lands back."

"He needs Clifford, but perhaps other lands. Something seized from Boyd or one of the others."

"I'd rather have Douglasdale returned to me, but if it's a good offer..." James shrugged. "Have you heard of any of the others in English hands? Bishop Wishert? Lady Elizabeth?"

"All close confined. They'll never see freedom although... I've heard that his orders are that they are to be held less harshly in their confinement. Lady Christina has been released at last from that..." The Keith's lips thinned. "...that cage where they kept her."

James ripped off a piece of bread. Curse them. At least old Longshanks had gone to the torments of Hell that he deserved. "Perhaps that means he hates us less than his father did. That would be good news for me." He took a drink of his ale.

"You'll need to offer them something. They don't love us Scots and you least of all. Could you give them the Bruce, do you think? That would put you high in the English regard."

James picked up an apple. It crunched when he bit into it, and he chewed thoughtfully. "I could try, but I'll make no promises on that score. He's too wily to be easily trapped, and he's never without Gilbert de Hay and the Campbell and their men. But Sir Edward Bruce or some lesser game... If the English make it worth my while. That I could promise."

"Sir Edward," Keith repeated. "He'd be a prize, but is it likely you could lure him without his brother?"

"I think that I could." James chewed some more bread. "He's often in the south and away from the King. He's impatient, hot-headed. Loves taking risks."

Keith snorted. "You're a fine one to talk of taking risks, cousin. But I've heard he's hot-headed. Dangerous. He's the type to fall into a trap. If I can promise, you'll lure him within reach..."

"I've no fondness of Edward de Bruce." James shrugged. "And perhaps I could lure Boyd as well."

"I could propose it to Aymer de Valence. He has the King's ear."

James started on the cheese. "Are you staying in Chester long?"

"Staying longer than I'd like," Keith said grimly. "The English want me in their sight and under their thumb. And I can't say it's safe for my family at home as long as Robert de Bruce is a free man. What about you? You're not staying until you have word, are you?"

James's mouth was full of bread and cheese, and he took a drink of the strong, dark ale to wash it down. He grinned wolfishly at Keith. "A bit close under their noses for me. No,

I'll be away for the border before nightfall." And he'd find some way to send a message to Lamberton, as well. "I'll send my man for an answer in a month's time." James wiped his mouth on the back of his hand and nodded to his cousin as he rose. The door banged closed behind him. Alone the news that Lamberton was freed from his dungeon had been worth the trip, but he might as well poke about a mite whilst he was here.

The guards glowered at him as he passed. "Bring news of King Hob?" one of them yelled.

James shrugged and kept going. An insult to his King wasn't going to draw him out. Those soldiers stumbling into a tavern might be in a mood to talk. If not them, then another. It looked like the kind of place that would draw the right clients for news.

James kept close to the edge of the street as he made his way back. The old madman had left or been dragged away. The body of the dog lay halfway out of the alley. From above a goodwife shouted before she emptied a chamber pot, and he jumped back to avoid the stinking splash. His lip curled. He'd forgotten the stink of a city.

The smell of ale, even stale, was a welcome relief when he pushed open the door. The room was long and draughty. A row of kegs stood at one end and a heart with a sputtering fire at the other. A pimple-faced serving boy ran back and forth with mugs that a grubby tavern keeper drew from the kegs.

Men crowded the benches. A fat merchant bent close to whisper in a priest's ear. A heavy muscled smith in a leather apron sat on a far corner, staring into his cup. But most of the places were filled with hard-faced soldiers. Three by the fire wore the yellow with starlings of Lord Clifford. Five, laughing drunkenly, wore polished mail topped with the red and gold of Aymer de Valence, Earl of Pembroke.

James stepped over the bench and sat near them, waving to the boy to bring him ale. When the lad held out a hand, James slipped him a single silver groat piece.

The oldest of Valence's men, lean-faced with a deep scar from eye to chin, narrowed his eyes at James. "What lord you serve?"

James shook his head and gave the man a bland smile. "Je ne comprends pas." When the lad slapped a mug down in front of him, James buried his face in it, slurping as he drank, keeping his eyes on the thick, dark brew.

"Good idea to wear your lord's colors hereabouts," the man muttered.

A younger one at his side said, "Ah, why don't you leave it, Adam? Probably some God-damned mercenary Clifford brought over from France too dumb to understand a word of honest English."

Adam upended his cup and drained it. He hammered on the rough boards of the table for the servant's attention. "Might be worth beating his head in after we have some more ale."

James slurped up some more of his ale, hiding his smile. They'd probably pass out first. If not, they were in for a surprise.

"We fight Clifford's men again. Mess him up, and his lordship will give us a lashing for sure. Anyway, we have a few days to stay drunk. I don't want to spend it locked up."

One of Clifford's men stood up, glaring. "You lot want a fight, you'll have it. Lucky buggers, you don't have to guard horse trains—nothing but rain and bogs and looking over your shoulder for King Hob." He snorted. "Soft duty you have, escorting the earl's get here and there."

Adam jumped to his feet, rocking the bench. James waved to the servant boy and raised his cup. He motioned to the cups of the other men and pantomimed filling them and threw down some coins. Grinning, he said, "Buvez, mes amis." He raised his cup in a toast to them. "Pourquoi se battre?"

The serving boy came back, his arms full of cups of ale. He thumped them hurriedly down, eyes cutting from side to side at the soldiers.

Adam grunted. "Won't beat his head in after all." He took a deep drink of the ale.

The man of Clifford's straddled the bench. "The youngster's right. A week until we're off for Buittle with a supply train. Rather do this than have my back flayed."

James threw a few groats on the table. It would be a good idea to have them rolling under the table before he slipped away.

CHAPTER 4

Sunlight twinkled on ripples on the murky current of the River Clyde as it surged through its way below. A thinly wooded ridge sloped down to the riverbed. Beneath spring green branches, James's men talked in hushed tones as they tied their horses out of sight of the road. James could hear the whinny of the rough-coated garrons and the stomp of hooves as they pawed at the leafy ground. He nudged his horse and turned it to ride back along the road a few lengths. The horses had to be well out of sight, but any faint noises would be covered by the sound of the oncoming supply train. Two of his men plodded past, carrying between them a full armload of fifteen-foot-long pikes. A dozen more men dragged up long willow branches to twine into a leafy barrier with the dense stand of trees on the higher side of the road.

Hew, a rangy man, copper hair flapping around his face, cantered around the bend in the road. "They're half an hour behind me."

"How many?"

"Fifty sumpter horses, heavily laden. We spotted two

23

outriders, so Keith and Gelleys stayed behind to see to them. They should have sent out more." He gave James a gap-toothed smile. "Guards aplenty, at least our number."

"You men," James called, "give them a hand with those branches. Make it dense so the horses can't force their way through."

Two more men trotted by, their load of pikes clinking. James followed them toward where they dumped their pikes atop a stack nearly as high as a horse's shoulder. The road here was straight for a goodly bit until it made another bend through the deep shade of willow trees. Past that bend, it climbed sharply for Bothwell Castle.

Wat strode out of the trees, leading his shaggy mount and wiped the sweat dripping down his leathery cheeks. "Almost done. The archers are in place."

James nodded. "They'll try to pass us more instead of attacking archers, I hope. The woven branches wouldn't protect them long."

"Some might get past. Bring help from the castle."

"I'm counting that they will try. Some could, so we must win this fight quickly. Form the men into the schiltron."

"To the pikes! They're almost upon us," Wat shouted.

Men streamed out the trees. Pikes clattered as the men grabbed them. Shoulder to shoulder, each planted the butt of his pike in the earth with a two-handed grip, a shield strapped to his back. In the front row, each man dropped to a knee. The second aimed pikes over their shoulders.

James watched for a moment as Wat swung into his saddle and harried the men into place, forming a square hedgehog of glittering steel. He turned to pace back toward where their enemy would come from. "Archers, hold your fire until they charge." He scowled at the branches woven into a barrier--slight protection indeed. "Your flights must bring down any who try to flee."

A falcon shrieked in the distance, a high scream. One answered. A third responded. Falcons do not answer one another's calls, except those belonging to him. He smiled. As he turned his horse to trot toward the schiltron, the woods grew quiet. In the distance, James could hear them, still out of sight around the bend in the road, moving closer: the tromp of horses' hooves and clank of harness, the clatter of swords and armor, the murmur of a man's voice, a laugh. A horse snorted.

Men parted to let him into the center of the pike square. "Plant your pikes hard, men. When the horses hit, they must be braced." He nodded to Wat. The other man unfurled James's starred, tapering standard. It hung limp in the still noon air. In such a schiltron, he had nearly died at Loudon Hill, but the schiltron had held.

He let out a breath he hadn't known he was holding as a rider cleared the bend. More riders emerged from around the bend, a dozen, more, three lines of them. A man carried the Clifford banner with its range of starlings at the head. Knights, men-at-arms, horses with their panniers laden with goods. Swords swung from belts. Shields caught the sunlight.

James stood in his stirrups. He raised a hand to his mouth and shouted, "This is Douglas land, and I am its lord. Return to your own country."

There was an instant, a heartbeat, when the Sassenach gaped at him. Then there was a shout, "We have the devil. Charge!"

The English whipped their horses to a gallop, shouting as they came. "St. George!" A wedge of enemy knights formed as they galloped, a broad knight in gray steed in the lead, shouting as he came. From the woods, a flight of arrows arched. A horse went down under tearing hooves. Behind the wedge boiled a swelter of warhorses and steel. The knight died, a sharp point ripping through his throat. His warhorse reared, slashing out with iron-shod hooves, as a pike jammed into its chest. A dozen horses shied at the last second. Pikes thrust into rearing mounts, ripped into chests. More plowed into the steel hedge. Curses and shrieks filled the air.

The charge was crumbling. The English reeled back from the hedge of steel points.

Men screamed, lashed their rearing horses as they fought to turn. From the woods, a flight of arrows arched. Another flight was in the air and another. "Hold!" James shouted over the cacophony. "They're ours."

Another warhorse hit, and a pike shattered into a horse's chest. Its rider went down, the pikeman crushed beneath its weight. The knight rose, covered in blood, laying about him with a war hammer. James thundered toward him through the gap in the schiltron, scything his sword in a huge arc as he rode. "Douglas!" his voice rang out. "Douglas and Scotland." A crunch and the knight was face down in the dirt.

James turned his snorting horse in a narrow circle, glaring down. The knight rolled onto his side and scrambled at the ground. "Yield." The man peered up at him, eyes unfocused and empty hands limp as blood dripped down his arm. "Yield or die."

"I yield." He fumbled his sword from its scabbard and cast it onto the ground. "I yield."

Horses snorted and reared. A horseman lashed at his horse's flanks as it scrambled up the slope and skirted the archers and schiltron. A flight of arrows rattled as a dozen horsemen galloped around the bend where they had come. The sound of fleeing hooves faded. James looked around for another enemy. No one remained on his feet except his own men, leaning wearily on their pikes; around them was a tangle of fallen horses and men. Someone groaned. Another voice pleaded for mercy. A raven squawked as it landed.

Long and faint, a trumpet's call drifted from out of sight.

James cursed. "Grab those sumpter horses," James ordered. "We need the supplies. We'll not wait for company from the castle. Parties of two. A single sumpter horse with each party."

The men scrambled for their mounts, grabbing the reins of the sumpter horses as they ran. James scowled as he looked his men over. Hew pulled Richert from under the body of a horse. His gashed arm from a shattering pike dripped red through Richert's grasping fingers. Were there no other wounded? They'd been well in luck. It would take the forces from Bothwell Castle a few minutes to mount and reach his spot, but not many. Wat chivvied the men to gather the pikes and lash them to horses.

"Richert, with me." James nudged his horse and leant to snatch the reins of a skittering horse. He jumped down and hoisted the man to his feet and into the saddle.

The English knight on the ground was cursing under his breath as he cushioned an arm against his chest. James gave him a hard look, but he was no danger. James picked up the dropped sword before he leapt into his saddle. He thrust the sword into a pack on one of the sumpter horses and grabbed up its lead.

CHAPTER 5

"*H*urry," James yelled. "Make sure you've lost them before you head for camp."

James sat on his horse, unmoving. He waited as his men threw themselves on their mounts. He took a deep breath to yell for them to hurry, but they were already moving. They melted into the forest. In three heartbeats, the road was empty of his men.

Blood dripped from Richert's hand. "Stay ahorse," James said. At Richert's nod, James kicked his horse and plunged into the forest. Shouts and the sound of hoofbeats followed from the road.

The trees were widely spaced here away from the true forest. The true edge of Ettrick Forest lay a two-hour ride ahead to the south and east. Their horses' hooves made no sound in the thick leaves underfoot. James frowned at the clank of his harness and armor. He'd cut their escape close.

He glanced over his shoulder. Richert swayed in the saddle, his freckles bright splotches in a white face, his ginger hair dripping with sweat. They needed space from their pursuers.

"Keep close," James said and clapped his heels to the horse's flanks. He plunged to a gallop. Behind a voice shouted, "Get them." Trees whipped by as he wove his way between the trunks, ducking limbs that slashed at his face. He spared a look to Richert, who hung on with a desperate scowl.

It was impossible not to leave signs of their passing, and drops of Richert's blood provided a sparse but clear trail. Somewhere ahead was a small burn, he knew. The rocky waterbed would hide their passage if they could reach it. Far to the left, there was another shout. Some of the pursuit must have split off to chase other of his men.

Ahead, water gurgled its way over a rocky course. The little burn might buy them some time. James plunged down the little slope and pulled up, water splashing around his horse's fetlocks. Sunlight dappled the waves as they rushed over the rocks.

Richert pulled up beside him and bent. He retched, spewing a thin stream of yellow bile. His horse snorted, dancing. James grasped his arm. "You've got to hold on." He took Richert's reins out of his hands. "Hold onto your saddlebow. I'll lead you." James shook his head. He looped the sumpter horse's lead around its neck as it blew through its nose. This would cost, but it couldn't be helped. He turned it and slapped its hindquarters hard. "Ha!" The animal snorted, dancing. He slapped its flank again and clattered up the opposite side and away at a run.

He tugged on Richert's reins and followed the middle of the burn. The shallow water foamed, splashing up the horse's legs.

"I'm all right," Richert muttered.

"Aye, you're a braw man. Soon we can stop, and I'll tie that wound up for you." James urged the horses to a fast canter. The sound of the water covered the clop of their

29

horses' hooves. Blood soaked in dribbles into the coat of Richert's horse, but perhaps not so much it would kill him. James hoped. The trees began to grow close to the edge of the burn and closer together. Branches formed a thick canopy.

James kneed his horse and led Richert up the little slope. The dense shade of the trees was crisp and fragrant of pine. He slid off his mount. "Let me look at that arm."

Richert grasped looked at him, eyes dull. "Not sure I can get down."

James twitched a slight smile. "Fall sideways. I'll catch you."

With a groan, Richert shoved himself out of the saddle, kicking his feet free of the stirrups. James caught him around the chest and lowered him to the ground. It took a moment rustling through Richert's saddlebag to find linen bandages. James slit Richert's leather jerkin, and wrapped the gash, pulling the strip tight. The man hissed a breath through his teeth, lips going even whiter. At least the bleeding had slowed whilst they rode.

James took his water bag from his saddle and knelt. He propped Richert up to give him a drink. "Rest for a minute, before we move on." If he could get far enough from their pursuers, he'd consider resting until the morrow. They still had a long ride to their camp in the depth of the Forest.

A snort from a horse brought James's head up with a jerk. He put a hand to Richert to shoulder. The man nodded, wide eyes, and James stood. For a moment, all he heard was the rush of blood in his ears. Leather creaked. There was a rattle of tack.

James pulled out his dirk. He pressed his back to a rough trunk in the dark shade of the close grown trees. One of his own mayhap? He eased around the tree and darted to the next in the direction of the sound. A horse stamped. Tack clattered. James peered around the huge trunk.

An English knight, back turned, looped the reins of his roan destrier around the branch of a deadfall pine. He pulled off his helm, dropped it to the ground at his feet, and muttered something under his breath in obvious disgust. He kicked a branch.

Lost? It didn't matter.

James lunged. The man grunted and started to turn. James grabbed his chin. Jerked it back. Slammed his dirk's point into the man's throat and ripped. A gurgle. Blood gushed, warm and sticky over his hand and up his arm. A hand tugged feebly at his arm. He kicked. James held on until the man went still and shoved the body away with a gust of a sigh. Rolled the corpse over with his foot. Dead eyes stared up at the canopy of leaves. Gray streaked hair draggled into a puddle of blood. He was old enough to be someone's father. Too bad his King hadn't let him stay home where he belonged.

James wiped his blade on the man's surcoat. He chewed his nether lip and frowned at the knight's mount. Shame to leave it, but it was hard too hard to sell a destrier. Time to ride.

He led Richert, bent over his horse's withers and swaying in the saddle, toward the forest of thick pines, under a heavy canopy of branches that turned daylight to murk. He kept to unmarked trails or no trails at all. He stopped twice more, but only briefly, watering the horses and re-bandaging Richert's wound before moving on at a slow, steady pace. The man grasped his saddlebow, swaying in his saddle, face twisted. Dusk fell. The uneven ground became dangerous even for their sure-footed beasts when James spotted a spot sheltered by a couple of deadfalls.

Silently, James dismounted, scanning the shadowy shapes

of the trees around them. There was barely room in the nook to hobble the animals and make a cold camp.

Richert slid from the saddle and collapsed onto his knees. James wrapped the man in both their cloaks and held his water bag to his mouth.

Richert shoved the water bag away. "You should let me make my own way."

"Get some sleep. We're riding at daybreak." James loosened the saddle girths, pulled off the saddles, and ran a cloth over the horse's coats.

He dropped a leather-wrapped pack beside Richert and sat down. There was a little dark yellow cheese, a bit dried but still edible. Using his dirk, James cut into slices. Richert managed a few bites before he drifted into sleep. James rested his back against the weathered trunk of one of the fallen giants and closed his eyes in a light doze.

Richert was steadier when they mounted and rode in the first light of dawn. Two hours later, a hawk's cry shrilled, sharp through the morning birdcalls. James pursed his lips and answered. The day warmed, and another hawk called to him. He answered once more and through the boles of the thickly grown trees was the edge of their camp.

It was a transient one, consisting of cowhides stretched over rough wooden frames, crude tents erected under the shelter of trees. A hart was roasting over the single fire pit in the middle of the clearing. Someone shouted, and his men gathered to greet their returning leader.

CHAPTER 6

TWO MONTHS LATER

*J*ames settled onto the floor, cross-legged, and leant back against the warm stones of the hearth. He closed his eye for a moment as his muscles unknotted, relaxing. He took a deep breath of the scent of pine fire and bread baking on the hearthstone.

Alycie took his hand and pressed a cup into it. "You're deathly weary."

He opened his eyes and she was kneeling beside him. "Weary enough, lass."

Wat groaned. "Your pardon, my lord. My bones are too old for floors." He hooked a stool, shoved it close into the yellow light of the fire, and thumped his bottom onto it.

James twitched the corner of his mouth into a half-grin. "Sit where you please, Wat, as long as I don't have to climb onto a horse tonight."

"Aye, but we've done right well." Wat knocked back a goodly swallow of the fiery uisge beatha. "Lost only two men, a handful hurt and cut off supplies to every castle near the Forest. A good season's work."

Will accepted a cup from his sister. "The problem is that it's stirred them like an angry beehive. We've been stung."

James sipped at the liquor in his cup. It eased its way down with welcome warmth. Alycie sat beside him and nestled close. He hooked his arm around her waist and settled her in the crook of his elbow. "How badly?"

She shuddered. "Young Copin. He had a dirk hidden."

James tangled his fingers into her hair, stroking softly.

Will cleared his throat roughly. "They found it on him and dragged him to the castle. He died from the hanging before they could gut him. Head's still over the gate."

James traced a finger down the long muscle of her neck as she pressed her face into his shoulder. "What about this new commander at the castle?"

There was a quick triple knock on the door. Will stood up and opened it a crack so that Iain Smythe could slip in. The man gave a half-bob in James's direction, bushy auburn hair half covering his forehead, bare arms dotted with scars from his forge. "My lord." He squatted, his heavily muscled shoulders resting against the wall. "I'm working the steel you brought as fast as I can, but it's nae easy to keep the Sassenach from catching on. They're watching us close."

"Do the best you can." James raised an eyebrow at Will. "This commander of theirs?"

Will drew his blond brows into a frown. "Sir John Webton by name. I've only seen him from a distance, but he's had his men out. Searching for weapons. Searching for you. For anyone helping you. Grabbing every mite of supplies they can lay hands on. Left us curst short on food and all."

"I'll have to try for the castle again. What the King has done, I'm not sure, but I've not taken even one castle. As long as they hold those, they hold Scotland."

Will scrapped a stool across the floor to join them,

leaning his elbows on his knees. "Did King Robert mean you to take them?" He shook his head. "They say that's a nasty business, besieging castles."

James closed his eyes again, stroking the silken length of Alycie's braid. "Sieges, no. Any we take must be in secret." He laid a kiss on the top of her head.

Alycie squawked softly and jumped to her feet. "My bannocks." She clambered over James's legs to kneel in front of the round hearth and grab a wooden peel from beside it. She shoved it under a round of the oaten bread to plop it onto a tray. A second and third followed. She slid her gaze to James with a wry twist of her lips. "You make me forget my chores. That's not good of you, Sir James."

James's stomach grumbled. "At least I brought bags of oats with me. Don't complain, lass."

She picked up the tray and carried it to the table.

The smith rubbed his mouth, looking hungrily at the oaten bannocks. "We need the supplies, my lord. No one has starved yet, but stomachs are lean."

Alycie wielded a large knife to cut the loaves into quarters. "You eat enough for two men anyway, Iain." But she held out a wedge of the steaming bread as Will sliced a piece off a circle of yellow cheese. Iain Smythe glanced at James before he took the bannock.

James grinned. "You're even bigger than I am. Go ahead." He got his feet under him and went to the table to pick up one of the bannocks. He broke off a piece and chewed it, frowning as he pondered the problem of food for the village.

"Copin didn't ride with me. Too young, but they'll take revenge anywhere they can. And cutting off the English supplies was bound to make them steal more from our people. Not a consequence I wanted, but I fear it cannot be helped. Still..." He took the pungent cheese Will held out and

35

ate it between two pieces of bannock, then washed it down with a drink of the liquor. "Since they're seizing supplies, if we show them something easy to snap up, we can be sure they'll take the bait. And the day after tomorrow is the Lanark fair, so someone taking hay to sell at the fair would be no surprise."

"Draw them out?" the smith asked. "Like you did with Thirwell?"

"Not exactly. I need to move my men closer to Douglas Castle, so we can take it. When I take it, I'll make sure no English hold it again. That I promise you. One castle. A start."

The smith crammed a hunk of bannock in his mouth. He nodded, apparently ready to take James's word for it. With a long-limbed step, James reached the door and cracked it. He pursed his lips, and a loud *shree* split the air. After a moment, he did it again.

Running footsteps thudded, and a low voice asked, "Aye, sir?"

"Send Gelleys for the men. I want them outwith the village by daybreak." The lad took a step back, but James held up a hand to halt him. "We'll need hay. Wat should bring fourteen bags of it." He closed the door as the young man pelted into the darkness. Smiling slightly, James picked up another piece of bannock. "Nothing wrong with your chores, hen. Best bannock I've tasted in many a day."

She tilted her chin up. "I should hope so. As though you men can bake as well as I do."

He put an arm around her shoulder to give her a squeeze. When he held the chunk of bannock to her lips, she nibbled at it. "I don't think the Sassenach will be watching you too closely after tomorrow," he said.

Iain Smythe grabbed another hunk of bannock and turned for the door. "That'll be a right relief, my lord."

Will cut off two more slices of cheese. He smiled at James and followed the smith to the door. "I'd take it kindly if you'd leave a bite of bannock for breaking my fast on the morrow."

CHAPTER 7

The scent of the early morning air was damp and green in the dawn light that filtered through the giant oaks. James squinted as he hoisted a bag of hay and looped its rope across the horse's saddle to the bag on the other side. The animal snorted and tossed its head. He patted its neck before he looped the rope around itself so that a tug on one end would release both bags.

The horse stamped and snorted again. It snapped at his arm. James laughed as he jerked back. "Easy, boy. It's only this once."

Wat strode up, sword in his hand, and tried a cut. "Would be better if I led them and you brought up the reinforcements."

James couldn't make out Wat's features in the shadows, but he could hear the scowl.

"No. This is how we'll do it."

"You get yourself killed, and we're crow's bait."

James shrugged. "I won't. You move the men into position in the trees. You'll be beside us soon enough."

Wat sheathed his sword. "As you say."

James tossed him his reins and walked along the line of men and horses. He patted Gelleys's shoulder as he checked the knot to be sure it would release. Hew was still fiddling with the rope, muttering curses under his breath, so James showed him again how the hitch knot worked. When he saw that the fourteen men who would bait the English out were ready, he narrowed his eyes and strained into the dimness. A hundred men were astride shaggy mounts, lightly armored with steel helms and leather, metal-reinforced baldrics. They massed like a hand ready to slap. James saw his blue standard unfurl as one of his men shook it out.

James turned and walked back to Wat awaiting him. "See that they charge on my battle cry." He jammed his hands on his hips and scowled. "Where is that tunic?" he barked. Wat handed it to him. James held it up. "It's not ripped down the side. How do you expect me to free my sword?"

He flapped into the rough woolen garment over his chain-mail hauberk. It came to mid-calf. He waved away the rope belt. "Give me your dirk," he said and ripped the side to the hem. He whipped out his sword, sheathed it, and whipped it out again.

He handed the dirk back to Wat, who stuck it into his belt. "If I die, you can nag at me then."

"What good will that do?"

"You'll feel better."

"I'll be dead, too."

"Then I'd best not get killed." James whipped out his sword again, saluted Wat, and yelled, "Let's move." He motioned ahead with the sword.

He picked up the horse's reins. The animal gave another snort and toss of its mane as they set off. Hooves plodded softly on the dirt road. They emerged out from under the heavy branches at the edge of Ettrick Forest. Pale golden waves of dawn washed up the eastern sky. Overhead the sky was still a dusty gray, and a sprinkling of stars strained to hold out against the light. Wisps of fog crept along the ground, playing a game of hide-and-seek with the road.

James sheathed his sword and shoved his hair out of his eyes. No helm. That was what had Wat in a panic, but they'd not look like innocent sellers on their way to the fair with helms. He'd left behind his shield. Couldn't be helped. Would some English knight split his head for him this day?

He took in a deep breath of the morning air. Douglas Water flowing nearby made it damp and fragrant. If he died today, it was fighting for home. That was worth dying for. He tugged on the reins and lengthened his stride, a smile tugging at his lips. He didn't intend to die. Not yet. Did anyone ever think they would die? Had Thomas thought he'd be sent in chains to his death?

Footsteps and hoofbeats thudded in the morning hush. A cock crowed, thin, in the distance. The shadow of the castle ate its way across the hill. At the top of a tower, a breeze caught a yellow banner, spreading it, so it flapped and rippled.

Perhaps it would look strange if he stared at the castle. That wasn't where they were headed but a few miles north-west to Lanark fair. He stared at his boots and kicked a stone that bounced into the heather. He cut his gaze to the castle and raised an eyebrow when he realized that the castle gate was already open.

"That gate is ours," he said loudly enough to carry back to his men. "Whatever happens, reach it and hold it. Let no one lay hands on the chains to close it. Hack off their hands if they try."

Behind him, there was a slap of steel on leather as someone loosened a sword beneath the cover of a tunic.

"They'll piss themselves when they hear the battle cry. Most likely hide in the cellar," Hew said. Someone laughed.

"Nae. The last place they'll go," another voice said, low. "Not after what Sir James left down there as a gift for them last time."

"Wheesht," James hushed them. "We're close enough for voices to carry."

The road divided; the narrower rutted track led up to the castle. James tugged his stubborn devil as it danced and took the way that wound halfway between the castle and the shadowy forest, the castle village out of sight past its edge.

The sun was well up, and a bead of sweat itched as it trickled down James's neck.

"What's taking so long? Mayhap the devils learnt from last time?" one of his men muttered.

Suddenly, the English were there in the castle gate, a dozen surging down the road, a wave of shields and swords, led by a knight with a waving plume on his shining helm, mail gleaming like a new cut coin. James gave them a moment to thunder closer.

"Now!"

He tugged the rope, and the bags of hay thumped to the ground. "A Douglas!" he bellowed. Wat had better hear him. "A Douglas!"

He vaulted into the saddle and jerked his sword free. The knight was upon him. His battle narrowed to the knight in front of him. He circled James, raining sword blows down. James caught them, wielding his sword two-handed. Steel whanged against steel. The sword hacked at James's throat, and James lashed out, knocking it aside. His enemy leant back to make room for another try. That gave James the room that he needed. He swung his longsword with all the strength that was in him. The knight's throat exploded in a shower of gore.

"A Douglas! A Douglas!" Wat yelled, thundering toward

him past an English guard hunched on the ground, arms flung over his head.

James whipped his horse to a gallop. He glanced up warily at the heavy grate of the portcullis, like the teeth of a monster. His men beside him swept toward the castle in a wave of shields and swords, his starred standard streaming. Shouts floated down from the castle walls as he galloped through the tunnel-like entrance.

The keep door stood open, the inside gaping darkness. A man-at-arms dashed across the bailey yard toward it. Wat leapt from his horse and slammed the flat of his sword against the back of his head. Fergus's horse plunged up the steps after a fleeing guard.

"To me!" a knight shouted, back to a wall. Men ran toward him.

Pointing with his sword to the door, James shouted, "Hold that," over the grunts and shouts of fighting men, shrieks of fear and pain. Wat planted himself, feet wide and sword raised, in the open doorway.

James paced his horse in a small circle. A mob of men-at-arms hunched against the wall, shields raised and swords ready.

James stood in his stirrups. "Yield! Yield and you'll have mercy."

The knight in a long mail hauberk and green surcoat braced his back against the wall and shouted back, "Mercy from the Douglas?" He spit. Blood ran down his cheek.

Fergus cursed. "Let's at them." Beside him, Philp swiped the blood from a slice on his round face as he stalked his horse toward the English mob, the other men hard behind him, dirty and dented and growling.

"Hold," James said. He nudged his horse a step toward the Englishmen. "My word on it as a knight. Surrender, and I let you live." A bleeding man-at-arms on the ground groaned.

The knight's eyes darted from James to his men and back again. "You swear it?"

"By the Holy Rude," James told him. He looked into the pale, sweating faces of the Englishmen, one by one. "Throw down your sword."

The knight's arm sagged down to his side. "I—" Even from where he sat, James heard his gulp. "I yield." He tossed his sword onto the ground.

James motioned with the point of his sword. "All of you. Now!"

A shield and then a sword clattered onto the ground, then another and another. James pushed his hair, dripping with sweat, back out of his eyes. "Philp. Hew. Gather the arms. Wat, we need a rope." He narrowed his eyes at his captives. "On your knees." He paced his horse back and forth, glowering at them as their hands were tied behind their backs.

The knight raised his head. "Douglas," he said from his knees. "You took an oath." Blood dripped on the ground from a gash across the knight's forehead, but the morning light glinted on his polished mail.

He swallowed a gush of bile at the memory of a bared neck bent below his sword and the gush of hot blood. "I did," James said coldly.

"Kill them, my lord," Philp urged. "Take their heads off like you did at the Larder."

"No." James sheathed his sword and peeled off his bloody leather gauntlets. "We have more important things to do than soil our blades with their blood."

Wat jerked the knight to his feet by his bound hands. "I'll set a guard on them. In the great hall?"

"Outwith the walls. Strip them of armor and make sure they have no weapons. Not even an eating knife. Then come to me. We have much to plan." He glared at the yellow banner

43

above the gate. "Philp, pull that Clifford banner down from my walls."

Philp, pale blue eyes in his leathery face, stared at James before turning to run up the steps to the parapet. James watched as he pulled down the pole and ripped the yellow banner loose. It floated like a dead leaf to the ground in front of the gate.

Gelleys was kneeling by the parapet steps, blood leaking through his fingers as he pressed it to his arm. An English guard lay still and unmoving in a red puddle nearby. Johne Rede knelt, holding himself up with one hand, the other pressed to his belly. James nodded to Richert, who trotted to his horse and untied his bag of healing supplies.

James swung from the saddle. "Wat, send one of the men for Will and Iain Smythe. And Alycie will have supplies for the wounded. I don't want the rest of the village here yet."

"Allane, Sande, see to the horses."

The men trotted to do his bidding, gathering reins of the mounts as men climbed from the saddle.

"Picket them. Wat, I want men on the walls but leave the gate open. Forbye, we'll have tooing and froing. Put a guard on the horses, as well. Move those prisoners out of here. On the far side of the castle away from the village with them." He sent Philp with a couple of men to find any English servants from within the keep.

The crowd of prisoners cast dark looks over their shoulders as they were herded out the gate. James gave them a last look. If they were fool enough to come back in his lands, he might not be so soft next time. Then he snorted. Easy enough to think they might not return, but their masters would have something other to say about that.

The yard was in chaos for a few minutes as the horses were gathered, snorting and skittering, still excited from the fight. The men were shouting and laughing, slapping shoulders, cursing their defeated enemies. The door of the keep slammed open, and two men in gray homespun stumbled out, Philp behind them. He shoved one down the steps to land on his knees, eyes wide with terror. James pointed to the gate, and they were shoved and prodded out to join the other prisoners. The last of their mounts followed, and the bailey quieted as the men were chivvied by Wat to their tasks.

"My lord," Will said from the shadow of the gate passage. Alycie was beside him, clutching a basket to her chest, plaid pulled tight around her shoulders. "I told her that she should wait. But she never listens to me."

"I'll help with the wounded." She smiled, but her gaze darted to the body that still lay on the steps to the parapet. Richert was bent over Johne Rede. The man moaned.

"Fergus, get that body out of sight," James ordered. He went to her and patted her shoulder. "You all right, lass?"

She nodded, but her mouth formed a tight, pale line. "There are men to care for." She thrust her pointed chin at Gelleys. "If someone will help him to the steps, I'll bind that up."

After she was settled, James put an arm around Will's shoulder. "You and Iain start emptying the stables. Picket the horses with our mounts. I'll share my plans with you later."

James smiled as Alycie flicked her long braid aside with a toss of her head as she sat on the stone step. Her head tilted, she daubed Gelleys's wound with a green salve and wrapped a strip of linen around the gash.

"Such a fight!" Gelleys said eagerly. His face was whey white below his thatch of dark hair, but that didn't slow down his tongue. "I was sure the damned Sassenach would get the gate closed, but Fergus put a blade through the man lowering it before it went even a foot. I've never seen such a victory. Beating them like that. Why we didn't lose a single man and five of the English dead. A knight captured and twenty men-at-arms—"

"One castle," Alycie interrupted. "And the English will be back."

"I know." He blinked at her, his face falling with disappointment. "But don't you think it was a great victory?"

James strode past a dog that stopped to lift its leg. He stood over them, arms crossed over his chest. "Gelleys, you'd talk the ears off a deaf man." The lad, as James thought of him of although they were of an age, looked up at him with a guilty grin.

"Of course, it was a thrilling victory. It's just—" Alycie tied off the bandage, patted his arm and stood up. "All done. It should heal, but if it gets hot with fever, come tell me. Or Richert."

James shoved fingers through his hair, pushing it out of his eyes. "You did well, Gelleys. Everyone did. See what food they've found in the great hall. Inside with you."

A horse neighed from the stable doors as Will and Iain Smythe led two animals out. James pointed out the castle gate. "Picket them. We'll decide which to keep." James crossed his arms. "I might make a trip into Buittle Castle tomorrow and sell one or two of the scrubbier horses. See what news I can gather."

Alycie frowned at him. "I hate when you do that. One day someone will recognize you."

"They won't, but I don't see how I have time. If Will took them, someone would know he doesn't raise horses." James stared through the walls with a brooding look, turning slowly to take in the whole of the castle. He'd expected the fire he'd set to it last year to have left more scars. Only a few streaks of black crept up the gray stone. "That will have to wait. Somehow, I must find a way... I may hold the lands, but power is yet in their hands as long as they hold the castles."

He could hear the bitter tone in his voice but couldn't repress it. "The King's own Lochmaben Castle. Buittle, Dumfries, Caevlaverock, Tibbers. If they dare not move through the Forest, I dare not attack them behind their stone walls."

Will paused on this way to the gate. "Couldn't Wat go to Buittle for you? Philp could give him a hand." The horse he led snorted and stomped, jerking its lead.

The thick oaken door of the keep creaked as it opened. "Do what?" Wat asked, shoving shut the door behind him.

Alycie put her hand on James's arm. "I'm done with the bandages, my lord."

"Will, have someone gather the women and the older children from the village. I want the kitchen and storerooms emptied. Empty the hen houses, too. After the horses are picketed, have the men haul out the grain and hay. There's no time to waste. They should take whatever they can carry. Pile the furniture in the cellar once it's empty."

He waited until Will was on his on their way out the gate to unloop his purse from his belt. Handing it to Wat, he said, "Give the damn Sassenach two siller each." He frowned as he decided which of his men hated the English the least and wouldn't murder them on the way. "Hew and David can guard them on their way. Have them follow them until nightfall and see they keep to the road to the south." He gave a brisk nod. "Allow the Sassenach no weapons, mind you, not even an eating knife."

Iain Smythe led two more whinnying, stamping horses from the stable. Two men carried lumber from a storeroom between toward the gates, and one cursed when he stumbled over a squawking rooster that flapped its way indignantly out from under his feet.

Wat tossed the leather purse in his hand and gave a wry laugh. "Siller from the Black Douglas?"

James's mouth twisted. "You want to ruin my reputation,

47

man? Don't say that it's mine. I just want them gone. Forthwith! Make sure they don't stop on the road before nightfall." He looked around and shouted, "Philp! Where are those shovels and picks?"

Richert looked up at James, shaking his head. James blew out a gusty sigh, but they were lucky to have only lost one man. He'd rather Alycie didn't see. She'd seen enough horrors in her life, so he'd spare her another.

Across the dusty bailey yard, Philp stood in the doorway of a wooden storage shed. "Where do we put them, Sir James?"

"Stack them outwith the gate."

James's stomach grumbled. No doubt they'd found food in the keep kitchen, but eating would have to wait. There was so much to do his mind reeled with it. He guided Alycie up the steps and pulled open the door. Inside, the great hall was long and drafty. Its stone walls were strangely barren, only a single banner draped behind the high table. Some of the stones still bore black streaks of soot, and the high-beamed ceilings looked raw and new. But the torches on the walls and the crackling fire in the hearth gave a pleasant light. A scent of bread and onions and meat wafted with the smell of the pine fire. James's stomach gurgled again, and Alycie ducked her head, mouth twitching a little.

He snorted. "No time."

He motioned to a doorway. "Most of the stores will be down there. Let's take a look." He smiled to himself. Eventually, they'd work their way through the castle stores to see what was in the Lord's chamber. And after, one night of his life, he would spend with Alycie in his own castle. The English be damned.

CHAPTER 8

A good distance from the walls, his men still in their leather armor stood gathered with the villagers in homespun, silent and gaping.

Sweat dripped down James's face. The day was hot and sticky with the summer sun a quarter-way up the morning sky. He swatted at swarming midges.

This is where he stood and watched the last time his lord father came riding home. He rode his gray courser that pranced as they came, and his starred pennant blew in the wind.

James picked up a broad, heavy grappling hook and peered down between the stone merlons that formed the uprights of the wall's battlements. Gelleys and Allane led two horses, the heaviest they'd found in the stables, harnessed, and stopped in front of the long pike of dirt where they'd undermined the edge of the wall. Philp joined them and waved to him.

"Ready," James called out. He dropped the long rope over the edge and shoved the grappling hook into place on the merlon. He braced a foot against it and shoved until it was

49

jammed into place. The wall shuddered under his feet. James caught his breath, ready to jump if he needed to. Yet he was sure it would take work to bring the wall down. He thought he was sure.

More hooks and ropes lay at his feet on the embattled parapet walk. He shoved and kicked the hook into place above the other as Gelleys pulled them to attach to a horse's harness. Two more went on the next merlon, and Allane fastened them to the horse he held. "Hold!" James shouted. He ran along the walk and took the steps two and three at a time to the bailey.

He ran for the gate. The wall would only come down at his word. Then let the English hold it if they could.

He emerged from the shadows of the tunnel-like gate. The two men had led the horses so that the ropes stretched taut. James turned to back away from the wall, breath coming fast. He wiped the sweat from his face as he backed up. Gelleys and Allane eyed him, ready to move on his word. He nodded. "Now."

Each man took a horse's halter. They urged the animals. Philp whipped the horses' hindquarters with a birch switch. "Hoi. Pull."

The horses strained. James frowned up, chewing his lip. They'd used tripled ropes, but they still might not hold. Still, the wall groaned. It cracked. Chunks of mortar showered from it. Stones thudded onto the ground.

"Move them," James yelled.

The horses gave one last heave and surged forward. The wall thundered as it shattered, horribly loud. James jerked a step back, and winced, forcing himself not to cover his ears. The wall was no more, just rubble and a billow of dusty debris.

There was silence. A loud gasp rose from the onlookers as

one. One of the horses snorted, shying. Gelleys hauled on its halter. Wat yelled to gather the hooks and ropes.

James felt a hand on his arm and turned his head. Alycie stood beside him, examining his face. "Jamie?"

He nodded slowly. "It's all right."

"Mayhap. But..." She pulled her plaid tight around her shoulders. "Where is your home if you destroy it? And how can you ever protect us?" She sighed. "No, I suppose it has never been protection since the Sassenach came. It's just strange to think of no castle in Douglasdale."

He put his hand on hers and ran a thumb across the back. "I can't think on it, lass." He took a deep breath and gazed with a twist of his stomach at the gaping hole and the pile of rocks.

His mouth tightened, and he called, "Wat, there's another wall to pull down. Set the men to work with the picks."

An hour of the thump of picks and grate of shovels undermined the edge of another wall. This time James stood nearby on the parapet walk and watched it crash into a pile of rocks. His ears were still ringing from the sound of that crash when another sound pierced its way through: a winding of a hunting horn. James grasped the hilt of his sword. Men dropped their tools. Another blast sounded, the signal of a friend approaching.

"To arms," James barked down to Wat. He'd never forget the lesson of Methven. Never turn your back if the English might have a sword at it. Never be sure that you might not be betrayed. Most like, it was a friend, but he couldn't think who. Any friend would be with the King in the north.

The men ran pell-mell for their swords, stacked at the foot of the slope.

The flutter of a banner... Horsemen, someone in the lead on a warhorse and a tail of men. James squinted a white pennant. Red devices. When he made out three red shields, he laughed. Boyd!

James stood on the tattered edge of what was left of the parapet, grinning. He'd missed his old friend and mentor. And Boyd would have news--news of the King.

Boyd clattered up and reined his dancing horse to a stop. James laughed. He jumped off the edge of the broken wooden walk, landing atop the rubble and leapt to the ground. "Robbie!" The hundred men in Boyd's tail clattered to a halt.

The tall, lanky knight dismounted. "Jamie," Boyd flickered a smile as James clapped him on the shoulder and then grasped his upper arms in his hands.

"You're a fine sight. What the devil are you doing down here?" He had to wonder where Boyd's grin was. As bad as things had been, Boyd had never lost that.

"I've word and orders." Boyd turned to wave his men from their mounts. "I do not suppose you could spare a mite of food for my men?"

James signaled Wat to take care of the newcomers. "God be good, I'm glad to lay eyes on you," James said as he motioned toward the keep. It was emptied except for a couple of benches and a side table but would do for a quiet talk. "Richert, bring us some wine, and there should be cheese and bread about somewhere."

At the open door of the keep, Boyd stopped to look over the destruction. "You always said they'd not hold it."

"And they haven't. They won't."

The inside was in cool shadow, only a glimmer of flame in the ashes of the great hearth. James dropped onto the bench and leaned back against the edge of the table. He frowned at his friend. "You have a grim look to you."

Boyd waited, jaw working, as Richert put a wooden tray with a loaf of bread, a round of dark yellow cheese, and a wine flagon on the table between them. Richert left the door ajar to let a shaft of golden light make a triangle of gold on the rush-strewn floor. "Aye, I was home to Kilmarnock raising men. And I finally got news of my brother."

James looked at his hands and waited, a chill wave washing through him.

"Executed a year past. Hanged, drawn..." Boyd shook his head. "I knew he was dead. But didn't quite know..." Boyd's scarred cheek twitched as he scowled at the far wall.

James poured a goblet full to the rim and put into Boyd's hand and filled a goblet for himself. He took a deep drink. "Like Thomas... Alexander..." James ran his hand through his hair. What could be said? "I'm sorry, Robbie." He'd seen Wallace and still heard his scream in his dreams. "They've killed every King's man they've captured, but until you were sure..."

Boyd gave a quick bark of grim laughter. "Not quite everyone."

"What? Who not?"

"Thomas Randolph still lives."

"They spared Randolph? But..." James frowned into his goblet. "The King's nephew? That's good news. But why did they spare him?"

"Because he's fighting for them now."

James stared at Boyd. "God have mercy. Randolph?" James shook his head. He jerked to his feet and paced fast to stare out the doorway into the sunlight and prowled angrily back. "A traitor? Does the King know?"

"Aye. I sent word."

James sat down his goblet and leaned his elbows on his knees, hands hanging between them. "That must have hit hard. That Tom Randolph would do that after they executed his own uncles, friends too many to count... Why? How?"

"To save having his guts ripped out, I should think. A

choice mayhap some others would have taken if they'd had the chance. So more to the point, why did they not kill him when they killed everyone else out of hand? Even the Earl of Atholl, old King Longshank's own cousin." Boyd shook his head. "Atholl and I kidnapped Streathern to bring him to Robert's coronation, remember? They hanged, drew, and quartered Streathern, too."

James looked around the nearly empty hall, walls with their streaks of soot where he'd fired it and beams still raw from being replaced. "I can't pull down the hall, but I'll fire it again. With the walls slighted, I do not think they'll rebuild it again."

"Probably not."

James took a deep breath and picked up his goblet. "Perhaps they thought a traitor in the King's very family was worse than killing the man. What of the King? When you saw him? How does he fare?"

Boyd ran a hand down his face. "Well, when I left. But you won't have heard. Last winter, he was ill. Coughing up thick gobs of slime, his lungs filled with it. Unable to breathe and near to death, but he led us into battle anyway." Boyd laughed again and for the first time sounded almost like his old self. "Damn the man. He had us prop him in the saddle. Gilbert de Hay and I held him up, and he led us." He grinned. "We chased the Comyn of Buchan all the way to the sea! Then the King sent Edward to ravage Buchan end to end. All Comyn's castles are destroyed: Slains, Rattray, Dundarg, Duffus. All of them. Buchan is ours."

James threw back his head with a laugh. "Betimes the King is a madman. Going into battle so ill. But we won."

"You're to bring your men north. As am I. We'll attack MacDougall of Lorn. That's another traitor who'll be paid. The King has not forgotten what he's owed."

James upended his goblet and gulped down the last drops

of wine. It was Lorn's men who'd given him his first wound. Iain Bacach MacDougall of Lorn, who had sent two of the King's brothers to shameful execution. Holding out the flagon to refill both their drinks, James said, "We'll share some braw fights then. That'll cheer you up, Robbie."

"That we will, lad." He downed his wine. "That we will."

"Have your men set to with mine slighting these walls. Two more must come down. And tomorrow I'll fire the keep, then we'll ride north." He raised his goblet. "Here's to Lorn. And vengeance."

CHAPTER 9

*S*moke billowed in a thick column into the sky, and the sight made the hairs on the back of James's neck stand on end. Monstrous shapes writhed in it as though to escape destruction. James gave a sharp cough at the acrid stench.

The rutted road from the castle turned and twisted under green trees. That was the road they had taken when he followed his father to war. He and Wat sneaked down that slope to find Tom Dickson. The kirk where Tom had died fighting the English lay past the trees. In the castle, he'd executed the English who'd killed Tom. Beyond in Douglas Water, James had washed off the blood.

Ghosts.

Boyd laid a rough buffet on James's shoulder. "You had to do it. Don't look so glum, lad."

A wry smile twitched James's mouth. He'd never be more than a lad to Boyd. "I'll have a word with Will and be ready to ride."

"Aye. I know it's Will you'll want to be speaking to. Not

that lass I saw you looking at." Boyd laughed. "You're a devil with the women, Jamie. I don't know how you do it."

"You're a fine one to say so." James grinned as he and Boyd turned their backs on the blazing castle and strode quickly toward Will Dickson's home. Boyd had always liked a woman who was an armful, and when there was a woman about, she was like to be in his lap. Women seemed to love that laugh of his. "Will said he had news of Sassenach moving near Peebles. I don't allow them free passage in my Forest, you know."

Boyd snorted and pulled open the door to duck in behind James. "Your Forest, is it? We've no time for hunting down English."

Alycie handed a ruddy-faced, shaggy-haired lad a bowl that wafted a ribbon of steam as he sat at the table beside Will. There was a scent of rabbit stew. "Hunt down the Sassenach?" she asked.

"This the one with news from Peebles?"

Will nodded. "Tell Sir James what you told me, Rane."

The lad started to rise, his eyes widening, mouth full as he chewed. James waved him back down and straddled a stool. Boyd squatted next to the door.

"At Easter Happrew, my lord," the lad said. "Near the Lyne Water. It's said they're hunting you—a couple of knights and a troop of English soldiers. But the knights..." He looked at Will and then back to James. "They're Scots."

"How do you know all this?"

"My father. His malting is there. They took it for a headquarters, so he sent me to tell you."

"And he is sure the knights are Scots?"

The lad washed the food down with a gulp of water. "He said so. He's not sure how long they'll stay, but the knight, the blond one, he sent out patrols."

"How many are there?"

The lad scratched his head. "Perhaps five score."

James clicked his tongue against his teeth. "Easter Happrew is only a short way from Peebles." He looked at Robbie Boyd. "A day's ride out of our way, but I'm thinking worth the time. It well should keep them from noticing for a bit that I've left the Forest, and we may find ourselves a prize. Worth it, I'm thinking."

Boyd looked at him silently for a moment and nodded. "You say your farewells whilst I check that the men are ready." He winked at Alycie, and she blushed, rosy-cheeked.

James stood up, smiling. "Rane, is it?"

"Aye, Sir James."

"Can you manage to sit a horse's back?"

"I rode here on my hobelar, but it's not fit to go back."

James put an arm around Alycie. "You follow after Sir Robert. Tell him I said you need a mount. I need you to show us where this malting is. You can guide us, can you not?"

The lad shoved his bowl back and jumped to his feet. "That I can, my lord." He dashed to the door. It slammed behind him.

James frowned at Will over Alycie's head. "I don't like this. Having to leave. I'd have her somewhere safe. Perhaps Alycie should go to one of the convents. Mostly they're not bothered."

Alycie shoved against his chest and stepped back. "But sometimes they are. There's nowhere that's safe, Jamie. You know that. At least here I'm of some use."

He pulled her close and wrapped her in his arms, laying his cheek on her soft hair.

Will cleared his throat. "Don't fash yourself, my lord. I'll see my sister comes to no harm. If the English come back, when they come back, I'll make sure she's out of sight."

She squeezed her arms tight around his waist and leaned

her forehead against his chest. "I wish there was somewhere safe. I wish we could go there. All of us."

He blinked hard. "Sometimes, hen," he kissed the top of her head, "sometimes so do I." He cleared his throat. Tears were unmanly. He took a deep breath, tilted her chin up. She brushed her lips over his, soft and sweet. "If I can, I'll send word when I'll return." He gripped Will's shoulder. "Keep safe."

He strode out into the mid-morning light. On the road, Wat was yelling amidst a clatter of tack and the snorting of the horses. The men, two hundred strong with Boyd's force added to James's, stood on the road, checking their horses' tack, chewing hunks of bannock, scratching, and talking.

CHAPTER 10

*J*ames mounted, wheeled about, and trotted to join them. He gave the command to move, the talk withered, and the men climbed into their saddles. Gelleys rode out first with the outriders he led, Philp and Hew. Wat nodded to James and called to the dozen men who would form the rear guard. They waited as James raised an arm overhead and signaled the main force to follow.

James rode into the Forest. He followed the game trails and shallow streams through the wilderness of gnarled trunks and branches that cut off the summer sun. That night they camped in a small haugh next to the Lyne Water. The next day as the sun set in ripples of rose and gold, they reached the outer edge of the Forest.

Gelleys emerged from the undergrowth so quietly that James's mount shied. James settled it and swung from the saddle. "English?"

"Guards around the edge of the village. Only two of them. Fools." He snorted.

Behind James, Boyd laughed. "The main force?"

Gelleys shook his head. "Nae seen a hair of their heads."

James chewed his lip as he looked over their men. "We'll go in afoot. Robbie, have a dozen men of your guard the horses. If things go awry, we'll split up and meet back here." He motioned to Rane and draped an arm around the lad's shoulder. "You'll show us to the malting and then hide, you hear?"

Rane gave a jerk of his head in assent. "It's just a mite past Torbank Hill."

James handed his reins to one of Boyd's men. They followed Rane up the steep hill shaped like a sand dune. James motioned to follow as he crawled the rest of the way. Robbie and Wat followed. He lay flat on his belly at the crest, looking across the purple and pink heathery stretch of land dotted with beech trees casting long shadows in the last rays of the sun. The braeside was speckled here and there with patches of yellow gorse. In the distance lay the village.

Rane scooted his way to beside James as he studied the welter of small houses with thatch roofs. A piddling gray stone tower stood only three stories high with no outer wall.

"It isn't big enough to hold the soldiers, so they took our place." Rane pointed to the long stone building with a slate roof on the far side of the tower. The village was oddly quiet, the enclosure where sheep would be sheltered at night empty. A guard was a black silhouette against the last ray of sunlight as he paced a path to and fro.

"Does the door bar from inside?"

The lad looked at him as though he was crazed. "Why would it do that? It's chained from the outside at night."

"Good man, Rane." James scratched at his narrow strip of beard. "Best you take the long way home. Long enough so they don't know you've been sneaking about at night."

"Aye, my cousin has a croft not far. I'll bide there for the night."

"Robbie, go back down and circle to the other side of the

61

village. Probably there's another guard for you to deal with. When an owl screeches a third time, come in."

Boyd nodded and trotted in a crouch down the braeside, leading his men. James lay flat to watch on the village as the blanket of night fell. The crush of heather under him scented the air. A bee buzzed near his hand. Wat whispered and sent two men to guard their flanks.

James studied the sprawling village. A few of the cots had spread to two or three rooms. A shaft of moonlight broke through a cloud to glint on the tower, but no light shone in its narrow, slit windows. There were slats of light showing in the windows of the malting though. Shutters opened, a figure momentarily silhouetted in the window. The light inside dimmed as though torches were snuffed. The night turned from gray to purple.

"Wat," James said softly, "Send Allane and Sande to see to our friend down there. One owl's hoot when they're done."

Their departure was a whisper of movement.

James slithered down to his waiting men. "Ready your weapons. On their signal, we move."

"Reminds me a bit of a night at Methven," Wat said.

James smiled. "Except we're the ones doing the sneaking this time."

"Well, I've heard the Sassenach want to meet that devil of a Black Douglas." Wat laughed softly. There were whispers of blades as they were drawn from their scabbards. "Might be I'll introduce you to them when we're there."

"Fergus, come with me on to kick in the door."

The man grunted assent.

On the *scree* of an owl, James drew his sword. "Mayhap they'll be glad to meet me."

He watched as the men spread out. All blooded under his command, they knew what to do. They would go in quietly and surround the building. He whistled to Wat to start the men creeping over the crest of the hill. In a crouch-walk, James led them forward, silence more golden than speed. A thud sounded as someone tripped in the darkness over a dark shape and a stifled curse. He froze, but nothing stirred in the oblivious village. The sliver of moon slid out from behind a fleeting the fleeing clouds. It's faint like gleamed on his face. He put his hand to his mouth. *Scree... Scree...*

A breeze brought the scent of rabbit cooking inside a cot as he slipped past, back pressed against the wall. James could just make out the dark shape of the building ahead, hulking black in this still watch of the night. How many English were yet on watch? Awake?

His very foremost men were at and around the walls, crouched and waiting. Fergus's bulk at his side, the two of them stooped as they moved through the darkness. At the building, James touched the rough stone of the wall as he moved low to the ground. It was impossible to see the door in the darkness.

From inside came a voice, "I'll lead a search tomorrow myself. Take half our men into the Forest. I swore I'll hunt Douglas down, the damned brigand."

James's breath caught in his chest at the familiarity of the voice.

"It's too risky, Randolph. We don't have enough men. Forbye, the Torwood is nothing but a trap waiting to snare a man."

When his fingers touched the age-slick wood of the door, James touched Fergus's arm. As the rest of the men waited, he whispered, "Ready?"

The man stepped two paces back and crouched. "Aye."

"Now!" James kicked with all his strength into the door as Fergus crashed his shoulder into it beside him. It gave with a thunderous crack.

James stumbled a couple of steps inside until he caught his balance.

"What the devil," Randolph said, silhouetted by the dim light in a hearth, gold hair catching the little light. So, like his uncle, King Robert. Randolph whirled and threw himself across the room toward a sleeping pallet where a sword lay. Beside James, his men thundered in, spreading as they ran.

The other man scurried backward, empty hands raised. "I'm not armed, man." Yelps came from groggy men in pallets as they were prodded, trod upon, and kicked into submission.

Randolph swept his sword up from beside a pile of blankets and swiveled.

"Randolph. Yield." James lunged after him. Their swords rang together. Again, testing. James backed off a step. Randolph followed, tried a slash. James jerked back, and the wind from the blade brushed his cheek.

"Honorless scoundrel," Randolph spat.

James gave way, a smile twitching his lips. "Fine words from a traitor." He circled backward, leading Randolph. The knight tried a hack at his legs; James leapt away, hopping lightly over a pile of blankets.

"Craven," Randolph said through gritted teeth. He came at James hard. Steel clanged on steel. James let Randolph drive him back, blocking each blow as he stepped over shields and blankets that littered the floor. He smiled blithely into Randolph's eyes. He almost laughed when the man growled under his breath. His blade swished by James's stomach, but James hacked a tear into the mail on Randolph's shoulder.

"Lost your skill at swordplay since you've kissed English arse?"

Randolph lunged, slamming the hilt of his sword toward James's face.

James dodged and caught Randolph across the stomach with the edge of his blade, scoring a gash into his mail. He sidestepped again and slid around the table where the two men had stood talking moment before. "Or mayhap you grew over-fond of the English King."

James drove out from the other side of the table, hard and fast. Randolph blocked. James jerked his sword upward toward the knight's head. Randolph took half a step back, braced himself, and slammed his sword down in a savage arc. James knocked it aside and slid away to the side. He brought his sword down into Randolph's elbow. The mail ripped. Randolph grunted as he half-turned and slammed James's sword aside. James bared his teeth in a grin as he stood his ground. A rivulet of red ran down Randolph's arm. James rained a flurry of blows. Randolph parried--again and again. Each parry was slower. James could hear the knight panting for breath. The crimson from Randolph's elbow dripped down onto his fingers and then the ground. He staggered.

James slammed his sword at Randolph's head. Randolph lost his feet. He lurched back, tripped over a blanket, and went down on his back. James knocked the sword from his hand with the flat of his blade. Beyond the rush of blood in his head, someone was shouting. He raised his sword, two-handed, aiming a swing that would split the traitor from neck to groin.

Hard hands grabbed him from behind, gripping his arm. He spun.

"James. No!" Robbie Boyd back-pedaled, raising his empty hands. "Not the King's kin."

James panted. Silence hung over the room. He let his arms fall. Around the edge of the room, kneeling amidst their sleeping blankets, the English gaped at him, still as could be with good Scottish steel at their throats.

His mouth was swollen and bloody where the hilt had

caught him. He took off his helm. His hair hung into his face, dripping sweat. He spit out a mouthful of blood. Leaning on his sword, he sucked in a deep breath of air. "Richert, tie the traitor up. And then stop his bleeding. He'll not die before he reaches the King."

Randolph propped himself on his elbow despite blood dripping down his cheek. He glared at James. "Brigand serving a brigand."

James sheathed his sword. "If he opens his faithless mouth again, gag him. We've no time for other prisoners. Bind them." He jerked a gesture toward the wary prisoners. "If they're in luck, someone will release them. Or let them starve."

CHAPTER 11

They rode in the dark through a scattering of towering Scotch pines. A sentry's horn blew one long, quavering note after they were recognized. Below, for miles like a scattering of fallen stars, James saw flickering points of light in an arc along the dark waters of Loch Tulla. Beyond hulked the black mass of Ben Crauchan. They had found the war camp they had traveled north to join.

A shout then more greeted them as they plodded into the camp. "Boyd's back. Tell the King," a voice shouted. Their horses' hooves padded softly in a thick layer of pine needles. The ground sloped down as they rode past smoky wood fires and lines of horses.

From one of the campfires came a plaintive song, a liquid sound that floated through the night air. James understood none of the Gaelic words but shivered as it faded away. Rough voices called for another. From another fire, laughter drowned out arguing voices. They rode past stacks of weapons, past pitch-pine torches and men squatting around sputtering fires where they roasted haunches of venison. The smell made James's empty belly grumble. It had been a fast ride with no time to bring down game.

Dark shapes strode toward them. James recognized the tall man in the lead, gold hair catching a gleam of the fire-light. He jumped from the saddle.

"Jamie. Jamie Douglas," Robert de Bruce called. Even in the torchlight, James could see he was thinner, his face drawn. He wore a simple circlet for a crown and mail that was as battered as any other man's, a simple plaid around his shoulders. He clasped James's arms.

"Your Grace." For a moment, words failed James. "You were ill, I heard."

"For a while." The King laughed, and his teeth shone white in his tanned face. "One too many nights in our good Scottish snow. But they nursed me like a bairn. I'm well enough now. Have your sergeant settle your men and tell me your news."

James stepped back. "Your Grace..." More bad news was the last thing he wanted to give the King, but the traitor had to be dealt with. "We took a prisoner. One that I had to bring to you myself." He thrust his chin toward Randolph, hands tied before him whom Wat was pulling from the saddle.

The King stared as Wat prodded their prisoner into the light of the torch. Robert de Bruce's mouth thinned. "Nephew..."

James grabbed Sir Thomas Randolph's elbow. Randolph tried to jerk free, but James gave the back of the man's leg a vicious kick.

Randolph thudded to the ground on one knee. He spared James a glare.

"So, you return to our company, lad. I am most glad to see that you did not share my brothers' fates. Unlike them, your head is quite firmly attached."

"Thanks to King Edward." Randolph's voice was shaking,

but James swore it wasn't with fear. "He forgave me for following you. For acting the fool."

The King gave a bark of laughter. "I will give you that at Methven we were fools. We trusted English honor."

Randolph glowered at James as he lurched to his feet. The man's chest heaved. "Don't you speak of honor. You! My own uncle. Hiding. Sneaking. Stealing upon knights in the dark. Nothing more than a brigand. Honor? The last thing you have."

"Ah. I see."

"I'm ashamed that we are kin."

James would not have liked the smile that flickered over the King's face turned upon him, but Randolph just braced his legs apart and glared at his royal uncle even harder.

"So, nephew, you find honor in men who lock your own aunt in a cage and tortured to death captured knights. A pretty notion of honor. But I'll let you have it. Whilst you stay as my guest."

Randolph's face twisted in a sneer. "King Hob—"

"Silence!"

Randolph clamped his mouth shut.

"Despite what you've done, I'll take your parole on your honor to make no attempt to escape. Or you can stay in chains. It is your choice, nephew. In Sir Robert Boyd's charge you'll remain. Until you remember whom I am. And your duty to your sworn King."

Randolph tilted his chin up. "You'd chain me? Your own kin?"

"Your choice, Nephew."

Randolph's gaze darted from his uncle's face to James. James narrowed his eyes at the man. Given a choice, he'd hang him and be done with it. The King was betimes soft to his enemies. Randolph glanced at Boyd.

69

Boyd gave an evil grin. "Don't look to me, pup. You deserve a good kicking."

"My word then." The arrogant tilt of Randolph's head never faltered as he swept his gaze back to the King. "I'll not try to escape. Not even from you."

James twitched his hand. Under the King's eye, he couldn't kill the man as he deserved, but it would have felt a laudable thing to do so. Instead, he jerked his dirk free. He grabbed Randolph's arm and slashed the rope binding his wrists. Then he held up the blade. "I could still be persuaded to use this."

"Lad, my sister would be wroth if I let you kill him." The Bruce squeezed his shoulder. "Come along. There's a tun of good wine that the Comyn gifted us with."

Randolph made a noise in his throat James decided to ignore. Wat was already taking care of settling the men and their horses, so James nodded to Niall Campbell and a red-haired youth. Gilbert de Hay pointed to some logs around a large campfire where a haunch of meat was spitted, sizzling and dripping fat into the fire. The scent made his mouth water. "Where's Sir Edward?" James asked. Not that he minded the King's only surviving brother not being there to give him looks like dirks to the heart.

"On his way to Galloway with most of my chivalry. If he can bring it to heel, I'll let him have it."

Hay handed James a cup, and he tipped the tun to pour. Boyd held out a cup for a share. If Randolph wanted some, that wasn't James's problem. Dripping fat flared in the fire.

"What about Lorn then? We won't need them?"

The King sat in the center of one of the logs and pulled out his dirk. He sliced off a chunk of the venison and chewed it, grease running through his fingers. James sprawled on the ground on a padding of sweet-smelling pine needles and bracken. After he had finished chewing, the Bruce said, "How many archers did you bring from Ettrick?"

Boyd cut off a slice of the dripping meat and tossed it to James, who snagged it in the air.

"Fifty," he said before he stuffed it in his mouth. He muffled a moan as savory taste filled his mouth, and juices dripped down his throat. "I keep my force small, so we can move fast."

"Those will be enough. You've never seen the Pass of Brander?"

James shook his head.

"Oh, it's a pretty sight." Sir Niall Campbell laughed. "My own lands are not so far. I've climbed it many a time up from River Awe. I hope you have a good head for heights, Douglas. And those men of yours."

"That won't be the worst." The red-haired youth spoke up. James frowned at him.

Gilbert de Hay leaned forward and poured a cup of wine from the tun. "Ross's heir." He nodded toward the lad. "Hostage for his lord father's behaving."

Huh. The King bringing the Earl of Ross to heel as well was news indeed, though considering Ross's treachery in turning the King's wife and daughter over to English imprisonment, it must have been a hard thing to swallow. Yet the lad looked happy enough.

"What will be worse then?" James asked.

"Climbing when you can't see a hand's span ahead in the mist."

Campbell nodded. "He's right about the mists. They clear mid-morning this time of the year when the wind from the sea reaches the pass."

"The Pass of Brander is nothing but a trap that Iain Bacach MacDougall waits to spring." The Bruce leaned forward and hacked another chunk off the haunch. "I'll

71

march along the river into the trap with my men. What say you to that?"

James frowned up at the top of the dark mass in the distance. "How high is it?"

"Think those Ettrick bowmen of yours can scramble up a cliff?" Niall Campbell gave him a bland look. "I told the King he should let me take my Highlanders to do it. Most like you lot will fall off."

James grinned, sure Campbell was thinking of the day he'd grabbed James as he tumbled down Ben Lomond. "Wouldn't be the first time."

Campbell laughed.

"I'd rather you didn't," the Bruce said. "My scouts say that Iain Bacach has two thousand men holding it, and if you fall on top of them, my plans will go awry."

Thomas Randolph jerked a steaming piece of venison from Boyd's knifepoint held toward him and glowered sullenly at his royal uncle.

"How many do we have?" James asked. It was hard to tell the numbers in the dark.

"Two thousand with yours and Robbie's," Gilbert de Hay said around a mouthful of food. He licked his fingers clean. "And if we're to be in position before the mist clears on the morrow, I'd say we need some rest. We'll have to move well before daybreak."

James nodded. The night was short in the Scottish summer. He stood and flexed, hands on the small of his back. "I'll not mind some rest. But what about him?" He glared at his erstwhile prisoner.

"The pine needles make a soft pallet. As for my nephew... He is an *honorable* man. His word is good." The King rose. He looked at the young knight with an odd expression on his face. "And Robbie will make sure of it."

Randolph jumped to his feet and opened his mouth.

Niall Campbell grabbed his arm, a hand on his hilt. "I suggest you thank your uncle nicely. Because your aunt—my wife—shivers in an English cage whilst you were free as a robin on the wing. None here is like to defend you."

"Enough," the Bruce shouted. He took a deep breath. "I'll have what is left of my family stay alive."

James stretched his back again, twisting to stretch weary muscles. Let the King deal with Randolph. "Jesu God, Gilbert is right. I'm finding a nice padded spot to sleep before we go mountain climbing." He walked slowly into the murk, feet leaden with weariness. After he shed his surcoat and armor, he sank into the needle padding beneath a pine. Battle on the morrow, an ambush, and you never knew what might go awry.

Letting his head fall back against the rough bark of the tree, he stared up through the soaring cathedral of tree limbs into the inky sky. He couldn't let himself think about Alycie. It was too much. If she needed him... If the village were attacked while he was too far too come to her aid... He couldn't stand the thought.

He couldn't even think of another such loss. He wasn't sure he would survive it. Better a sword in the belly than losing her.

No. Tonight he must only think only of his duty to the King and the coming battle.

CHAPTER 12

*J*ames lurched awake, heart thudding as he grabbed his sword. Where were his men? He took a deep breath of the scent of pine needles that made his bed and remembered where he was. In the gray half-light of near dawn, thick mist wrapped the trees like winding sheets. He staggered to his feet. "Robbie," he called. "You awake?"

Boyd groaned nearby. "I could use a featherbed. With a nice soft lass in it."

"Didn't you find one whilst you were home?"

Boyd laughed, groaned, and laughed again. "Mayhap." There was some rustling in the darkness. "Randolph. Don't think you're staying abed."

"I'm awake, man," Randolph groused.

James flapped his way into his hauberk. He searched the ground around his feet for his surcoat, donned that, and buckled his sword belt. "I don't think I'm looking forward to the King's plan." He grinned to himself. "Or not the climbing in the murk part anyway."

"James. Boyd," Gilbert de Hay called. "Time for a council."

The torches formed a halo of light where Maol Choluim, the Earl of Lennox, his elegant head thrown back with a scowl, faced the King. "The risk is too great, Your Grace. They could tear us apart."

"Ridding the kingdom of the enemy is worth the risk. I can't fight the English with a Scottish sword at my back, Maol." He motioned to James to join them.

The earl nodded to him, glumly. "I'll see that my men are ready to march then."

Niall Campbell appeared through a curtain of mist as Boyd strode out from the trees, Randolph at his heels. "My men are at the mouth of the pass," Campbell said.

"You'd best have your sergeant join us, Jamie," the Bruce said. He started into the foggy gray of dawn. "Robbie, you'll lead your men along the river bank with the rest of us."

James whistled the scream of a falcon.

Wat shouted, "You want me, my lord?" He trotted through the fog to James's side and blinked at the King, giving a startled bob of a bow.

"Are the men roused and ready?"

"Aye."

"Then come with me to look where we're leading them." He walked behind the King down a narrow, stony path. Pale shimmers of dawn fanned out to the east turning the mist ghostly. The western sky was still black, sprinkled with stars. Through breaks in the mist, dark, jagged peaks rose high and wild. The King stopped next to the river, a short way down from the path. Strands of white drifted, writhing, from its foamy water as it rushed by.

The Pass of Brander yawned before them, stretching into blank darkness.

James raised his gaze to the track to the summit, up and

up, to stones and trees and a looming mass of a mountain shrouded black under the damp pall. James strained to see the through the murk. He tightened his sword belt to cover a shiver.

"Our scouts place the MacDougall's caterans halfway through the pass, where the river bends. I'll lead our men into the pass alongside the river once the sun is full above the horizon."

James chewed his lip. They'd fought MacDougall's Highland warriors at the Battle of Dail Righ, where they had all nearly died. Attacking them with so small a force was no light matter. "I don't have enough archers to do that many of them much harm."

"No. It will come down to hand-to-hand. But archers can break their attack first. Then we have them in a pincer."

James bit his lip as he leaned his head back, still searching for the summit. "Wat, bring up our men. It will not get better for waiting."

Wat waved an arm over his head and shouted. "It's time! Move you."

Gelleys and Hew led his men toward the track, steep and narrow, that wended its way upward. There were near two hundred men: some fifty-odd archers in the green of foresters with Ettrick bows on their backs and the rest foot in motley armor with swords and axes on their belts, shields strapped to their backs.

"You're our eyes in this soup," James said. "Gelleys ahead; Philp to the right flank. Hew to the left. A single rockfall could give us away, so silent as you go. Anything moves more than a mouse, give a falcon's cry." He thrust his chin toward the mountainous way they would take. "They say Iain Bacach's men lie in wait halfway through the pass. So those, you'll watch for. Two calls when you spot them." He slapped

Gelleys's shoulder and watched as the men trotted ahead and were swallowed up into white nothingness. Then with a wave of his hand, he followed. Wat walked beside him.

Behind them, there was a moment of uneasy murmurs, and the men came after them. The bowmen bunched in the center. Andro and Richert walked together as they'd been lads together in Peebles. Fergus walked a bit away from the others. Even his men feared Fergus, who always seemed a bit crazed in battle, his eyes wild with fury.

As they ascended a twisting path between giant outcrops, mist wrapped them like a blanket. When James brushed a clump of bracken, a raven flapped away, cawing angrily. He paused and gulped in a breath, listened. Silence. Mist deadened the air like the grave. James let out a breath he'd not known he was holding and walked softly on.

James watched each place that he set a foot, stepping over scree that would slide underfoot and hollows to stumble over. The climb took two hours through air, so still they seemed in a ghostly white world apart.

Beside him, Wat was panting softly when they reached what James thought must be the summit. A breath of air brushed his cheek. He swiveled his head. In spots the mist wavered. Soon they'd be as exposed as a priest at the altar. Where were the hell-spawn MacDougalls?

He held up a hand. "Hold here," he whispered.

Wat passed the word back to Richert, and it went from man to man.

James eased his way to the edge of the cliff and knelt on one knee, peering down. The wind brushed his face, and the fog split and writhed. He dropped onto his belly. Through tatters of white, all he saw was gray rocks, brown bracken poking up between them. A falcon shrieked and then again. He jerked over onto his side when at a touch on his arm.

77

Hew knelt beside him and whispered, "Just ahead, my lord. Gelleys sent me back. He's keeping watch."

"How far down are they?"

The man wrinkled up his ruddy face as he thought about it. "Less than a bow's shot. But not far from that far."

James huffed, far enough that it might be possible to lie in wait without being spied. Perhaps. He stood up, and a stone moved under his foot, not so near the edge that it went over. "Could you tell how many?"

"More than I could count in the mist. Lying quietly in wait, it seemed to me."

An echo of a shout from the depths of the pass repeated and died away. The King must have begun his march into the trap. A drape of mist broke away and floated off like a ship's sail.

"Come." James spun on his heel and walked as fast as he could, looking down at every step for scree on the bare rock. Around a crag, his men still awaited, bunched nervously.

Standing close to Wat's shoulder, James said, "Two lines in front of the archers, kneeling. Swords at the ready. Wat, form them up where Hew shows you. I'll bring the archers after they have their orders."

Wat nodded to Hew and motioned to the men to follow him. James watched as they silently filed past. "We've little time. The King is walking into the trap. You must keep him alive. The moment they begin their attack, fire. Every arrow must count. You understand me?" He looked from face to face, meeting each man's eyes. "Everything depends on you. The King's life. Everything."

He gave them a moment to absorb his words before he said, "A double line behind the foot. And quietly." He turned and padded carefully into ragged wisps of fog quickly blowing across the yawning chasm of the pass.

His foot knelt in two lines, sword gripped in their hands. Shields up. The archers scurried into place, spacing themselves so that the man behind would have space to aim. Sweat pooled under James's arms as a last long strand of mist sailed into the chasm. Brown bracken stuck up between rocks. Patches of heather clung to the steep empty slope. But halfway down teemed with men. Bare-shanked men, clad in homespun tunics beneath piebald cowhide coats but a few in mail hauberks, all in helmets and rawhide brogans. Men ready for battle. Hooked Lochaber axes to bring down horses. Claymores. Round highland shields. No. Not quite teemed, for they were still as a stalking cat, ready to spring.

The bowmen braced their bows to string and eased arrows free for firing. One of his men strangled a cough. James stood there amidst scraggly patches of heather that struggled through the rocky terrain, straining his eyes down the fair pass for the glint of sunlight on steel. Above a pair of gulls wheeled and squalled, lost from the sea. Long minutes he chewed his lip, barely breathing. Should the MacDougalls spot them before time...

Beside the undulating blue river far below, a glittering snake of men appeared around the far bend. Points of sun shone on helms and hilts. They couldn't go more than two abreast in so narrow a space. More and more came into view, too far to make out detail. A gold banner fluttered in the rising wind. A blue and white Saltire flew beside it. Ten minutes and the King would be below. Less... Battle was nothing. But the King...

A gull screeched overhead.

James wiped the sweat from his palm on the front of his surcoat. He drew his sword with a whisper against the leather scabbard. He gripped the hilt hard, heart pounding in time to a war drum only he could hear.

One of the MacDougalls leapt to his feet. "Thoir lonnseagh agaibh!" the man bellowed. A long wail of a horn sounded, echoing from the rocky sides of the pass, followed by wild shouting from thousands of throats. Rocks smashed down, bounced, and crashed toward the army below. Three men shoved at a boulder the size of a horse. It thundered down the mountainside.

Beside the shimmering river, the King's horse reared. A wall of men turned their horses in a pantomime of war. The stone landed with a tearing crash amidst of the horsemen.

"Fire!" James shouted. The bows thudded. *Twap. Twap. Twap.*

"Lonnseagh!"

The Highlanders ran, bounding down the side of the mountain, screaming their war cries. Below the King's banner, the line of wheeled, horses reared, a thin shrill of a trumpet cut through the battle's chaos.

Twap, Twap sang the bows. Screams mixed with the cheers. A dozen bodies tumbled forward and then slid down the braeside. A bearded man knelt, arrow in his back, screaming. Another boulder tumbled beside them.

James heard anguished screams. A trumpet blasted. On their hocks, the horses labored to scale the steep slope.

"Fire, damn you!" he shouted. "Over our heads! A Douglas!" He ran. His sword's song was sweet as he swung.

His men shouted only a step behind him. "Douglas! Douglas!"

Arrows sailed over their heads, hissing death. The MacDougalls spun to meet them. Men hacked at them with long axes and broad-bladed swords. The battle shrank to the man in front of him. Red hair flying, a cateran swung his hooked axe. James ducked under, swung, and the man went down in a fountain of blood. Then another. Men fled down the braeside or stood and died. "Douglas!" he shouted as he killed. "King Robert and Scotland!" *Let them stop us now.*

A swordsman came, screaming a war cry. James lopped his arm off at the elbow. James ran on. A cateran raised a rock over his head and heaved it. James barked a laugh as he dodged. He chopped into the man's belly. He ran past the King, standing in his stirrups and hacking in wide right and left swaths at a mob of shouting Highlanders, Robbie Boyd and Earl Maol Choluim beside him. It was a chaos of rearing horses and desperately fighting men afoot. A cateran drove a Lochaber axe into the chest of a man-at-arms' horse. The screaming animal crashed to the ground, trapping the man's leg underneath it. James swung at the cateran's neck as he ran by.

The MacDougalls broke and scrambled, plunging down the braeside before them. A few tossed aside axes to run faster.

"After them," James bellowed. The mouth of the defile opened before them. A MacDougall dashed up and lunged at him. James caught the blow with his blade. Their blades clashed again. James knocked the man's sword aside and buried his blade in the man's chest.

As he jerked it free, he caught sight of a long, slender bridge over the river. On the far side of the shining, rippling river, a MacDougall lifted an axe over his head, red hair gleaming in the sunlight. He brought it down on a wooden piling. The wooden span shuddered. A trickle of MacDougall caterans pounded onto the bridge.

"The bridge! Seize it." He bolted toward the narrow span. Sweat dripped, stinging, into his eyes. Fergus ran beside him, hacking at every MacDougall they came to.

James reached the foot of the bridge; his steps rang hollow on the planks. A cateran, bare-headed, bald as an egg but with arms that rippled with muscle, spun and swung at him. He blocked the powerful blow. The bridge shuddered under his feet. "Fergus!" James called as he swung a stroke. The cateran brushed it aside. They hacked at each other, raining desperate blows. Fergus's dirk sank into the man's side. The man twisted and tried a hopeless thrust. James slashed at his throat. The blood gushed as he fell. James leapt over his body. "Hold this side. I'll take the other," he said over his shoulder, not bothering to look.

He raised his sword as he dashed over the rocking bridge, footfalls sounding like drum beats. A man ran at him, screaming. James slammed the flat of his sword into his head and tipped him over the railing into the river. Ahead, a short, smash-faced man paused, axe raised above his head, then he lowered it, tossed it aside, and fled.

James thrust the point of his sword into the ground and leaned on it, panting. He pulled off his helm and dropped it at his feet. Pushing his fingers through his dripping wet hair, he took a deep breath. The glittering waters of Loch Etive spread before him, and on the shore, a thin stream of men ran, fleeing. The river air was moist and cool as he sucked it into his lungs. He looked up the brown twisting track that led to the castle high atop the promontory.

But on the other side of the bridge, men were still screaming. MacDougalls hacked and slashed at his bunched company, blocking the foot of the bridge in wild, bloody hand-to-hand fighting.

He strode toward the ragged remnants of the battle. "Richert. Fergus. Hew." James pointed to the far end of the bridge for them to guard. They peeled off from the melee and trotted past him. Blood trickled down Fergus's neck. Somewhere he had lost his helm and one of his ears.

The King galloped up, Robert Boyd, Niall Campbell, and the earl still beside him, tailed by hundreds of their men. "Yield!" the King shouted.

One of the MacDougalls ran at the Bruce, grimly silent, Lochaber axe flashing. Earl Maol jerked at his horse, it reared, lashing with hooves and the man's head shattered in a splatter of gore. The MacDougall's resistance shattered with it.

The King met James's gaze. He nodded. They held the Pass. Now for Castle Dunstaffnage.

CHAPTER 13

Within the bailey, the yard was in an uproar. Barrels of ale were being carried out. A whole steer roasted over a massive makeshift firepit whilst a lad turned a crank. Fat spattered down, filling the air with the scent of meat. Men shouted and laughed. Boards were being laid across sawhorses to make a long table against the gray stone outer wall. A young gilly clattered down the steps of the keep, a platter piled with bread clasped in his arms. A lone sentry stood atop the battlement, cloak pushed back and head bare in the heat of the late summer day.

Wat was in the middle of it, shouting commands beside one of the King's sergeants, a burly man, red-faced under his beard. "Sir Robert Boyd was looking for you, my lord."

"I'll find him shortly." James smoothed his blue tunic and hose, the only one in the castle's stores that would fit his height though tight over his broad shoulders, feeling a bit foolish in borrowed finery. Forbye, his hip seemed light without his sword or dirk. He'd left them in the tower room he'd claimed along with Gilbert de Hay, Robbie Boyd, and the young Ross. Space was scant in the castle with their whole army crammed into it. "Have they sent out enough for the men?"

"One of the cooks said they'd send two sheep roasted whole out from the kitchen hearth," Wat said over the other sergeant's shouts to hurry with assembling the table.

James leaned close to speak privily to Wat, "Change the guards on the hour, so they all have some of the feast. But make sure that they are sober on watch." The old MacDougall had surrendered, but that didn't mean he could be trusted.

"I'll see to the guards. Don't fash yourself."

"Who comes?" the sentry shouted.

The reply sounded angry and arrogant, though James couldn't make out the words, and the sentry called permission to enter. Half-a-dozen men tromped through the louring gateway into the bailey, burly men wearing polished helmets, saffron tunics tightened with gemmed belts, bracelets of engraved gold on their massive arms and an elaborate pin held a plaid over each man's left shoulder. Instead of beards, their faces sported massive mustaches that drooped to their chins.

The man in the lead was younger and thinner than the rest, though the tallest of them. His head was bare of a helmet exposing his golden-red hair, but his armor was polished bright enough to rival the sun. Angus Og MacDonald. Hawk-nosed and ruddy complexioned from spending most of his life on his clan's galleys that ruled much of the western sea. He grinned when he saw James. "Douglas. I heard you gave Iain Bacach's men a right doing." He held out his sword-calloused hand that James clasped in a double grip.

"My men did indeed, Angus. But did you lay hold of the sleekit weasel? I saw those sea-wolves of you on the loch."

Angus Og scowled, thin nostrils flaring. "He slipped past us in the night." He spit on the ground. Iain Bacach

MacDougall had beheaded one of Angus's cousins on the beach after the disastrous battle at Strathfillan when the King's brothers were captured. "We chased him as far as we could, but he reached the English fleet before we could bring him to bay."

Ranald MacRuarie, in finery even brighter than Angus's, growled what sounded much like a curse.

"Too bad." James ran a thumb across his mustache. "But that means he won't have a chance to make his peace with the King."

Angus's eyes gleamed, and he threw back his head to laugh. James grinned and then laughed and threw an arm around Angus Og's shoulder. "I'd rather meet the man on the battlefield than in court, my friend. As would you. Let's go watch his father crawl."

James pushed Angus toward the narrow door of the keep, and they sauntered into the Great Hall of Dunstaffnage Castle. The hall was immense with a high-timbered ceiling. A minstrel was plucking a harp in the gallery, barely heard above the male laughter as the crowd eddied and flowed. Gilli Colium MacLean was roaring at some jape from burly Malcolm MacGregor whilst the MacPhersons, and the Shaws kept their distance. The air was heavy with the smell of sweating men, of roast pig and fruits stewed with spices, of wine and of wood-smoke. Above the raised platform at the head of the huge room hung the gold of the royal banner with its rampant lion. Sir Edward de Bruce's red saltire, his own blue starred standard, Boyd's pennant scattered with red shields and a dozen others draped the walls.

Gilbert de Hay tugged at his embroidered green tunic as though he'd forgotten what it was like not to be in armor. Hay watched as two pikemen took their places behind the lord's chair that would serve the King. Below, long tables were loaded with silver cups engraved with Lorn's crest, silver flagons of wine, and pewter trenchers.

The Earl of Lennox and Sir Niall Campbell, Lord of Awe, were laughing. Both had managed to find clothes in the castle's stores fit for a feast. In fact, the whole room was filled with men in a festive mood in clean clothing and at peace, even if only for one night.

Lennox and Campbell nodded to them when they saw Angus Og MacDonald and strolled to greet him.

"I don't see Robbie about," James said.

Campbell shrugged. "Saw him a bit ago. He's making sure old Alexander Lorn does his role properly."

"Think the old man can remember it long enough?"

"He's not so doddering as all that. A pity we didn't catch that son of his, but the King will be right pleased with this night's work anyway, I think." Campbell bared his teeth in a grin and stepped aside to make room for young Ross to join them, but the lad didn't seem eager to say much in their company, so Campbell went on. "As am I. Curst MacDougall's have borne hard on my people whilst I've been with the King."

"Old Lorn on his knees will please us all well enough." James plucked up a flagon and filled cups for the four of them. He frowned for a moment, thinking of what would please him to do with the men who'd sent Thomas, injured and bound, to foul execution.

Angus Og sniffed suspiciously at his wine cup. "The MacDougall dogs are too stingy to have good wine in their cellar."

"I've had worse the last year, Angus. And none at all ofttimes enough." James drank deeply. "It's not so bad."

William de Irwin, slender and dark, the King's armor-bearer, stepped out of the narrow doorway that led to the stairs and shouted, "Be upstanding for Lord Robert de Bruce, King of the Scots."

It was rare enough to have occasion for ceremony, and James gave a shout, laughing as he cheered. The room was in an uproar as the Bruce stepped past through the doorway, still in armor but topped with a gold surcoat worked with an embroidered lion, a simple gold coronet on his bare head. He grinned as he strolled through the immense hall toward the table on the dais. When he stepped onto the dais, he turned and motioned for quiet.

"Your Grace," Robert Boyd said from the same doorway, "Alexander MacDougall, erstwhile Lord of Lorn, begs permission to approach."

James saw that the King took a deep breath before he answered. "So be it."

Alexander MacDougall's head shook, the wattles on his neck swinging as he walked, gaze fixed on his feet, toward the King. He was dressed in dark velvet tunic and hose, but his feet and white-haired head were bare as was only right for a penitent. Lorn stopped at the foot of the dais and carefully lowered himself to first one knee and then the second. "I come to beg Your Grace to accept me and my people into your peace," he said, voice wavering. "I offer my fealty."

"Offer?" The tendons on the King's neck stood out as though he ground his teeth, but his voice was level and calm. "You offer what is mine by right, Alexander MacDougall."

Lorn looked up, gaping. "Your Grace, I surrendered my castle on your word that you would extend mercy."

"Mercy such as you did not show my brothers, sirrah, but my word I keep. I accept your homage as it is my due. You and your lady wife will be offered no harm. I will hold your lands of Argyll in safety until I receive the same homage from your son and heir. Until such time, Sir Niall Campbell will give you escort to his own good castle where you'll be kept in all dignity."

King Robert extended his hands and accepted MacDougall's within them as the man hurriedly muttered his oath. From the sour look on the King's face, he was sorely tempted to wipe his hands as Alexander MacDougall climbed creakily to his feet.

The King turned his head and opened his mouth to say something when Thomas Randolph stepped out of the crush. The two men looked at each other for a long moment, so alike Randolph could have been the King's younger self, tall, golden. But now the King's face was sun-darkened, and lines radiated out from his eyes. The King closed his mouth and tilted an eyebrow as Randolph gracefully dropped to one knee.

The chatter stopped, and the only sound was the thump of a hound's tail under a table.

"Will you forgive me my ill words, Uncle?" Yet Randolph begged with an arrogant tilt to his chin.

"Ill words." The Bruce nodded as though he were thinking of something else, then lowered his gaze to the man kneeling at his feet. "Ill-thought out, certainly. And have you other words for me now, nephew? I will hear them."

Color crept into Randolph's face. "I do, sire. I wronged you. Will you accept me into your peace? Accept my fealty? I swear by my honor, I'll serve you well."

The room held its breath as the King looked thoughtfully at his nephew. At last, he nodded.

"Then, my forgiveness you have and my peace." He held out his hands.

Randolph placed his hands within those of his royal uncle. "I acknowledge you, Lord Robert, by the grace of God, King of the Scots, and I will henceforth and always be a faithful vassal to you, and I will defend you, Your Grace, against all malefactors and invaders. Before all God and the Saints, I swear it."

"I, Robert, do hereby receive your homage and promise that I will be a good and faithful lord."

There was applause and laughter. James twitched a raised eyebrow at Niall Campbell, who shrugged. The King had lost too much. James could hardly begrudge him offering peace to the few of his family still alive, but how true was the oath Randolph had just taken? James wondered.

The King motioned to James to join them. "I'll have peace between the two of you as well," he said.

"Of course, sire." Peace did not have to mean trust. He'd not be in a hurry to trust Randolph whatever the King said.

Randolph offered his hand. "I still owe Sir James a blow or two. Perhaps one day on a jousting field."

"Mayhap, someday. For now, Jamie, Angus Og's ships will speed you to Galloway. My brother has orders to capture Rutherglen Castle, and you're to aid him before you return to hold Ettrick Forest."

CHAPTER 14

Three days later, James's horse slid down the rocky bank to the River Clyde, his three hundred men in a triple column behind him. Gulls wheeled, squalling overhead. Only a mile inland from where Angus Og had landed them, the wind still carried a scent of distant burning, and a thin snake of dark smoke crawled into the winter clouds. They splashed across the shallow ford rimed with ice and up the other side into the wide valley.

James sharpened his gaze at a shout as one of his forward scouts cantered down the icy braeside, waving an arm over his head. "Armored men riding this way," the man yelled. "Flying the Bruce banner."

James reined in his snorting and prancing horse. His men spread out behind him, dismounting to water their horses and squatting to scoop up icy water. Most had lost their green tinge from being tossed in Angus's galleys.

The wind caught James's fur cloak and whipped it around. His horse snorted and sidled until he reined it in with one hand and caught the edge of his blowing cloak with the other. "Gilles, take two men and be sure that is Sir

Edward." It had been a hard school that taught him to take no chances. James waited, mounted, frowning until Gilles galloped back ahead of the chivalry of knights riding under the flowing red and gold Bruce banner.

"Well met," James called, and his words were on puffs of white. He spurred his horse to a trot to meet the King's brother.

Edward de Bruce, clad in a handsome suit of mail under a surcoat of red and gold, a plumed helmet on his head, rode at the head of thirty knights in polished armor riding strong chargers. James swung from his horse and strode through the brown bracken. "Sir Edward." He bowed, making it his most courteous and keeping his expression bland in the face of Edward de Bruce's scowl.

Edward de Bruce dismounted and stood, arms crossed over his chest. "I can use your men for the siege, but do not mistake who is in command. Because my brother favors you, don't make any error on that."

"Of a certainty. I've no quarrel with your command." No point in sighing. Edward's dislike was not new. He thrust his chin toward the rising smoke in the distance. "Was there much resistance?"

Sir Edward snorted. "Ingram de Umfraville and Aymer Saint John tried to hold at the ford of the Dee. Now they're shaking and quivering inside Buittle where I can't get at them. Left me to collect taxes in cattle and grain." He bared his teeth in a grin. "And burn anyplace that resisted."

James rubbed his chin thoughtfully. "Then our backs should be secure for a siege."

"We'll move on Rutherglen today. If we take it by spring, we'll be lucky." Sir Edward grimaced. "It will make a grim winter, but my brother commands, so we must."

James nodded. The King's brother might be in command, but if he could think of a way to take the mighty castle of

Rutherglen without a winter-long siege, he would certainly take it. He swallowed a laugh because he didn't intend to say any such thing to Sir Edward. Instead, he nodded. "Your greater number of men follow not far behind, I suppose."

"An hour behind on their slower mounts."

"The English will have ample warning from the burning." James swung into the saddle, and Sir Edward did the same. "Wat, bring the men in the van behind Sir Edward's men," James called out. Amidst the creak of leather and clatter of armor, James's men mounted.

So, they rode on. James kept his gaze ahead, occasionally glancing at his morose commander from the corner of his eye. He'd try his best to be civil to the man for the King's sake. "Do you know if they can bring supplies in from the sea?"

"It backs to a high cliff. No way up unless you've wings."

James nodded. He couldn't think of anything else to say. They'd never gotten on, but he had no desire for the man to be an enemy. He'd speak softly and keep his own counsel.

Scouts rode back with word that the town of Rutherglen near the castle was empty of people. They clattered through the empty streets past cots with doors agape. A single chicken clucked and pecked at winter brown heather beneath open shutters. James ordered scouts to circle the town to be sure no armed men lurked.

A rutted road led up the hill to Rutherglen. Its great stone wall rose twenty feet high against the westering sun that made the low clouds glow red and gold behind it. James dismounted and stood, frowning upwards. "I've heard its walls are as thick as a man is tall."

Sir Edward grunted. "This is the only road up the castle mount. That will make a siege easy to hold."

"I'll keep my scouts out. Make sure they don't steal a march on us from Buittle to relieve it."

Sir Edward spun on his heel. "This will make a good enough base camp. Convenient." He laughed. "Have your men hold the road out of bow shot."

No surprise to be given the dirty work, but he bowed and motioned to Wat. "I'll see if I can find a building or two large enough for our men." He lowered his voice although Edward de Bruce had already walked away. "Before most of his men arrive, we'll settle our own. And send enough to hold the road well out of bow range. Fifty should be enough."

"A siege so near to Glasgow. It's risky," Wat said, glancing around to be sure they weren't overheard.

"The King wants it taken, so we take it. But see if anyone has a better idea than sitting here whilst we starve them out. Give out the word, I'll reward any good plan. After dark, we'll take a ride. See if we can think of something a bit more..."

Wat grinned. "More like what the Black Douglas would do?"

A whole winter in Edward de Bruce's company would have him the Black Douglas indeed. Drive him to murder most like. And wouldn't that please the King? James headed toward a long, low stone building. He pushed open the door and breathed in the scent of the malt he expected it should hold. They must have emptied it as they fled, but the rich scent was pleasant. And it was large enough for most of his men when they weren't holding the siege. Forbye, it was made to be easily heated. Holy Jesu, that would be welcome. Already the air smelled of snow.

He stuck his head out the door. "Richert, find some tables and stools. Wat, get the men in here once the horses are stabled. Fergus, we need wood for the fire."

Soon his men were filing in, stomping their feet from the cold, clapping and rubbing their hands. They threw blankets into piles in the corners and cursed the cold. Richert and

Hew carried in a table, and a couple of stools whilst Fergus lumbered in with his arms piled his with logs for a fire. "I looked, and they didn't leave a scrap of food anywhere," Hew grumbled.

James paused his pacing. "Sir Edward's men are driving cattle with them that they've levied. They've grain, too. For tonight we'll make do with the oats in our bags for bannocks."

When Wat opened the door, the wind caught it out of his hand. It crashed against the wall. "It's ugly out there." He shoved the door closed.

"Don't settle yourself yet, Wat. I want to take a good look at our task." James nodded toward the door. "We'll ride as far around the castle as can be. Perhaps it will spark some idea in this slow pate of mine."

Wat snorted but followed him around the long building to a couple of storage sheds they'd taken for stables. The horses danced a bit at being re-saddled, but soon they rode through the early dark, the wind burning their cheeks. The moon made a smear of light in the heavy clouds.

Their horses' hooves thudded against the frozen ground of the road. Near the top of the steep climb, his men piled logs into a blockade. James turned off the road and at a slow walk around the dark, hulking bulk of the castle, skirting bog pits and clumps of bracken. "We'll need a patrol," he said to Wat as they made their careful way. Near the top of the castle mount, he dismounted and knelt to peer down.

"That's a sharp slope for a charge," Wat said. He sniffled and wiped his running nose on the back of his hand.

"It's steep all right," James agreed, squinting down into darkness. "There might be a path though." Scree shifted under his feet and bounced down the side of the mount, splashing into bog pots on its way down. He slithered a few feet down on a patch of ice.

"Jesu God! Careful!" Wat's hard fist grabbed his shoulder and dragged him back.

James sprawled on his arse. "Curse this weather for a siege." He knocked Wat's hand away. "I have to send the patrols out. We can't afford to be flanked."

Wat peered cautiously down.

"How many?"

"Ten should be enough." James clicked his tongue against his teeth as he did the math. "We'll be hard-pressed. In this weather, we should switch them... Do you think twice a night will be enough?"

"Better three times. Twice during the day unless the weather worsens."

James grunted in agreement as he stood and broadened his stance on the icy ground.

"And keep fifty men on the road?" Wat asked.

"No, twenty-five. Sir Edward has enough so he can make up the lack." Hell mend the man. "And scouts to our rear, as well. Ten should do. I want them out at all times." James shook his head. Edward should take some of the load, but James wouldn't count on him except in a battle. The man had no patience except for a sword in his hand. "We have to find a better way than a winter-long siege. But we're stuck for now." He grabbed his reins and mounted. "Back to camp then."

CHAPTER 15

*B*y the next day, the ground was covered with a thin crust of snow. Flurries blew in the sharp wind, and men came in went with reddened, wind-chapped faces and cold-numbed hands and feet. Every few hours, James slid and skated his way to his horse and rode to the blockade to glower at the castle. Pennants that snapped in the wind and a flicker of movement through the crenels of the embattled parapet were the only signs of life in the great fortress.

The hoofbeats of a heavy mount on the road behind him jerked James from his reverie.

"What think you?" Edward de Bruce said, close wrapped in a heavy cloak. "They could try to break through."

"They might. I'm surprised that they haven't even made an attempt. It must be they're short on men for a fight."

"I hate this. Sitting on my arse. Waiting." Edward's horse shook its mane and snorted as though in agreement.

James laughed. "Not a pleasure in this cold. At least we could have a summer siege instead of freezing."

"We could try scaling ladders." The man leaned forward,

squinting at the castle. "How many do you think it would take?"

James rubbed a hand over his beard. "Let's..." He caught himself. Best to be diplomatic. "What would you say to a sally? I'd like an idea of how many archers they have. Longbows? Crossbows? Hard to judge."

Edward nodded. "A feint to test their strength. Not a bad idea, Douglas. Give me half your men to join mine. That will make it look good."

For once, he was in agreement with Edward de Bruce, a miracle of itself. He twitched a smile. "Tomorrow?" At a grunt of approval, James said, "We'll need at least fifty ladders. I'll set some of my men to cutting wood," and turned his horse's head for camp. It would be hard on his men; they'd had little rest. But it would help make a better plan if they knew what they were up against inside the walls of the castle.

Hammering came from behind the building where his men ripped down a cowshed for the wood. They carried in long, thin logs cleared of their limbs. One of the men bent over a board, the saw grating as he cut rungs. A quarter of a steer roasted over a roaring fire in the huge hearth that normally heated the barley for turning it into malt. James sat, back propped against the wall, on a stool, legs stretched out. Hammering blows nearly covered the comforting *whish, whish* of his oilstone as he sharpened his sword.

Wat pulled up a stool. "You think an attack is really wise, my lord?" He pulled out his dirk tested the point on his thumb before he also began to sharpen the weapon.

James shrugged. "No, but we must know what we're up against. Make sure the men know that as soon as they counter-attack, we're retiring. In good order, mind." He twitched what he intended to be a smile but realized was more of a grimace. "Even Sir Edward, hot-head that he is, doesn't think we'll make it to the walls."

"We might could at night—in the dark."

"Aye," James said. "I've thought of that. Do we have enough black and gray cloaks? That would make the men hard to see until we were at the walls."

Wat paused the swish of the oilstone. "No. But in the snow... could they see the men anyway?"

James let out a long sigh. "There is no way we could carry the ladders to walls, even in the snow and not be spotted by lookouts." He leaned his head back against the wall. "We'll have to think of something. What we did at Douglas wouldn't work here. There's no way we'll tempt them to open the gate."

Philp sidled up and hunkered between the two men. "I heard something that..." He shook his head. "I didn't think it made sense, but you might want to talk to him. One of Sir Edward's men had an idea for a different sort of ladder. The man said it was ladders could be carried secret like, but Sir Edward called him a fool and sent him away with a kick to the arse. Probably right, but mayhap it wouldn't hurt to hear the man out."

"It never hurts to listen." James winked. "If it's a terrible idea, I'll not have your hide for it. Can you find him?"

"May take me a mite of time, but I'll find him. His name is Syme the Ironsmith."

"Good man. Find him for me. The worst that happens, I waste a little time talking to him."

After Philp went out looking for his man, James checked the ladders, thirty feet long, twenty of them. It wasn't likely they'd be used, but he could be wrong. If they made it to the walls, he'd not turn down the chance. At least, come morning light they'd find out the English strength.

But morning brought little light, only dark heavy clouds

99

blown before a sharp wind. He left half his men at the blockade and riding patrols whilst he led the rest against the sea wind laced with sleet that whipped and stung his face. No horns to be blown, he'd agreed with Edward de Bruce. Frozen bracken snapped under hundreds of feet. Men grunted and cursed as they slipped on the icy, sleety ground. The Douglas pennant snapped in the wind.

Moaning notes of a horn came from inside the castle. Voices shouted garbled commands carried by the wind.

An arrow thudded in front of James; he lifted his shield. Another thudded and bounced off it. "Wat, how many do they have on the walls?" He stepped forward a pace, squinting in the dim light. Cursing, he used a hand to shield his eyes from the blowing sleet. One of his men screamed. Another arrow whistled past James's head as he flinched. On the parapet, through nearly every crenel, threatened a long-bow, dozens of them. Another flight of arrows clattered around them. He silently thanked Saint Bride for the stiff wind spoiling their aim. "Blow retiral!" James shouted. The horn winded twice. "Retire! Leave the ladders."

The wooden ladders clattered as they were thrown down. James spun and leapt over one, shoving one of his men ahead of him with a hand to the middle of his back. His men slipped and slithered on the icy ground. Hew, arrow buried in his shoulder, was being half carried by Fergus. Another lay face down on the white-sheeted ground. James knelt. Arrows rattled around him. He rolled the man over. An arrow buried deep in the chest, the man coughed up a spume of blood and lay still. Wat grabbed James's arm and jerked him to his feet. They tore down the slope to catch up to the others, James sliding down the braeside every second and third step. Behind them, another horn blew within the castle.

James stopped and looked back. Out of bow range, he glared at the dark walls wrapped in the blowing white of the storm. "That answers any doubt. We can't take it with an assault."

Sir Edward's men were trotting past, and the man swung from his horse, his face knotted into a scowl. "As we feared."

"Did you lose any men?"

"A couple. Not enough to be a problem."

"After dark I'll see the bodies are retrieved," James said.

Edward arched an eyebrow. "What good when they're dead?"

"I don't leave my men to English *mercy*," James spit out before he could rein in his anger and frustration. "Dead or alive."

Edward paused his mouth tight. "You hate the English no more than I, Douglas. It was my brothers they foully murdered. Tortured to death." His jaw worked. "Three brothers dead, tortured and beheaded. A sister caged no better than an animal."

James's anger flowed out like a tide. "I know." He looked closely at Edward de Bruce, so like his brother in looks, broad-shouldered, blond hair, face weathered from years in the field. He was hot-headed, and James prayed he was never king, but Edward de Bruce was a fury in battle. "I meant no disrespect, my lord. They've done enough evil to go around. To all of us."

Edward gave him a hard look, grabbed up his reins, and stamped after his men toward camp. James scrubbed his face with his hands, trying to rub away his frustration. Somehow, they would take this castle. The problem was that he had no idea how.

He crunched through the thin crust of snow and ice toward the long building, thumping his hands together, fingers numb.

"Sir James," Philp called. Behind him stood a man of middle years, chest big as a keg of ale with streaks of gray in his bronze hair and a heavy bag slung over his thick shoulder. Philp thrust his head toward the man. "This is Syme that I told you about."

"Then bring him in, and we'll warm ourselves whilst we talk." James stomped to work some feeling back in his feet. He hit the door with the flat of his hand and strode inside. Richert squatted in a far corner as he adjusted a blanket. "Richert, how does Hew fair?"

"Arrowhead went all the way through his shoulder, my lord. Pulling it out wasn't too bad. If he doesn't get wound fever, he'll mend."

James nodded and went to hold his hands out to the fire that blazed up from the stone pit in the floor that served as a hearth. The door slammed as the two men followed him in. James looked over his shoulder, trying to ignore the prickle as the blood flowed back into his hands and feet. Curse a siege in such weather.

"Syme, is it?"

"Aye, my lord. A smith and..." Syme cleared his throat and dropped the bag on the floor with a loud metallic clatter. The man scratched the back of his neck, and he shifted from one foot to the other. "The thing is, my lord, these ladders we use. It just seems to me there doesn't be any way to sneak them to a castle wall."

James gave a bark of a laugh. "I'll not argue with you there."

"So, I was thinking on it and made a different sort, but Sir Edward... Well, he's a right proud knight, King's brother and all. Said he wasn't one for sneaking." Syme nudged the bag with his foot. "Philp here said you might want to take a look. I think it would work. If a man didn't mind sneaking." He knelt to pick up the bag and dumped a mess of ropes and boards and metal onto the floor. "Look, my lord." He pulled out a heavy, squared iron hook in each hand and stood, stretching out the mess.

Frowning, James shook on the rope where it went through wooden rungs a couple of feet apart and came to the third one down that had an iron fender across the back. He turned it. "This would...?" He blinked and grinned. "This would hold it off the wall whilst you climbed."

Syme held out one of the hooks. "See, I made a hole in each of the hooks. You could stick the point of a pike in, and a tall man could lift it high enough to hook over the wall. If he sneaked up, quiet-like."

James took the hook, heart thumping in his chest. "By the Holy Rude," he said softly. "Syme, how long would it take you to make more of these?"

The man beamed. "I'll make as many as pleases you. Hardly any work to make if I have the rope and a mite of iron."

James's men had gathered in a circle around them, muttering and peering over each other's shoulders.

"I'll see you have as much as you need. And a handsome reward to go with it." James was chuckling as he straightened out the rope ladder. "That no one ever thought of this before... By all the saints, what we can do with such a thing."

Wat squatted and straightened out the bottom portion. "We'll need a good amount of rope—forty feet for each ladder. Or fifty more like. And iron for the hooks. Wood for the rungs." He scratched his head. "Not sure where we'll find that much. It'll take doing."

Syme put in, "I saw a good pile of rope in the stables. And there's iron at the smithy they left there. Not like it takes very much."

"Wat, have someone search the town. Find every scrap of rope and iron in the place. Let's hope this miserable weather holds. We'll need it to cover a night attack. Tear down the rest of that cowshed for the wood."

"You going to tell Sir Edward what you're planning?" Wat asked.

James grimaced. "He's in command. I can't attack without his say so, but I don't know that he has to know what we're planning exactly." He nodded to himself. "I'll tell him that we'll make another feint at the walls by night and ask him to have his men ready in case we can open the gates."

Syme frowned at him. "He fought hard at the Dee. He's no craven, you know."

"Only a madman would question his valor." James grinned. "But I'm not the King's brother nor nearly too proud to sneak an attack."

The man examined his creation, nodding thoughtfully.

"So, get to work on what we need for these ladders--all of you. Syme, do you think you can have twenty ladders made in two days' time? Before the English in Buittle find their courage and decide to come to their aid."

CHAPTER 16

The second night, James leaned on the wall outwith the malting door looking at the scattering of stars in a clear winter sky and cursing. Clear weather held for three more days until clouds blew in late in the afternoon, so dark that it turned night an hour before the sun set. When James made his way to the house where Sir Edward crouched over a cup of wine with another knight, the King's brother grunted and shrugged when James told him that he was going to make a night attack on the castle. "If we make it over the walls and open the gates, we could use a company of your men."

"If." Edward snorted. "But I'll send a company to the barricade." He waved to his unarmored companion. "See to it."

"I'll wait till the English are snug inside, hiding from this snow. My men will be at the castle walls in three hours' time." James let the door bang closed behind him.

Flakes of snow, as big as oak leaves, tumbled in the wind as he squelched his way to the malting. "Four men to a ladder," he ordered as he stomped inside, unbuckling his sword belt. He tossed it onto the table. "It will be dirks and dirty work in the dark. No noise. Not a sound from the lot of you."

Richert spoke up. "The pikes are the hard part. We must have them for the ladders."

"No help for that. You men carrying those, try to put them down silently. Don't let them rattle against the walls." Twenty men with pikes to put the ladders in place, forty all together for the attack. Richert had the right of it that those made sneaking harder. James pulled his mail hauberk over his head. "No armor. No swords. Our weapons tonight are dirks and our ladders." He stuck his dirk, as long as his forearm, into his belt. Clattering and clanking and muttering of men shedding their armor filled the room. Plunging his hand into a bucket of ash next to the hearth, James pulled up a handful and smeared it over his face.

Syme folded a ladder into one of the rough bags and nudged the pile of bags beside the door with a foot. "My lord, a favor."

James twitched a smile. "I owe you at least one. What's that?"

"I'd like to be first up."

"No reason not. I'll be behind you." He looked his men over. There was always the worry he'd forgotten something. Something that would mean his men would die. He picked up his heavy cloak and pulled it around his shoulders. "We'll be exposed out there for a long while getting to the walls. Put on every stitch that you have. If your cloak is dark, then wear it."

Fergus shouldered one of the bags and took a pike from the other side of the door. "Too bad we can't climb with these."

James slapped the man's shoulder. "You're good enough

with your dirk for tonight's work." One last look. Either they
won, or they died--just another night of war. "Let's go."

James led an odd group of warriors through thick,
blowing snow up the rutted road to Rutherglen Castle. They
were unarmed except for their dirks stuck in their belts, in
wool tunics and trews and flapping cloaks, faces and hands
smeared with wood ash to make sure they didn't stand out in
the murk. They moved silently through the dark. One man
grunted when he stumbled into a hole. Bracken crunched as
James shoved his way past, but the noise blew away on the
whistle of the wind. James sucked in a breath as he slid down
the edge of the dry spike-lined moat. Someone grunted
softly. "Spread out," James whispered. They knew their part
now, to scramble up the far side of the moat. James squeezed
Syme's shoulder and then prodded him ahead. Wat was
panting on the other side as he tried to climb and handle the
sixteen-foot pike he carried.

Spread out the few feet between the edge of the moat and
the stone wall, James gave a low whistle, his signal to hoist
the ladders. Their task, to raise the hooks on the pike tips
and catch them on the edge of the parapet, they'd had no
chance to practice. He'd chosen the strongest of his men for
the job. Syme grunted as he hoisted the pike overhead. Wat
panted as he lifted. There was a faint clank of metal on stone.
The man sucked cursed under his breath and lifted the pike
higher. "Got it," he breathed out and jerked on one of the
rungs. James leaned back against the wall, closed his eyes,
and let his hammering heart slow. James pulled his dirk,
clasped it between his teeth, and signaled for Syme to go.

The ladder rocked as they climbed, clanking faintly
against the stone. James grabbed the merlon and hoisted
himself through the crenel, breathing a sigh of relief. If any
guards had seen the hooks, they'd cut the rope through and

send his men crashing down. But the snow and the cold had kept all the defenders inside.

James waved Wat to the other side without speaking. The man already had his orders. They split the party in two. The square six-story keep was surrounded by the high, thick curtain wall with the embattled parapet walk. The subsidiary buildings in the bailey yard, stables, and warehouses were coated with snow. Wat led half the men at a trot to the far gatehouse tower where half the sentries would be sheltered. James hurriedly led half the men down the stairs to approach from the near side tower. There must have been at least a hundred defenders in the castle, judging by what they'd seen three days before, but only a few would be on night duty.

A dog barked once and yelped. Then there was silence.

James pressed his ear to the tower door. A snore snorted on the other side. A voice raised softly in a night song--a cursing complaint. He threw open the door with a crash and dove for the nearest guard, head down on a table. With a hard hand, he grabbed over the guard's mouth and jerked back the head. A hard slice across the throat followed, and blood pooled on the table. James spun. The small, stark chamber was filled with unarmored men, and four more bodies sprawled on the blood-soaked floor.

There was clanging as something metal was thrown off the wall. "What is that thing? Where are the other guards?"

James stepped into the doorway. They'd missed a guard, and he'd found one of their ladders. Trying not to sound Scottish, James shouted, "Some fool thing the smith was trying out. I'll be right up. God damn, it was freezing up there."

"What kind of fool thing?" The man didn't sound overly worried.

He bound up the twisting stairs to the parapet. The guard strode toward him. "What the devil's going..."

James plunged his dirk deep into the man's throat. Blood gushed, warm and sticky, over his arms as he caught the body and lowered it. No help for it. By the time he ran back down the stairway, Wat and his twenty men were streaming out of the tower. Wat nodded his success.

Across the wide cobbled courtyard, the keep was dark, the door closed. James motioned Fergus to him. "Take three men and check the stables and outbuildings. If you must, silence anyone that you find." Opening the gates would be sure to rouse the castle. He couldn't afford to bring help. "Wat, once the fighting starts inside, raise the gate and sound the alarm," he said and ran.

He threw open the door. A dying fire flickered on the hearth, throwing flickering light over men wrapped in blankets on the floor. A man rolled to his knees, fumbling for a weapon that James kicked away. He slammed the flat of his sword on the man's head. "Fight and you're dead men," he yelled. His men rushed through the room, grabbing up weapons as they went. A dark figure threw a blanket back as he rose, swinging a sword, but he went down with a groan. James scooped up a sword from the floor.

Outside, the gate squealed metal upon stone as the grate was raised. A trumpet blew. "A Douglas!" Wat shouted. The lord's chamber would be higher. "With me," James called to half a dozen of his men and took the stairs two and three at a time. The door to a room flew open, and a man stumbled out, bare-arsed with a blade in his hand. Within the room, a woman whimpered. The man backed against the wall, raising his sword. James batted it aside and held his blade at the man's neck. "Best you yield," he said softly.

Half a dozen more men dashed down from an upper story. A woman above was screaming. One of the men ran full tilt into James's sword. The others threw their blades clattering on the stone floor. "Check the upper floors. I especially want the hell-spawn archers if you find any." He motioned the prisoners ahead of him and followed them down to the great hall.

Only three men had been killed there. The others sat, hands bound behind them, staring in terror at the Scots who had come seemingly out of nowhere. In a moment, Sir Edward threw the door open with a bang. He shook his head as he looked around the hall. Finally, he said, "Hell mend you, Douglas. You are good at sneaking."

James smiled. "It's a skill I have, Sir Edward."

The man snorted and strode past the prisoners to the lord's chair at the head of the hall. "Someone throw wood on the fire. It's hellish cold out there."

CHAPTER 17

SPRING 1309

ames paced, glowering over the waste of the Moor of Rannoch before smacking his fist into his palm. His men glanced his way but kept their distance. It had been a two-day wait, and he could delay no longer than daybreak on the morrow to leave for Saint Andrews. Even with his tail of only two score men, he'd been hard-pressed to find decent ground to camp. Behind him, they sat on rocks and logs around two campfires, the scent of roasting quail and rabbits cutting through the smell of the dank pools, burns, and peat bogs that dotted the landscape where trees twisted into monstrous forms from the winds. Yet it was broken by massive ribs of dark rock. The high, blue mountains beyond, Mount Rannock and the vast maze of the Mamlorn, made him feel small and alone in this vast, wilderness remorseless desolation, even with his men at his back.

From the top of the stony ridge, his lookout shouted, "Incoming!"

Three horsemen cleared the crest, riding at a walk toward

them. James squinted, walking toward the incomers. Three were black friars on simply palfreys. With them rode handsomely equipped knights, two men-at-arms, and two women.

James took a step toward them, drawing his sword. Behind him was the sound of dozens of swords being drawn.

The friar in the lead kicked his horse to a faster pace.

"Bishop Lamberton!" James shouted and ran toward them. Lamberton, in his simple friar's robes, climbed haltingly from his horse, sinking to his ankles into standing water. James brushed through knee-high reeds, splashing, and would have dropped to his knees to kiss the Bishop of Saint Andrew's ring if the thin, bony man hadn't grabbed his arms in a fierce grip.

"Jamie—lad..." William Lamberton's voice broke. "To lay eyes on you again..." The bishop's mouth worked, but he couldn't seem to find words.

James shook his head. "Thanks be to Jesu." He returned the bishop's grip as hard as he dared, almost afraid to loose him. "I feared you'd never come home. Are you...?" But he obviously was not well. How he had aged, gray streaks mixed with his brown hair, his face thin, deep runnels carved around his eye and mouth. He had moved like an old man, aged by years chained in an English dungeon.

"I am free and in Scotland. And the long years make seeing you all the sweeter." He held James at arm's length. "Let me look at you. A man grown."

James frowned past the bishop's shoulder. "Though you come in strange company."

Robert de Keith twitched his reins and rode to dismount beside the two of them. "Less strange than seeing you in Carlisle Castle." His laugh was a harsh bark. "Less unlikely than you swearing fealty to the English King."

James shrugged. "I might have. It is possible. Not likely. But possible."

"I heard the Bruce has taken the Earl of Ross into his peace. The man betrayed the Queen. By the Holy Rude, he's more likely to forgive me. I served the English—not quite so well."

James expelled a long breath. "He'll take you into his peace if you give him your oath. But you'd do well to mean it, Keith." He looked over his shoulder to his men. "Guide the ladies and the friars into the camp and take care of the horses." James put a hand on Bishop Lamberton's back and urged him carefully toward the campfire. "Come and sit. Tell me how you fare."

"Not so ill now, James, so don't look at me like that. And even better now to smell the air of home again." Lamberton gave a wry laugh. "Even the peat stink of the moors makes my heart leap with joy."

The men were leaping up, bowing respectfully, moving away to the other fire to give the nobles men some space. The black-clad friars followed whilst Robert de Keith helped his lady and daughter from dismount.

"I don't mean to drive your men from their fire. But I need to sit for a while." Lamberton lowered himself stiffly to sit on one of the rocks. He groaned softly. "Days in the saddle come hard now."

"And I need to hear what news you can tell me." James pulled his dirk and speared one of the quail. "But eat first." He motioned to Richert to bring ale from the little cask that sat nearby. "Keith, help your ladies to some food, though it's simple camp fare." James had forgotten the lass's name if he'd ever known it. Her downturned mouth gave her a sullen look. The Keith split a bird and gave half to his lady wife. She thanked him in an undertone. The lass first put her hands behind her back, but a raised eyebrow and glower from her father caused her to take it. Her thanks were as sullen as her look.

Lamberton blew on the brown, dripping bird to cool it. "There's little news that you won't already have heard. Edward of Caernarfon is in trouble as always with his nobles. Near as at war with them as you might guess. He has to invade, to crush Scotland to try to make them ignore their anger at him."

"Yet, he freed you."

"Well, Anthony Bek hates me." Lamberton's thin mouth twitched. "And Edward hates Anthony Bek."

"It's one time I'll thank Jesu for an Englishman's hatred then. But have you word of the others? Have you seen any of them? The Queen? Little Margory? The King's sisters?"

"Thanks be, I was allowed to visit them. They are... as well as one can expect. Closely guarded. But the lass... she is with nuns who could not bring themselves to treat her harshly. That is well. The Queen has been treated less kindly, but they dared not harm her for her father's sake." Lamberton took a cup of ale as James held it out and sighed with pleasure as he drank.

"You can imagine the King's thoughts... What he's feared."

"I was there when Thomas and Alexander were... killed. Forced to watch. Allowed to offer them no comfort." The bishop rubbed his face. "At least they were not long dying. That will be a little comfort to the King. It's all I can offer."

In the long silence, James stared at his hands. He'd lost many friends since, but the thought of Thomas's terrible death still twisted something inside his chest. The silence was too painful to allow to last, so James said, "But to know that the Queen and the Princess are well is good news indeed."

The bishop tore off a leg to eagerly suck the meat from it,

swallowed the mouthful of food, and wiped greasy lips on the back of his sleeve. He gave a slightly bitter laugh. "I'm not so fine as you once remember me, lad."

"A finer sight than I've seen in many a day." James squeezed the bishop's arm, hardly able to believe he was actually back after so long. "Finer than a scraggly orphan lad you took in when I came to your door."

"Well that I did, Jamie. Well that I did. One of the better things that I've done." He tore off the other dripping leg from the small fowl and ate it, smiling a little around the food.

"You think the invasion will be soon?"

"Not this year. Perhaps not the next, for when they come, they will bring an army meant to crush Scotland for once and for all. So, the King must make plans. And deal with angry barons."

"Our first parliament since Lord Robert was crowned—it will be a good chance for planning. He'll be pleased beyond words to see you." James smiled. "Even you, Keith. I didn't tell him the bishop had slipped the English noose. It will be a surprise."

Lamberton shook his head. "Well, as to that, I am going back once I've talked to him. Given him my advice."

James's face blanked with horror. "Why?"

"The English King trusts me, at least somewhat. I can act as your eyes on the English movements, send you word of their plans. Send word on the prisoners they hold. Perhaps give them some comfort and carry messages. I'll do more good there than here." His face was determined. "Don't look so appalled, lad. I'm not ill-treated now. I give you my oath."

James swallowed. "But you were. And will be again if they know that you spy for us. We can use every aid we can get, but no one would ask such a thing of you. To put yourself back in their hands."

"I do what I must. As always." Lamberton tore the bird in

115

two and looked at the halves as though bemused. "But I can rest by a warm fire with a full belly tonight. That will be good after days on the road. And tomorrow we ride for Saint Andrews—and home."

CHAPTER 18

*J*ames nodded to the guards as he dismounted in the cobbled bailey yard, dampened by the spray from the surging waves below. Walls, half rubble, surrounded on all four sides. Tired and hungry but suppressing a grin, he strode into the one remaining corner tower of Saint Andrew's Castle. Putting one over on the King was a hard thing to manage, but he was sure that he had done it. The King stood at the foot of narrow stairs, speaking to the Bishop David de Moray, both in the finery of office instead of their usual armor. James twitched a pleased smile at the King's gold tabard with a lion picked out in jewels and gold coronet, a gold belt about his waist. He straightened his expression and bowed deeply before he interrupted them.

"Your Graces," he said, creasing his face in a frown. "Forgive me interrupting you. I fear I brought someone you must see, my liege, outwith the doors."

The King raised his eyebrows. "James Douglas, you're late to arrive for the Privy Council. I wanted you here two days past."

"Your pardon, sire. You'll understand the necessity for

delay when you see what I've brought. A most urgent matter, on my oath."

Moray nodded toward the door. "I'm sure Lord Douglas has his reasons. Mayhap we should see them."

"Very well, Jamie. Let's see what grim news you've brought me." The King first looked from James to the bishop and then walked to the door and flung it open. In the court-yard stood James's men under his blue standard, fluttering in a stiff sea wind, but before them stood a friar in a dark trav-eling cloak. The King frowned, looking puzzled. His eyes widened, and he gave a wordless cry of astonishment. He ran down the steps of the tower. "William Lamberton! William!"

James couldn't help his laugh as Bishop Lamberton's face alit with joy. "My liege." He lowered himself stiffly to one knee before the Bruce reached him. He grasped the King's hands and kissed each. "My liege."

The King pulled Lamberton to his feet and threw his arms around him in a tight embrace. "My dear friend." Keeping an arm around Lamberton's shoulder, he turned to James. "What secrets have you been keeping, James Douglas?"

James laughed. "Most dire ones, Your Grace. Dire indeed. The Bishop of Saint Andrews is returned to Scotland." His laughter faded at the thought that Lamberton would not stay. This was something the King would indeed consider dire and must be discussed. "Another is here who craves an audi-ence with the King of the Scots." He shot Robert de Keith a cool look. The man stood with his chin high, but the way he was chewing his lip hinted at a little fear at his reception.

The King's gaze skated over the man who was hereditary Knight Marischal of Scotland. He turned his shoulder.

William de Irvine clattered down the stairs, his young face red with distress. "Your Grace, you must be ready for the procession to the parliament."

"That will wait." Robert the Bruce put a hand on Lamberton's shoulder, and his face twisted into a grimace of pain. "I thank Holy Mary and the Saints for your safe return, but... Have you seen my wife? My daughter? My poor sisters? Are they..." His voice broke. He took a deep breath, and James could see him forcing himself into a mask of calm. "How do they fare?"

"I saw Lady Elizabeth and Marjorie and was allowed to visit, if only briefly. They are in good health and..." He seemed to search for words. "They are not treated as badly as might be. They are treated better than your sister, I am glad to say, and even Christina is released from that foul cage where she was held. Your sister suffered, but now she's in the hands of nuns who have sworn to me that they will treat her gently. They are all in fair health. Given no honors, kept in close confinement, but not..." Lamberton frowned. "...not quite ill-treated."

The King closed his eyes, his lips pale he pressed them together so hard.

"They think of you, pray for you daily. They know you would rescue them if it were in your power."

"Is it what I have done, William? Is that why they've suffered as they have? For my sins?"

Lamberton gripped the King's arm. "You know better. Who invaded our lands? The fault is not yours."

James cleared his throat, gave the Keith a hard look, and thrust his chin toward the King. The man strode to stand before the Bruce. He bowed and knelt on both knees.

"Your Grace," he said evenly. "I seek your royal pardon and to be received into your peace. I swear to be your true man henceforth if you will have me."

The King looked past Keith to the woman and girl who accompanied him. "You and all your house? And where is your son and heir, Sir Robert?"

Robert de Keith flushed red. "He is at Merse. Forgive me,

119

Your Grace, but until I was sure of your mercy, I could not risk him. He is still a small lad, but he'll serve you as I will. You won't regret your mercy, sire. I give you my oath."

Robert de Bruce studied him with a long, cool look. "Then here is my hand, my Lord Marischal, and I will take your oath." The Bruce extended his hand, which the Keith took between his.

"I take you as my liege lord and swear by all the saints to serve you and your heirs well and faithfully until my life's end."

"Then your oath I accept and will defend your rights as your lord. I so swear."

The Keith stood up, letting out a rather noisy breath of relief that made the King grin. He slapped the Keith's shoulder. "Welcome home." And suddenly, there was a buzz of activity as though everyone had held their breaths.

David de Moray walked toward Lamberton, holding out his hands. "My dear friend." He pulled the bishop into a brief grasp.

Irvine cleared his throat. "Your Grace, I beg you. The parliament will be delayed."

"Am I not fine enough for you?" the Bruce growled with an expansive gesture that took in his bejeweled tabard over a red velvet tunic and hose.

The door to the tower opened with a forceful thud. "It's almost time for this damned procession," Robert Boyd said as he strode down the steps. He looked James up and down with a satiric twist to his mouth. "I think we'll have to leave you in the scullery though, my Lord of Douglas. No member of the Privy Council could possibly be so mud bejeweled."

"Do I have time to make myself presentable, William?" James asked of Irvine. "And what of my lord bishop? He should return to his own cathedral in state."

Lamberton shrugged. "What matter that I'm not in finery? I am home."

David de Moray already had a hand on Lamberton's arm. "I have spare episcopal robes in my rooms. Water to wash the dirt of the road will refresh you." He was urging to the steps that led into the tower. "Your people will be overjoyed to see you healthy and returned to us."

Across the bailey yard, Niall Campbell was shouting to ready the banners. A priest herded a covey of chattering boys into lines, hushing and yelling for order in turns. Gilbert de Hay and Bernard de Linton argued loudly with the Provost of the city about the order of proceedings.

"Robbie, I must at least wash and put on a clean tunic," James said, grabbing a bag from off his horse.

He left behind a smiling King Robert de Bruce as horses were led up for the cavalcade to the Cathedral of Saint Andrews, and the bailey descended into a chaos of stamping horses and shouting men. Sir Edward de Bruce thundered in and pulled up his snorting steed, laughing heartily at some shouted jape as the tower door closed behind James.

There was time for nothing more than splashing soap and water over his face and chest, running his razor over his cheeks, and pulling on a red velvet tunic he'd saved for the occasion. It was time to run down the winding tower steps to join the throng that rode with the King. The wind off the North Sea brought a saltwater scent and whipped the banners over their heads as they rode down the twisting way, lined on both sides with a crowd of burghers and priests. Lamberton, in exquisite if borrowed blue vestments edged with gold, rode at the King's side.

"The King! The King!" someone shouted. Others took up the cry. Robert de Bruce waved, grinning broadly as the chant grew louder.

"Bishop Lamberton!" An elderly priest elbowed his way

through the crush. Lamberton reined in his horse for a moment to press his hand to the man's head before he rode on. The crowd cheered.

James nodded to his uncle, James the High Steward of Scotland, only recently returned to the King's peace. Beside his uncle rode young Walter, laughing and chatting to the men around him. As usual, Sir Edward glared at James without speaking, but this was too fine an occasion for that to be a worry. James twitched a smile at the King's brother, which he knew would irritate him. The bishops of Ross, Brechin, Dunblane, and Dunkeld in their gleaming finery out from its hiding joined David de Moray behind the others. James bowed briefly to Maol, Earl of Lennox and the glum Earl of Ross as they passed to take the lead behind the bishops. Then came noblemen by the hundred and James joined the throng. Niall Campbell waved to James from the other side of the stream of mounted men. Alexander Lindsay shouted a greeting.

Before them rose almost into the clouds the triple towers of Saint Andrew's Cathedral. The sun gleamed on stained glass windows, spared from the war by Saint Andrew's distance from the usual route of the English armies. Behind them, the choirboys raised their voices in a song of thanksgiving.

The cathedral doors were thrown open for the King's procession.

A hidden choir raised their voices. The Master of Arms and heralds bowed and led the King of Scots through the great cathedral to the cloth-draped dais. With the noisy throng, James followed the King into the great vaulted nave, bathed in light from hundreds of high windows. Swaths of greenery and tapestries screened the front and the high altar. The place echoed with hundreds of voices. James elbowed Boyd and they pushed their way through the crush to the chairs that had been brought in for the Privy Council. He mumbled an apology when he stumbled over John Graham's feet as he edged past. William de Irvine trod on James's toes as he squeezed through. Randolph gave James a lukewarm nod.

The King stood before his throne, beaming as heralds pointed and guided the company to their places. Behind the nobility, the west end of the chancel filled the hundreds with townspeople who pointed at the returned bishop. The lean, black-robed Chancellor of the Realm, Bernard de Linton, with his fiery hair and freckle-splattered face, stood at the base of the dais.

"What a crush. Even more than the coronation," James muttered as they stood waiting for the King to take his seat. Gradually the uproar lessened. The air smelled of incense, pine greenery, and hundreds of men sweating in their velvet finery. The King stood for another moment and sat down.

The Herald cried, "Hear ye! Hear ye! All persons having business before the King of the Scots are called to draw near for the parliament of the Kingdom of Scotland is now in session. God save the King!"

The King raised his hands for quiet. "As the first order of business in this parliament, I welcome my beloved friend, Master William, Bishop of Saint Andrews and Primate of the Realm returned from captivity."

James grinned and joined in the shouting as the room broke into cheers. He had not told the King that the bishop intended to return to England. He took a deep breath. Mayhap that was news that would better come from the bishop himself.

The chancellor bowed to the King and requested permission to address the parliament. At the King's nod, the cleric went into a long speech concerning how the clerics had agreed that Edward Longshanks of England had stolen the crown of Scotland. James sighed as the man listed the crimes of the English at length in support of the puppet king, John Toom Tabard, and listed the ancestry of Lord Robert's grandsire from the long line of Gaelic kings. As though that was something they didn't all know. Then Maol, Earl of Lennox, gave another speech repeating exactly the same thing on behalf of the nobility.

Robbie Boyd muttered, "Did he have to tell us what we already signed our names to?"

James grunted. "All to convince the Pope, I suppose. Remind me why I prefer this to fighting battles?"

Boyd made a choking sound as he stifled his laugh.

Once the restless muttering in the immense nave quieted, the chancellor stepped to the foot of the dais. "Your Grace." He held out a parchment to the King. "This letter requires your royal attention and that of the parliament."

The Bruce took it and bent his head over it briefly. At last, something that wasn't old news. James crossed his arms, and Boyd raised an eyebrow at him.

The King scanned the throng, his face bland. "From Philippe le Bel of France. It is addressed to Lord Robert, King of the Scots."

James took in a sharp breath. That was a victory all in itself and one not to be ignored. Forcing the rulers of the realms of Christendom to recognize the rightful king would help more than anything except the recognition of the Pope himself. Ignoring the discourtesy to speak over the King, the room buzzed with whispers.

The Bruce held up a hand for silence. "The King of France asks me to join my realm with his in a crusade to retake the Holy Land."

On the other side of the room, someone gave a single loud bark of laughter. James blinked and shook his head. Absurd. They were hard put to hold the kingdom. To be honest with so many castles still in English hands, one could hardly say that they did so.

To empty the land of its fighting men for a foreign crusade? Was the King of the French mad?

"This is a request, however mad it may seem, which we may turn to our good. Let us think on it. It is no secret that Philippe le Bel of France has his own concerns with Mother Church..." The King gave a wry smile. "...as do we." That the Pope had excommunicated the entire Kingdom of Scotland was more than a sore point. "A crusade would benefit him with the Pope, besides serving God. So mayhap we should agree to aid him in such an endeavor."

A low murmur of protest ran through the room. The Bruce waved away their concern. "All the King of France need do is send us such aid as will help *us* clear Scotland of our enemies first."

"Not in a hundred years," Boyd grumbled softly. "The damned French King betrayed us before."

The herald shouted down the tumult, so the King could continue. "I see that you, as do I, have doubts that we may count to the French to remember their treaties of aid with us. But with such an answer, none can say we Scots are loath to help the Holy Mother Church against the infidel. Indeed, were it possible, I would lead a crusade. I pray that the day will come when I may do so."

David de Moray sprang to his feet. "Your Grace, I beg you, let me speak."

The King nodded. "My lord bishop."

"We fight a nation that despoils not only our people and denies, nay, would slay our rightful King, but despoils and robs our churches, abbeys, and monasteries, as well. Has held two of our bishops in *durance vile*. Killed priests in every part of the nation. Nuns homeless and raped. Churches burned. Long since I've declared the war against this invader—this cruel oppressor—to be a crusade, and I tell you today, so it is. We already fight a crusade." The bishop gave a brusque nod of his head and sat down.

"Yes!" James shouted, jumping to his feet. Then he realized the entire parliament was shouting and cheering alongside him. Boyd bumped his shoulder against James's. Irvine raised his clenched fists over his head as he shouted. "Scotland! Scotland!"

The master of arms and the herald were yelling for silence.

"Hear me!" the King shouted in his battlefield voice. James sat down in a hurry, and the cathedral filled with the rustle and scrape as hundreds did the same. "We have a holy duty to protect the realm. Accepting this proposal from the French King—or saying that we do—will only aid in performing that duty. Our crusade, as the good Master David says, is to our kingdom and people. Our first duty is to protect Scotland. I will lead no man on another crusade until the crusade to secure my realm and the church within it is done." The King held out the letter to his chancellor. "Master Linton, I believe the parliament is agreed. Answer the King of France that we shall be most pleased to have him send aid to us in order to clear our enemy from our lands. Then we shall most heartily join him in his holy endeavor."

Once Linton had taken the letter, the King leaned forward, hands steepled before him. "Now to other matters. The earldom of Carrick is mine to confer, handed down from my mother and her Gaelic line. Not long since, I promised it to my dear brother, Sir Edward, as a reward for his valor in defending our realm. I, therefore, require that this parliament confirm my gifting of it to Sir Edward de Bruce. And because my only child, my dear daughter Marjorie, is in the hands of the English, he must also be declared my heir. I'll not chance the kingdom falling prey to the vultures of England should God so ordain that I die."

James poked at a back tooth with his tongue. Edward had disliked him since the first day they laid eyes on each other, but he could hardly protest. Forbye, the man had fought for the King as bravely as anyone could. If he was a bit of a fool and greedy, well, they hadn't much of choice. Most people liked the man well enough, especially the ladies. James snorted in amusement and added his shout of agreement to the rest of the cathedral that rang with it.

The King waited until they quieted to continue. "Another urgent matter before us is the lack of a Lord Warden of the Marches. In the past, there have been three Lord Wardens, of the Western, the Middle, and the Eastern March, to protect the realm from encroachment from our enemies to the south. The lack is dire in these times. We have no doubt that the English King intends to lead a new invasion to secure the castles they still hold. To reconquer our lands and people. Whoever is Lord of the Marches will hold all our lives in his hands. My lord of Douglas holds those lands now and to him that I give this heavy duty. Does my parliament agree?"

James's face burned. His chest seemed not to work as though a band compressed it. When Boyd elbowed him hard in the ribs, grinning, James took in a breath with a whoosh. He laughed as everyone around him shouted. Irvine slapped his back. Even Thomas Randolph turned and nodded to him, smiling.

There were more speeches, but it all passed in a buzz. Lord Warden of all Scotland's marches, the entire border under his command—if he could win it. No man had ever been named to such power in Scotland. He was drunk with the honor and wondered if wine would sober him. The thought made him laugh.

CHAPTER 19

*J*ames ran a hand down the front of his tunic. He'd sponged it and donned velvet hose, doeskin thigh boots, and a short satin-lined cloak slung over one shoulder. It was lucky that there were at least a few English tall enough for him to help himself to their finery. He let the flow of the gaily-dressed crowd carry him toward the door of the Priory. Angus Og, one shoulder draped with a multi-color plaid over a saffron tunic, upper arms bound with gold bracelets, gripped a hand on James's shoulder. "Bedecked like a swan, my lord warden."

James eyed Angus's finery and twitched a smile. "You're one to say so."

"If you think I'm bedecked, wait until you see Lady Christina. I swear the woman brought every gem in the isles." Angus raised his eyebrows. "I think she means to renew her acquaintance with Lord Robert, forbye that she didn't trust young Raurie to attend the parliament without her oversight."

James scanned the crowd that was filing through the wide-flung doors. "Are they here?"

Angus Og, who overtopped even James by an inch or more, gave him a light shove by the back of his neck. "She is already inside, making sure the musicians will play music fit for our dancing."

James took a stumbling step with a laugh. "Jesu God, you Highlanders are ruffians."

Angus snorted. "I'm an Islander, you heathen of a Scot."

Indeed, the Lord of the Isles, as he styled himself, wouldn't claim to be a Scot if the devil himself demanded it, even if he did fight at the King's side. Strange people, the people of the isles. James shook his head as he passed into the high-beamed Great Hall of the priory. Servants scurried carried huge platters heaped with food to fill tables that lined the walls, scenting the air with cinnamon and apples and savory smells of roasted meats. Playful notes of a lute drifted over the chatter of hundreds of voices. James, the High Stewart, as glittering as the rest of the throng in blue so dark it was almost black, and a hat with a peacock's feather and young Walter at his heels, called for James to join him. James looked longingly at the wine flagons, but the High Stewart had been his mother's brother and was his own god sire, so strolled in that direction. "My lord uncle, you're looking well," he said with a slight smile. Considering his long stay in the English King's peace, he was more well than many others.

His uncle shook his head. "Don't use that tone to me, James."

"Your pardon, uncle. I meant no tone at all. I'm pleased to see you in good health." He tilted his head and smiled at his cousin. The lad was well-grown and in his twelfth year if James's memory was true. "You serve as your father's squire, Walter?"

Walter pulled a sullen look. "Still a page. And I shouldn't be. No other my age is better on a horse or with a sword at practice." The High Stewart made a sound of protest, but his son turned his glower upon his father. "You know it's true, my lord."

The High Stewart gave a fatherly sigh.

James patted Walter's shoulder. "I'm sure you'll make a braw squire. I was squire to Bishop Lamberton and learnt much in his house though he's no knight."

The lines in his uncle's face deepened. He studied his son for a moment and shook his head. "The danger... but I suppose you're right."

James almost laughed at the look of shock on the lad's face. "You... you mean...?"

"I'll talk to James tomorrow. I'd trust him with your safety, and he can teach you what you need to know."

James opened his mouth, but nothing came out.

Walter let out a short yelp of laughter. "Thank you. My lord, thank you!" He was bouncing with eagerness. "Sir James, when will we leave? I swear, I'll be a good squire. The best. My word on it."

He had well and truly walked into that one. His mouth twitched. "You'll need to go home for your gear, I suppose. I'll ride with you and talk." He grasped Walter by both shoulders. "It's no game. Don't mistake."

The High Stewart cleared his throat. "Have you seen Bishop Lamberton tonight? He's an old friend."

James was happy to seize the change in topic and scanned the eddying crowd. "No, I don't see him, but there's Master David de Moray." James raised his eyebrows. "And a very lovely lady on his arm." David de Moray might be more warrior than a priest, a leading light of the Church Militant, but his attention to the woman beside him was most particular. Moray patted the hand tucked into his arm. The woman's full, silken rose-colored gown brushed about her as they strolled; her head was bent, listening to something the bishop was saying to her.

"She's a beauty," Robert Boyd said as he joined them.

James bit the inside of his cheek as he studied her. Truly, she was lovely. Perhaps even more so than his own Alycie. Her hands wouldn't be roughened from caring for villagers. Not strong enough to rub out the pain of shoulders knotted from the weight of his armor. Her hair wouldn't Alycie's sweet scent of green grass and herbs when he held her against him—

A fanfare blared out. A herald next to the door announced, "Lord Robert, by God's grace, King of the Scots and Lord of Annandale."

James bowed as King Robert de Bruce swept into the great chamber. He was smiling, talking to William Lamberton who walked by his side. To the soft strains of the lute, he strolled toward the throne at the head of the hall. He paused his progress to speak to Christina MacRaurie, bowing over her hand. The head of the MacRauries was a handsome woman in the fullness of her power, striking in a velvet gown of black with red underdress peeking out. Her neck and arms were gold and jewel bedecked. James sputtered a laugh as the King peered down her bodice in open admiration.

His uncle cleared his throat. "They say the King is free with his attentions to the ladies these days."

"He's no monk," James said. "And his lady wife has been stolen from him for too long. What can you expect?"

The King took Christina's hand and drew her along as he and Lamberton continued through the throng. As soon as he reached his throne, the King called for dancing. The lute faded away, and the sound of the musicians tuning took its place. The King led Christina onto the cleared floor. He turned and frowned at the glittering crowd. "Don't stand about like dolts. I said we will dance. Tonight is a time for gaiety."

James looked about for a partner as they pressed back to give the dancers room. The fact was he knew few women of noble birth.

His uncle nudged him. "James, here is Isabel de Strathbogie, and the lovely lass has no partner yet. You'd best make up the lack." As James bowed over the dark-haired woman's hand, over her shoulder, he saw Edward de Bruce scowl at him and then turn to another woman to take her hand. Typical. James smiled and led the lady onto the floor. The musicians struck up a reel, and the King led them through the twists and turns of the dance. As they wove past, James noted that Boyd's eyes followed the lady in pink. Boyd was right. She was beautiful.

The dance ended, and James ran a hand over his dripping brow as his partner returned to her brother. "Give over this dancing," Boyd said. "Let's find some wine." But a herald edged up to them and said the Lord Warden and Sir Robert were to attend on His Grace.

The Bruce was seated on the throne at the end of the hall with Christina MacRaurie seated on one side. David de Moray and his companion stood on the other.

"Ha! Lads, you remember Lady Christina, I vow."

James bowed. "I can't imagine a man in the kingdom who could forget her, sire."

"But this lovely lady with Master David, the two of you may not know. Lady Caitrina has been in France for several years past. Master David's good-niece."

Robert Boyd's mouth dropped open. He snapped it closed, his face flooding with color. James raised his eyebrow as the normally cool-headed Boyd stammered. "Lady Caitrina? Jesu God forgive me. I didn't recognize you after such a time."

"Robbie Boyd." She swallowed. "Seeing you brings back... happy memories."

Boyd took both her hands and kissed them. "You look..." He laughed. "You look wonderful. I'd heard that you were in France."

The King beamed. "Musicians," he called, "another dance." As they struck the notes, he motioned a peremptory hand to the two. "Take yourselves off to the dance floor. And do the pretty to the lady, Robbie. I'm going to talk to my new Lord Warden for a moment." He cut his eyes toward the bishop whose mouth was twitching in a wry smile.

Once the two were swirling through the pattern of a dance, Moray said, "I confess it, Your Grace. You were right. It's been too long she's been a widow but finding her a good husband amid a war... one who might be killed as poor Andrew was. It has been a hard thing. She can be stubborn as a mule and wouldn't consider a husband from the French."

"After the man who was her first husband, you couldn't offer her hand to just anyone, my friend. But death will come to all of us," the King said. "We'd best find what joy we might between our labors. And I expect my nobles to do their duty. That includes marrying and having heirs." The King gave James a pointed look. "I do mean you, Jamie." The King snorted. "And that brother of mine."

James turned to watch Robbie Boyd laughing as he and Caitrina glided past. "It may be you're right, sire. I'd not thought of marriage. Or an heir."

CHAPTER 20

AUGUST 1311

*J*ames slithered his way up the hill across a padding of old pine needles rubbing into his chest. Wat bumped his leg as he struggled behind. Beyond the flat top of the hill, sounded a crashing tide of noise, a rumble that blotted out any other possible sound. Everything had fled from the coming flood. Not just the people, but animals, birds. Nothing was left.

He sucked a breath through his teeth. Jesu God have mercy on us. Not that God seemed in a hurry to grant such a prayer. An army spread across the vale below James, moving in waves of divisions, one after another. On in on. An ocean of men and horses. To past the horizon. Like sunlight shimmering on wavelets, it caught the armor, the weapons, the harness. Banners flowed about it like brightly dyed sails. The leopard banner of the Plantagenet King was so large he might have reached out and touched it, beside it the red on white Cross of Saint George. He picked out John de Warrenne's smaller black and gold checky banner, the red and gold of Aymer de Valence, the starling banner of the Cliffords, and the gold cross of the Earl of Ulster. Between

them danced smaller banners too far away to make out—
hundreds of them. No. Thousands.

"How many you think?" Young Walter muttered in a tone
of awe.

"It doesn't matter. More than we can hope to take on."

On the other side of Walter, Wat grunted.

James twisted his neck to peer at the rear of the army,
where it flowed out of sight. "Damn Sassenach breed like
rabbits." How far back could the English army go? There was
no sign of the wagons that must be there somewhere out of
sight in the van of the army. Wagons with what supplies they
carried with them that soon must run low.

A stick thumped to the ground next to his head. James
jerked around, dirk free in a breath. Gelleys motioned from
the foot of the hill. James nudged Wat and squirmed backward until he could slide down. He gained his feet and
crouch ran to Gelleys. "Anything?"

"A group split off an hour back."

"Scouts or foragers?"

Gelleys shrugged. "Two-score. Moving south and west."

"Foragers then. We can cut them off. Let's move the men."
James gathered his reins. His horse snorted and bared its
teeth. He swung into the saddle.

"They'll skirt the Forest," James said. "Look for anything
they can loot."

Walter pushed his overgrown hair out of his eyes. "They
could go into the forest after game."

Wat spat. "Take too long to kill enough to do any good.
Faster to find barns to loot."

Gelleys gave a harsh laugh as they mounted. It was near
dusk when they passed a place where a village had stood. The
fields around it were trampled, the cots blackened ruins.
Crows covered the body of a stinking animal, rising cawing,
as James and his men passed.

135

At last, they reached the forest and its green fragrance enfolded them as they followed a deer track into its edges. A lookout waved as they passed, and they rode into a clearing. Men sat quietly, whisking whetstones along the edges of blades. One snored, and low laughs came from a small group. Two were grooming horses in the picket line. One pissed against a tree. Two hundred in all, his best men, honed like a sword in the past year.

"Mount up," Wat called. They scrambled for the horses.

"Gelleys, scout ahead," James said. "David, two bowshots on the left flank. Philp, you take the right.

As James led the men, their horses' hooves padded in the heavy layer of pine needles. They rode through dappled shade and breathed the scent of pine sap and horses and sweat and leather. Leather creaked. A startled bird flew in a rustle of feathers. But on the hunt, the men were quiet. Waiting for prey. A slight breeze creaked branches high overhead and carried a faint scent of distant smoke. They rode slowly as they hunted.

He loved Ettrick Forest and the cool shade of the great trees. James twitched a smile. He snorted. The King said it was his when the day came they could hold it. That day would not be fast coming. A slow fading of the dusk turned the light a smoky gray and then was gone dark.

A whistle turned James's head. He spotted David and signaled a turn. David pointed through the trees to where the forest thinned.

A moon-cast shadow crept back and forth on the ground. A rope creaked as a body swayed gently in the breeze. James stood in his stirrups and grasped the rope with one hand as he sawed at it with his dirk. The body stank already—of shit and piss. The rope parted. The body thudded to the pine needle covered ground with a thud.

He climbed from the saddle and turned it over with his foot.

Wat leaned over his horse's neck, peering down. "Stupid to be here, but some just won't leave."

Walter was bent over his horse's withers, gagging. There was the sound of men twitching uneasily in their saddles.

James bent a knee and peered at the dead man in the pewter moonlight. Thin, rags on his back. Blood streaked the swollen, empurpled face. "Perhaps. Or looking for loot, as well. If so, I would have hanged him myself."

"Aye, but you'd have the right," Fergus said.

James turned the head with the tips of his fingers. One cheek had been beaten in. "I wouldn't have beaten him first." He swallowed to keep down his gorge from the stench of shit and blood. James slowly moved his hand to the rags that covered a still, sprawled leg. Still wet with piss. "Beaten near to death before they hanged him," James continued softly. "For information he wouldn't have had."

James stood up and looked back the way they had come. "Take the horses back to that clearing we passed. Picket them." He pondered hoof-prints in the mucky ground. The rains had stopped, but water still oozed through the padding of needles under the trees. "I'll follow these. You come after. Spread out. Wat, give me the hoot of an owl when you're set."

Wat started to say something, but James cut him off. "Do as I command." He'd do better ridding them of any lookouts by himself. Wat hated when he did things like this, convinced one day he'd get himself killed and his men would soon follow. Such was war.

He followed the hoof tracks, dashing from tree to tree along the edge of the forest. Suddenly, a faint gleam of light broke the darkness to his left. He lifted his head, breathing deep. A hint of smoke, but from a campfire or from a burned field or house? It smelled fresh. He crouch ran from tree to tree.

The English were sitting by a low-burning fire. Beyond them was a dark bulk of massed, picketed horses. There was a red glow against the dark horizon. A single sentry stood, silhouetted against the red light, swaying a bit from weariness. James dropped to his belly and wriggled through the wet padding of pine needles and mud to between two thin saplings. A thick stick lay under his hand. He grasped it.

Nearby an owl hooted. Beyond, the land turned to clumps of bracken and heather. A bird swooped across the moon, dove to the ground, and something screamed. The sentry whirled. At the fire, someone muttered. A figure started erect.

The wind moved the trees, and scattered shadows whispered across James's face. He lay motionless. All was silent. The sentry slumped once more, still. A rattling snore began by the dying campfire. The sentry's head bent, probably half-asleep. The moon settled behind a fleeting cloud.

James stood close to the thin tree trunk and threw the stick past the sentry.

"Wha...?" The man turned his back, shaking his head.

James ran, drawing his dirk. Plunged it in and twisted hard. He slapped his hand over the man's mouth and clamped down. Left the dirk in and grasped his waist. He lifted him. The man's feet moved, barely kicking, against James's shins as he backed up into the shadows and lowered the body softly to the ground. James wiped his hands on the man's cloak and pulled the dirk from his throat. Now was the time.

After drawing his sword, James sprinted toward the sleeping camp. "A Douglas!" he shouted. Behind him, his men attacked, screaming. The first man James encountered died as soon as he opened his eyes, James's sword plunging straight down. Men were scrambling onto hands and knees. Jumping to their feet. His men overran them, hacking as they went. One ran flailing his sword at James, the faint light catching terror in his face as James shouted his war cry. James smashed his face in with a swing of his blade. He fell backward into the fire, and the stink of burning meat rose up. One fled to the horses and threw himself onto its unsaddled back, galloping away.

Fergus was bellowing, "Scotland!" as they took their revenge for the army they could not fight. There were forty English bodies scattered around the fire. James grabbed the legs and pulled a dead man from the remains of the campfire.

Suddenly, it was quiet. James felt limp with exhaustion. He hadn't slept in two days. Water dripped down his chest and legs. His muscles quivered. He would give a great deal for a featherbed and Alycie in his arms. Instead, he said, "Richert, loose those horses. The rest of you check the bodies. See what they have we can use. And hurry. We must reach Douglas village and have much to burn when we're ahead of them once more."

CHAPTER 21

The rain had eased to nothing more than a gray drizzle. Dark clouds hung low and thick, threatening another downpour. Mud splattered up to James's knees as his horse sloshed through the muck. A patter of raindrops on the wet ground accompanied the sucking sound of hooves pulling free of the mud. Weeks of unseasonable summer rains had made the ground treacherous, all bogs and hidden rocks. The packhorse he was leading reared on the lead and whinnied; it jerked him half out of the saddle. He wrestled his horse into a circle. The pack animal snorted as it splashed and scrambled in a hole it had stepped into beneath the water. They were lucky more hadn't done the same.

Wat, riding behind James, wiped dripping water from his cheeks. "Feels like Angus has dropped us into the sea."

"That might be drier." James forced a laugh.

Half a dozen of his men were strung out behind him, each leading a packhorse loaded with bags of barley. James shook his head, wondering how much of it would be ruined before they reached the village. He jumped from the saddle and led the snorting animal free. It limped, its right forefoot well off the ground. James cursed as he bent to run his hand down its leg. It would never make the distance.

The other horses were too heavily laden to take more weight. He jerked the ropes that held the sacks in place. Peat-stinking mucky water splashed to his chest when they hit. "Devil take this rain."

He pulled his dirk from his belt. "Easy, boy." Wat climbed from the saddle and grabbed the harness. James gripped the halter and shoved the dirk hard into the vee at the base of the throat. The beast screamed as it thrashed for a moment. Blood splashed into the mud and unfurled like smoke in the pool of rainwater. It went down. He remounted as Wat stripped the tack.

Another half-hour to Douglas village, if they were lucky. He prayed to Saint Bride that they didn't lose more horses and barley on the way. It was the only grain the village would see. James squinted upwards through the mist wondering when they'd see some blue instead of the murky gray that had graced them these past months. A hacking cough rattled behind him. He should have left Richert behind at the camp, but lying out wet had half his men as ill. Forbye, Richert would be a help if any of the villagers were ill.

Smoke from the houses wrapped itself into the mist as they rode between the stone cots. Up the hill, mist twisted around the ruins of the castle. A single scrawny dog barked before it turned tail and fled. Ragged children ran from every corner of the village, splashing through puddles, muddy to the thigh, laughing and squealing with excitement. A thin-faced woman opened a door, stepped out, and waved. Two men strode in from the woods, carrying bows. Iain Smythe shouted a hallo from the open front of the smithy.

James pointed toward the building where the smith stood. "Gelleys, unload it inside." He frowned. He should keep the barley for later, but too many were already hungry. "Open two bags and hand out a measure for each person, including the bairns. Hold the rest back."

He set his horse to a canter past the woods toward the house where he'd rather be than anywhere else in the land. Alycie wouldn't know he was here. But she was waiting in the doorway. He flung himself out of the saddle and bound up the stone step to press a kiss on her cheek. "I'll not touch you, lass. I'm muck from head to foot." Her face was parchment pale and purple shadows stained under her eyes.

Inside, someone whimpered. She put her hand on his arm and urged him inside. The house smelled of the oak fire and herbs but below that the feverish smell of a sick child.

"Iain's wife died four days ago from a croup." A sudden cough sounded like a bark, hoarse and tearing. "Now their wee Forsy has it. I'm nursing him." She shook her head with a jerk.

Will was bent over a small pallet in a corner near the fire. He straightened. "He swallowed a few drops of the honey water."

"It's the coltsfoot in it that might help." Alycie handed James a cloth to wipe his face and hair dry.

Iain was a braw man, steady. Losing a wife was bad, but James couldn't imagine if Iain lost the bairn too. "Any others? This has been the worse curst summer I've ever seen." He threw his dripping cloak across a stool.

"Many a cough, but this is the worst of them. Every field flooded, drowning the crops. Some sheep lost."

"Bad enough then, though I suppose it could have been worse. Will, there's barley at the smithy. Once everyone has a measure, I'll bring Iain and the provost over. We've plans to make. The village will flee on the morrow."

The child hawked and coughed. Alycie took the cup of

herbal mixture from Will and knelt beside him. She lifted his head and dribbled a bit into his mouth.

James made his voice hard. "I'll burn everything behind you."

Alycie looked up at him, eyes wide. "Everything?"

"Any cows or sheep that are in the village must go or be slaughtered. We'll leave nothing for the damned Sassenach."

"The King?" Will asked in a choked voice. "Where is his army?"

"He's retreated beyond the Firth of Forth into Moray. My men are all our army left in the entire of Lothian."

Alycie's lips had turned white to her lips. "Is it the English King then? Is he leading them?"

"So my spies tell me. With Aymer de Valence. And Lord Clifford, devil take him."

Her hands were shaking hard enough that a bit of the tonic slopped over the rim. "They'll take it all back. Everything you've won."

James's laugh felt tight and grim. "That may be. But they'll be hellish hungry doing it."

Will frowned, looking puzzled. "But..."

"Go on. Get the barley. Everyone will need a full belly for what must be done. We'll talk later."

Will gave a brief nod, picked up a bowl, and bolted out the door. James watched after him for a moment.

"Jamie." She stood and put the cup on the table. "The bairn is too ill to travel."

She knew better, but this was a hard thing. He pulled her close and laid a cheek on the top of her head. "He has to, lass. We haven't any choice." He ran his hand softly up and down her spine, feeling how thin she had grown. "I..." He almost said he was sorry. He should have taken better care of her. Taken care of everyone. But all the crops had failed in the unseasonable summer storms. What good did sorry do when people were hungry?

She pressed her head into the side of his neck and wrapped her arms around his waist. "There must be some way." Her voice had half a sob. "He'll die."

He opened his mouth and closed it again. He could tell her that a child with croup most likely would die, even if she could nurse it with every herb that she had. But she didn't want to hear it. Hell mend the damned English.

The bairn's breathing was noisy, but he seemed to have fallen asleep. Alycie should rest whilst she could. She'd worked herself half to death, taking care of the others from the look of her. He patted her shoulder and gently nudged her onto a stool. "You need some food and drink. What is there?"

Her laugh was shaky. "Jamie Douglas, you don't wait on me. It isn't your place."

"It is today." He squatted in front of the fire and picked up a pot of some watery stuff to sniff. "What's this?"

"Chamomile tisane."

He gave her his stern look, the same one he used on his men. "Don't you move." He found a pottery cup. There was only a dollop of honey left in the jar, but that went in, and he stirred it into the tisane that was still warm. Kneeling on one knee next to her, he pressed it into her hands. "You'll need all your strength, Alycie. You have to rest."

She flicked a quick glance toward the pallet.

"There are others who'll need you, too. I mean it. Drink and rest."

She let out a drawn-out sigh and sipped the warm drink. "I'll need to gather what herbs I have dried." She stared through the wall, as though she were seeing something else. He knew not what. "What clothes we can carry. But food?"

James stood up to pace around the warm room, impatiently kicking a stool out of his way. "We brought in horses loaded with every bit I could spare from my men. You'll keep the horses to carry it. And I'll send a few of my men so the lad can ride."

"Forsy is too small to ride, even if he..."

"You'll hold him whilst you ride pillion behind one of my men. You're light enough, it won't overburden the horse. It'll be easier on him than being carried afoot." And easier on her. She'd used up too much of her strength already. He was sure of that from one single look.

When Will returned with the bit of barley, Alycie took it out of his hands. "I'll make gruel. It will feed the three of us." She cast a quick glance at Forsy. "He might manage a bite with it thinned."

"No, the two of you eat. I need to see to the horses and men." James tilted up her chin and brushed his lips to hers.

"There's enough," Will protested, but his heart wasn't in it, only courtesy.

"I'm not hungry. Forbye, I'll be back in camp soon enough. Even with the rains, there are deer in the forest we can bring down. Both of you need a good meal." James smiled though it was stiff. They needed to see that he knew what he was about. "I'll be back in an hour's time with the others. We'll talk about what has to be done."

His men had seen to the horses as James had known that they would, wiping them down. There was room in the smithy and the nearby shed for all the horses. James tied his at the end well away from the others. It would as soon take a bite out of another horse that bumped it as not. After he unsaddled it and wiped it down, he found his men had settled in a corner of the smithy and looked happy enough just to be out of the damp. The heat of the forge was a welcome warmth

Iain Smythe put down his hammer and came to meet him. James squeezed his arm. "Your wife, Iain. Alycie told me."

The man's throat worked as he swallowed. "It's hard, my lord. And the lad..." His face worked as he blinked for a moment and then shook his head. "It's good you brought food. Thank you."

James stifled the sigh that almost escaped. "You'll not be grateful when you hear my news. Eat first. I want Alycie to have time to get some food down before we talk."

The man studied his face grimly. "How bad?"

James looked at his feet and then back to his vassal. God, hadn't they already suffered enough? "Bad. Another army. One too large for King Robert to defeat."

"I've no taste for food." The man looked around the smithy as though he were lost. "I... I'll bank the fire. And put away my tools."

James checked the bags of barley stacked against a wall and patted them to see how wet it was. He thought the bags had kept the barley dry. Sometimes he wondered if God had turned his back on them--crops failing and now this. But he'd not believe it. They'd been through worse.

James sent Wat for Gavane Anguson. The man's leathery face was knotted like a fist, his long hair mostly gray. Once Iain Smythe had his fire banked in the forge and his tools racked on the back wall, they walked together through the trees to the house. He suspected the two men had already guessed, and he made short work of the news. More important was deciding what they could carry into the hills. What mattered was how they would survive with winter and an army upon them.

Alycie sat by the sleeping child, gently stroking his red hair back from his forehead as she watched. James leaned his shoulders against the wall, his arms folded across his chest as he studied the men's faces and waited for questions.

"How many? The damned Sassenach?"

James grimaced. "Four times the King's numbers at least. Better armor and weapons. More knights. Hundreds of longbows. We haven't a hope to beat them on the field. But we can starve them. No such army can bring enough food. I'm burning all the way to the sea." He looked from man to man. "Everything. Houses. Barns. If a field still stands, we'll burn it. Trample it into the ground if we must. And we have little time. Tomorrow you'll flee into the hills."

Will chewed his lower lip as the other two men stared at their hands. Iain turned his head to stare at his son asleep, breathe rasping. "I... I'll have to carry the bairn."

"The guards can help with that." Iain made a sound of protest, but James cut him off. "I'll be easier on the lad."

"He's right," Will said. He chewed a lip as he thought. "Even hand barrows would be stuck in the muck of the roads the way they are this year. If we slaughtered the animals, the meat would spoil too fast anyway. So they must go, too."

"I'll bury my tools. No use for them with no forge," Iain said. "I'll carry part of the food. Won't do me harm to play pack animal. Not much else I'll need to take... except..." He glanced toward the sleeping child.

"We have one free mount from the barley we gave out today," James put in. "Some food and supplies people can't carry on their backs may go on that. It's not much. Alycie can ride pillion behind one of the guards so she can carry your lad. You may have to slaughter some animals on the way. If there's been even a bite of harvest brought in anywhere, it's more than I have heard."

"Where did you find the barley?" Gavane asked.

James laughed. "Where do you think?"

Gavane stared into the tiny fire on the hearth. "Only five cattle in the village. A dozen sheep. We'll herd them the best that we can." He looked at James. "You say you'll give us guards, my lord?"

"I can only spare four." He'd thought to say two, but two more would make little difference to his harrying the English, and there was always danger upon the road. "I stay behind with my men. If there's a straggler behind that army, we'll have him. This won't be free. They'll pay."

"Not much I can think on needs to be said." Iain lumbered to his feet. "Best we just tell everyone. We have the night to prepare. I say we go from one door to another. We'll spend enough time in the rain. No reason for standing out in it for a meeting." He bobbed a respectful nod of the head to James as he headed for the door. Gavane and Will mumbled in agreement and followed.

"Blessed Saint Bride," Alycie murmured as she rose. "How can the King make you face an army by yourself? When he has men..."

James pulled Alycie into his arms. "Not enough to defeat them, hen. Not nearly enough. I won't face them. I'm not so stupid. I'll burn ahead of them, and then I'll nip at their heels and take a bite from their arse if I get a chance. But you have to be safe. Away." He dug his fingers into her thick blonde hair. Her lips were soft. She carried the scent of honey and thyme. Then he was nibbling her lips, thrusting his tongue into her warmth. Hot and sweet.

"Tell me you'll miss me whilst you're gone," James whispered. He knew what she would say, but he needed to hear words.

"I miss you always. When you're gone. Fear for you."

Her hands held him tight, and James was stroking her hair, kissing her face, kissing her neck. "I've missed you," he said, and he found her mouth again. Alycie opened her lips to that delving kiss and called forth everything hidden inside him beneath the anger.

He broke the kiss, and Alycie swayed against him, arms around his neck for support. She made a little sound in her throat and drunk on the moment, he lifted her up and carried her through the door to her bed. He stripped her kirtle over her head and tossed it aside. He loved her breasts, the way they filled his hands when he cupped them. He put his lips to one pink nipple and sucked, feeling it harden against his tongue. He moved to the other teasing it between his lips.

"Jamie." Alycie unfastened the tie of her underskirt and pushed it down over her hips.

He stripped, tossing down his armor, sword, and under-tunic. It didn't matter that they were wet and needed cleaning. She lay down and held his hand to pull her toward him. They lay together on her bed, light from the doorway playing shadows over their naked bodies as they moved together, rediscovering each other with mouths and with hands.

James nuzzled his way up her throat, panting a little, and she opened her mouth for him. Their tongues touched and withdrew. He raised his head, and they smiled at each other.

"I'll make it safe for you to come back. I promise."

She brushed his hair back from his forehead. "I know."

James examined the soft features that hid such determination. Her eyes held his gaze.

"I love you, Alycie."

James opened his mouth to say more, but she kissed him, a butterfly's breath of a kiss. "I've always loved you," she whispered. She opened her mouth to his tongue, claiming him as he claimed her. The muggy afternoon, his horse stamping outside, a crack of thunder in the distance, the hum of voices planning their flight made a distant background that no longer mattered.

"Trust me," he said. "It will be all right."

"You know that I do."

It had been too long for both of them, but they soon found the ancient tidal rhythm, like the crest and fall of waves on the shore. Pleasure built like a swell running in from the sea. He moved faster, and Alycie rose to meet him, lifting with his rhythm.

Alycie whimpered, eyes shut tight, straining against him. A pink flush spread up her chest and neck. He could hear the rush of her breath, feel the slippery leak of pleasure between them. Release roared in from the depths of the sea, crashing through every doubt, every resistance. He slumped onto his elbows. She dug in her fingers as her back arched. "James," Alycie cried.

Time blurred. James shifted into a place where there was no need for pride or titles or glory. He felt what he felt for Alycie. Here was his deepest pleasure. When he was completely spent, he stroked her face as he pulled out and rolled onto his side. She curled into his arms with a satisfied murmur. He buried his face in the sweet heathery scent of her hair, closed his eyes, half weak with pleasure. This was truly loving. He'd give whatever he had or might ever have to hold onto it.

"When you return, we'll wed. No one can stop me. Like my father. I marry whom I please."

When he looked at her, her eyes were wide, shining in the faint light from the other room. "The King... He'd never allow it. What will he do?"

"There's nothing he can do once we're wed at the door of a church." He narrowed his eyes into the half-darkness. The King would indeed be angry. Furious would be a better word.

"Jamie..." She tilted her head back to look into his eyes. "You can't. You... you'd die for him."

"He'll be angry. Eventually, he'll forgive me."

When she didn't answer, he pulled her closer. "I would die

for him. Probably, one day, I will die for him. But until then, why shouldn't we have a few moments of happiness? God knows we've had little enough." He kissed her forehead. "I'll have you and anyone who doesn't like it, hell mend them. Even the King."

"Do you think you might ask me first?" Alycie whispered. There was a smile in her voice, and her cheek pressed into his neck.

He laughed softly. "I'll court you with roses. When you return, lass."

CHAPTER 22

*B*arking like a furious hound was near at hand. James awoke with a thudding feeling, then he realized the sound was a cough. He was mashed against the wall, muting his usual sprawl because he was in Alycie's narrow bed. He slid his hand across the coverlet and found her gone. Pottery clattered in the other room. A voice softly murmured words he couldn't make out. It felt like near morning though outwith the window was still the almost-light of a summer night.

He crawled to the foot of the bed and gathered the armor and clothes he'd thrown there. He pulled on his hose and tunic. A fire burned in the hearth beneath a steaming pot that sent up the scent of some medicinal herb. The bairn Alycie held in her lap, a cup to his mouth, was older than James had thought. Perhaps three years or four.

James flapped into his tunic and hose. He eyed his mail with disgust. It needed a good cleaning, so he got a cloth and wiped at it. That wouldn't be as good as it needed but better than naught.

"I..." Alycie cleared her throat. "I need to pack herbs I can use. There will be hurts to tend. More illness, most like."

"I'll go make sure they're readying to leave." James tossed the cloth on the table and tugged the hauberk over his head. "Isn't there a woman who can care for him whilst you do what you need?"

"They have to ready what they can, as well. I'll manage."

He cupped her cheek. Under his palm, it was smooth, warm. He stroked the blue and green plaid that covered her shoulder that had the velvety feel of having been washed a hundred times. He tried to think of something to tell her, but what they'd said in the night was all there was. "When you return..."

She nodded and he walked out the door. He passed the trees into the village proper filled with pale light. A sheep bleated. A lank-haired lad of twelve poked at it with his crook as the animal tried to circle past him. "Get back you, barmy thing."

A horse blew and nickered as Gelleys led it out of the shed. Iain and Will walked toward him, gesturing as they quietly argued some point.

"We need another day," Iain said. "Will it make that much difference?"

James wondered if he hoped the child would be better for another day's respite. "It's too much risk. Everyone must be gone today."

Will gaped, open-mouthed, staring into the distance. "Look."

Black billows rose on the horizon, writhing to mix with the gray clouds.

"I told you. We'll burn everything ahead of the English. It's started."

Iain shook his head. "You said... but it didn't sound real.

It's bad enough when the English loot and destroy. But our own?"

"I'll burn the whole land before I let them have it." He glared at Wat, chatting to one of the women who had her arms around a bundle. "Wat! Load the horses. Now!"

As Wat trotted to carry out his orders, the three of him watched for a moment. Iain said, "I've buried my tools. Best I see to my lad now. Alycie will have to ready her medicines to go."

Will scowled. "The cattle should be here. I'm a mind to wallop that lazy David Kintor. He's naught but a layabout."

"Will you see to it, Will? My men seem to think it's a holy day as slow as they are." He took a deep breath as he strode toward the pack animals and his men throwing sacks of barley on their backs. He wouldn't shout at them or not much. They shouldn't pay for the tearing pain of doing this. "Gelleys, see Gawane for what food might be loaded onto the spare horse. Wat, I'm sending four guards with them. All but you and Richert. Gelleys should lead them. As long as they're on the road by midday, with the late dusk, they'll have time to be well away."

"Fergus? In case they're attacked?"

James nodded.

Confusion and noise was a swelling tide: a man cursed as he led two cattle, horses whickered, women traded shouts about what to carry with them, sheep bleated, Wat yelled at the men to hurry. Gawane swatted at a filthy-faced lad and told him to run to his mam. Will carried a cask of ale on his shoulder to be loaded.

Scuttling clouds streaked the sky, but at least it wasn't raining. He motioned Gelleys over and told him to fasten padding behind his saddle for a pillion for Alycie to ride. He'd not tell her that it was as much for her as the sick lad she was tending. She'd be sure to think she should walk with the others.

It took a full three hours, but when Alycie came out of the trees that separated their house from the village, the chaos had turned into an order of march. His face felt like stretched leather, tight and grim, as he handed her up behind Gelleys. He moved his mouth into a smile. "It won't be so bad. Soon you'll be back."

She looked around. Her throat worked. "Keep safe," she said in a husky voice.

The day had grown warm when Fergus led them away from Douglas village, men and women bunched together. Children hung onto their mother's skirts. Wailing from a bairn, sheep lowing, a thin dog ran after them barking. With one arm, Alycie clung to Gelleys's waist, the other cradled the lad to her breast. She didn't look back. The thud of hooves faded into the distance.

James narrowed his eyes as he watched the roiling black smoke on the horizon. Five years that he'd fought. And more his father before him. Would it ever end? Well, it would not today. He picked up his horse's reins.

Wat dropped an armload of torches, an oily cloth wrapped around the end, at his feet. One flickered and smoked as he held it aloft.

James held out his hand. "Give me one." How many times must a man destroy his own home? He studied the torch for a moment and gave an impatient shake of his head. No time for being maudlin. "Richert, take the horses clear of town, so they don't spook. You know what to do. The forge is still burning for fire. That should go last. I'll be back." James thrust his torch up to Wat's. It caught with a sigh.

As Richert gathered the reins to his horse and Wat's, James swung into the saddle. He cantered into the trees, and the house was before him, a simple thing though larger than

155

most in the village, three rooms instead of only one. A gift from to their family from his father. Sturdy thatched roof. Stone walls. Windows with strong shutters.

He tied the reins tight to a branch. No time for chasing down a spooked steed. Then he strode in through the front door, banging it open with the flat of his hand.

His footsteps were like drumbeats in the empty house. The bed where he'd slept last night with Alycie, the coverlet still crumpled, the dents of their bodies in the mattress. It wouldn't catch so easily. He slid his dirk from his belt and plunged it in, ripping a slash. It gaped like a wound, bleeding straw. He thrust the torch into it. Held it.

The straw caught. Flames curled and spread across it to snake-like a live thing up the wall toward the open window. The fire crackled, sending up ribbons of smoke. He spun on a heel and thudded into the main room. He knocked clay jars about and found one filled with uisge beatha. He tightened his hand around it until his arm shook. James went to the door and dashed it into the fire. It went up whoosh. Heat scorched his face. He tossed in the torch and backed toward the open door. Flames followed, wrapping the rafters, eating hungrily into the thatch. Smoke boiled out. James backed out the door. The thatched roof flared. Flames danced across it.

He loped to the horse, jerked loose his reins, and mounted. He squeezed the reins so tight they cut into his hands as he watched. The roof collapsed with a gush of flames as high as the treetops that outshone the gray daylight. He turned the horse's head and rode toward billowing columns of smoke.

CHAPTER 23

A cold wind cut at James's face, and black clouds like fish scales slid across the high morning sky. He settled on the edge of a low boulder and fumbled his whetstone out of the leather bag that hung from his sword belt. He pulled the stone along the edge of his dirk with a nervous *whisk*. He flexed his neck and shoulders, aching from the weight of armor he'd not been out of in long weeks.

Ice glazed the dry heather, glittering like a jeweled crust in the pale morning sun, tiny flashing gems of blue and white. It had been three days since they'd picked off a handful of English stragglers. A man needed to keep busy, or he'd think of things better ignored. A man might think of burned villages and cold, hungry people sheltered in caves in the hills. Think of a bairn coughing his life away. Might think of Alycie torn from her home. He might wonder... He pushed the worry away. He must trust that Tom would take care of Alycie. He had enough to worry him here.

The men bunched in small groups over tiny fires, plaids pulled tight around their shoulders. Fergus's thumped the hilt of his sword to bang a dent out of his helm. Richert rifled through a bag. One of the arches muttered under his breath as he ran his hands over his bow. But most of the two hundred men rubbed their hands together over the fires.

James raised his head, sniffing. There was no doubt. The wind carried the scent of coming snow.

The dry, scrubby heather rustled as Wat wended his way past through the camp. He dropped onto the boulder beside James. "Gelleys and the scouts have been gone longer than I like."

"It's a good way to Dumbarton. And no point coming back without news." James tested the point on his thumb and stuck the blade back into his belt.

"Think the English will retire all the way to Berwick?"

James grunted. Wat was nattering on like an old henwife, but he got like that when he was nervous. "You know they will. It will be snow fly soon enough." He grunted a laugh. "They're near enough eating their horses now."

"Might be they'd winter at the Linlithgow Peel."

James shrugged. "How are we on grain for the horses?" What they had, they'd taken from the English, and that was getting scant.

Wat opened his mouth to answer, but a horn winded a long note. He snapped his mouth shut and stood up.

James dropped his hand to his sword hilt, but another note wound its way through the air. "Good." He stifled a sigh of relief.

Allane stood up and rubbed his lean belly. "Wouldn't mind if there was news of some Sassenach with food for us."

Fergus barked a loud bray of a laugh. "We've already taken it all."

"Nae, they must have some left."

James listened quietly to the clatter and mutter of men rising, adjusting weapons and watching the braeside for riders. He stood up with Hew cantered into sight up the slope.

James strode toward him. "Are they moving?"

"Aye. They'll be into the Fells tomorrow. But they sent some ahead." He frowned as he climbed from the saddle. "Ready for plunder, it looks like. Welsh archers and English foot. Two hundred or near enough. Fifty horse with them. Gelleys was tracking them and sent me ahead."

Wat shouted for the horses.

A wind flapped James's cloak. "How far?"

"An hour behind."

One of the men led up his devil of a mount, looking wary when it bared its teeth at him. James took the reins. "Not much cover for an ambush that way," he said more to himself than the scout.

"Not much in the way of trees, but they're into Campsie Fells."

James nodded thoughtfully. It might be possible to attack the English from both flanks. The Fells were hills with sharp, narrow glens between. Not so bad as where he and the King had been caught in an ambush at Dail Righ, but bad enough if they could catch the English unawares.

James nudged his horse to a walk and led them down the braeside amidst the creak of saddle leather, the jingle of bridles and thud of horses' hooves on the hard earth. As he passed a thick clump of bracken, a grouse leapt into the air with a *whirr* of its wings. It was nearing noontide when Hew pointed down a narrow glen with a small stand of scrawny beeches.

As they approached, Gelleys stepped out of the shadows. He motioned north with his chin. "Philp is keeping watch up there."

Philp stood and waved an arm over his head. "They're still

a bit to the north. Horse in the van and the rear. Near two hundred. Mixed Welsh archers and English pikes."

"Must be mad sending out a small force like that," Wat said. "You're sure it's not a trap?"

Gelleys's face turned as dark as his freckles, and he gave Wat an indignant look. "Been at this long enough to know a trap when I see one. We scouted in all directions. It's just this one division."

James made a noise in his throat. "I trust you to scout. That's your job." He twitched a smile. "Wat's to make sure I'm not a fool for trusting you."

Gelleys nodded. "Would seem mad. He's right, but they're looking to plunder food most like. Horses look bad and men no better."

"Our horses can make it down the slope of the glen?"

"Oh, aye. It's steep, but they can make it."

James thrust his chin toward the brae out of sight beyond the glen. "Wat, you take half the men to the other side of the next ridge. Move into position fast, out of sight, and attack their rear on my shout. We'll take the van. Gelleys, you watch on the far ridge. On your way, tell Philp to give me a wave when the English are in sight."

Wat bellowed for his men and whipped his horse to a run. Scree flew from the hooves as the horse scrambled up the slope, men trailing after him. Gelleys paused to speak to Philp and then followed. The thud of hooves faded into silence.

James trotted his horse halfway up the braeside and motioned for his men to form a wedge on him. Fergus took his left, his tangle of red hair and beard jutting from under his dented helm. Allane muttered a *Pater Noster* as he took James's left. Another formed on them and then another until they'd formed a deadly spearhead. Then they waited. A horse whinnied. James drew his sword. He worked his arm

160

through the straps on his shield. Leather creaked behind him as his men readied. His mouth was dry, and he smiled to himself. It was always dry before a battle. He adjusted the reins in his shield hand.

A gust of wind rustled the heather, and blowing needles of snow stung his face. Come now, James thought ruefully. Let's get this over with. And he tried to count the battles he'd been in...large ones...small ones. Tonight he'd try to number them when this one was over.

Philp waved an arm high over his head. James kicked his horse into motion. He kneed his horse from a walk to a trot, wheeling wide around the crest of the brae. The ground was frozen and slippery under the heather. His horse's hooves sliding on the icy slope; James kicked its flanks, and it surged forwards, churning the earth. They rounded the braeside and ahead of them were the English, a mob of foot soldiers surrounded by mounted knights and men-at-arms. A shout went up. They were stopping and bracing for attack.

James lifted his sword and shouted, "Douglas!" Voices took up the cry, "Douglas!" He kicked his horse to a gallop, and the spearhead of thundering hooves and blades flew. Ahead he spotted a knight in a yellow surcoat scattered with starlings. A Clifford, James thought, but too young. Not Sir Robert, Baron of Clifford. A pity, but still, he could die. James slashed the man in the throat beneath his helm with all the weight of his charge, taking his head half off.

Wat and the men he led thundered, screaming over the opposite ridge.

An arrow thudded against James's shield. Fergus galloped beside him, hacking every enemy they passed. James wheeled to the left where the arrow had come from. An archer raised his bow. James rode him down. A pikeman came at him, and James opened him from neck to belly.

"Retire!" a knight was shouting, standing in his stirrups.

The man whipped his horse and galloped away. The knights were fleeing.

"Let them go!" James shouted. The wedge broke apart in a chaos of killing. James spurred his mount over a body slashing off an arm that swung at him. He cracked a head with his shield. He smashed a raised shield and cut down the man who held it. His men were shouting, "Douglas! Douglas!" and "Scotland!" Shot through the shouts were the screams of dying men and the song of steel upon steel.

In front of him, a pikeman buried his weapon in the belly of Fergus's horse. As Fergus tumbled free and scrambled to his feet, James hacked the man's arm. He dropped his pike as Fergus turned to another man-at-arms running at him. Another pikeman came at him, but James had no more time. A man-at-arms grabbed his bridle and swung a sword at him. James kicked him in the chest, and his rearing mount also kicked the man's chest. Blood gushed into the gory, ice-slick ground. Snow flurries floated around a sea of madness. He slashed and hacked. Men came at him, or he rode them down. His horse jumped over a body and stumbled to its knees. It lurched to its feet again as he slammed his shield into the face of a screaming enemy.

He looked around for another enemy to kill. He wheeled his snorting, dancing horse in a circle. The churned ground was rimed with red ice. Wat rode toward him, blood dripping from a gash on his cheek, past bodies thrown down like broken dolls, past his men slumped wearily in their saddles, some afoot, leaning on their swords. Richert knelt next to Allane, pressing a rapidly reddening cloth against his chest.

James nodded. "Well done," he croaked. He cleared his throat, worked spit into his mouth. "Very well done."

CHAPTER 24

*T*he snow squeaked underfoot as he trudged toward Sean Smith, bundled in plaids in the black opening of the cave. Snowflakes feathered their way lazily through the air.

"Sean, is Alycie inside?" He jerked his thumb over his shoulder to his men unloading a hart they'd brought down and few bags of barley. Pickings from the English had been scant since the invaders were near out of food. "We've supplies and need to talk about plans."

Sean's face wrinkled up like a fist. "She's past the ridge..." His mouth worked.

What was wrong with the man? "Why is she out in this weather? Is Will with her?"

When Sean nodded, James said, "Get the men together to bring in the food." The cold stung his wind raw cheeks as he turned and tromped past the cave opening.

His feet slid on the icy ground as he clambered past gray rocks that stuck up through the glimmering white. A dozen steps and his toes were icy numb. He chewed his lip, trying to decide what to do about his people. The trip to the village through ice and snow to destroyed homes might kill some of them, but so might the rest of the winter sheltered in brae-side caves. He'd give Alycie a good scold for being out in this.

"Alycie! Will!" he called as he topped the ridge.

Down the braeside, Will, wrapped tightly in a faded plaid, turned. He stood still, a big gray stone in his arms.

James half ran and half skidding down the slippery brae. The cold air burned his throat. "Where's Alycie?"

Will's voice was thin in the icy air. "She's... here."

James frowned, looking back and forth. Will kicked the snow clear from a spot and knelt to fit the stone into place against another. He looked up. His eyes were red-rimmed. "We must have a wall. Or the priest won't consecrate the ground." His voice broke.

James's chest tightened so hard he could barely speak. "Where is she?"

A blanket of snow-covered mounds. Six. No, seven. One very small. Will pointed to the nearest. James couldn't breathe. He gasped for air, heart thundering in his ears. Little lights flashed behind his eyes. His knee hit the ground. He plunged his hand into the snow. So cold. Oh, God. She must be so cold.

A raw sound ripped out of his throat. Out here alone with no one to comfort her. No one to hold her. In the dark cold and alone. How could he leave her so?

"After the lad died... We tried to nurse her..." Will's voice was hoarse with grief.

James nodded. He had sent her into the hills. Sent her to die. What else could he have done? God! He slammed his fist down on the frozen ground. Drops of red from his split knuckles splattered onto the white snow...

Damn the English for the mongrel curs that they were.

CHAPTER 25

JUNE 1312

*J*ames looked down at the tumbling waters of the River Esk from the top of a beech-topped rise, riding silent beside Robbie Boyd. Behind them a dozen banners whipped and snapped in the summer breeze over their well-armed and armored troop.

In the long shadow of Hadrian's Wall, where it dipped down the slope, King Robert de Bruce raised his arm over his head to call a halt. He turned his prancing mount in a tight circle as he looked back over the long file of men-at-arms, a thousand strong. "Lightly water the horses. Commanders to me," he called as he swung from the saddle. He tossed his reins to a squire and strode into the shade of the high beeches beneath a flurry of fleeing larks.

James jumped from the saddle to follow. He shouted for Wat see to the men whilst the King finally divulged his plans for bringing a thousand men to the border with England after a year of dodging battle with the English army that still sulked at Berwick-upon-Tweed.

Thomas Randolph sent a cool glance James's way,

walking beside Boyd. Gilbert de Hay trailed after the two men.

Boyd nudged James with an elbow. "Turnabout that we invade England. I've known a plump English lass or two I wouldn't mind looking up."

James snorted what he hoped sounded like a laugh and shook his head.

Boyd smirked. "Just because you have a lass waiting doesn't mean I don't like a nice armful."

"We're about business here," the King said. "I'll give the English something to think on other than invading our land. And Clifford's priory of Irthing is near here. As often as he's burned Douglasdale and my own Annandale, we owe him a turn."

James felt his shoulders go rigid under the weight of his armor.

"He burned my Nithsdale this summer past," Randolph said.

"Moreover, James has word that much of the church goods they stripped from our own churches are at Lanercost Abbey. By the Rude of Saint Margaret, we have every reason to see that abbey isn't enriched at Scotland's cost. How much of our downfall was plotted in its walls..." Bruce's face closed like a fist, and he stared for a few moments beyond the stones of the long wall.

James's lip curled in a snarl. "We'll give them a taste of their own foul deeds, my lord."

"James," the King snapped. "You're like a hound with a burr under its tail these days."

James felt a flush climb up from his neck as he scowled at the King.

"I'll not repeat Wallace's mistake. He let his men pillage and rape when he raided into England. He could not keep them under control. Instead of fear, he left boiling anger. But no one—" The Bruce gave each of them a searing look. "—no one will say that of me. We're here for policy, not for revenge."

James folded his arms and stared sullenly at his feet. Then why the hell are we here?

"You understand me, my Lord of Douglas?" A ray of sun gleamed on the King's golden surcoat.

"Aye, Your Grace," James said through stiff lips.

"God knows we have cause for revenge, but it would use gain nothing but more bloodshed. I mean that for all of you. Keep control of your men. No rapes. No killing, except those who resist."

"Why?" Randolph asked, sounding truly baffled.

"I have two purposes. We'll convince the English camp at Berwick that they cannot leave the North of England undefended so that they don't march against Scotland again. And we'll regain at least some of the riches they've stolen from us. They enriched themselves to our cost." A grim smile twitched the King's lips. "Now we begin to take our own back. Today, Lanercost Abbey and Gilsland. Tomorrow Hawtewysill. They to serve those purposes. Robbie, you with me to Lanercost. Jamie will go to Gilsland and Thom second in command. We must do what we came for before there is time for word to reach Chester Castle or Berwick."

"I don't think I..." James frowned. "We're to attack but not kill them?"

"Sweep in. Give them no chance to resist. These aren't knights or fighters. Take what plunder you can carry, destroy and burn what you can't except for the holy precinct itself. I'll join you at Gilsland, and we'll ride for Hawtewysill."

James sucked in a long breath. "We'll let them see how it feels."

"Remember. It is for the Lord Treasurer's use so that we can fight the damned English. Not in your purses. You all

167

understand." The King gave him a long, considering look and nodded brusquely. "Heed my commands. Questions?"

"What of Thirlwall Castle, Sire?" Randolph asked. "They'll see the smoke from the burning if nothing else."

"They've not a large force," James said. "Not enough to be a threat."

"We haven't time to spare." The Bruce strode toward the river where the horses were being led from being watered. "My horse!" The King mounted and yelled for half the ranks of the men to follow.

The men were ranged along the bank, watering the horses, chewing hunks of hard bannock, talking, pissing, laughing, and shouting. At the command, the talk died, and amidst the creak of leather, they climbed into the saddle.

"Come on. We've work," James muttered to Randolph. He swung ahorse and spurred his black devil toward the ford. James kneed his horse to a canter through the bracken, brown already in summer's heat. Randolph rode beside him. Dense stands of beeches cast long shadows along the high stone wall. A covey of partridge took whirring flight from under their hooves. James's horse snorted and danced, and he gave it a sharp tug.

"Think they'll fight, Douglas?" Randolph asked.

James grunted. How did the man expect him to know? "The King said not."

They topped the hill and below stretched a rich patch-work of fields and pasture in the golds and greens of early summer. The River Irthing made a narrow blue-green ribbon that meandered to a score of gray stone houses and the priory spire catching the noon sun a little beyond. In a field, two men threw down scythes and ran. A dozen brown flanked cattle scattered, lowing, as the Scots cantered by.

"Philp, take a couple of men to round those up cattle,"

James called over his shoulder, and the man shouted, as he peeled away to thunder after the fleeing cattle.

Near the shadow of the woods, a swineherd stood gaping, his sounder of dun-colored pigs snorting around him.

"Keith, Hew, take care of those. Then start firing the fields."

A yellow dog darted out from behind a field hedge, snarling and barking behind James. His horse lashed with its rear hooves, and the cur ran yelping. He pulled up his dancing mount and stood in his stirrups to shout, face stiff and grim. "Quiet. Now, you lot listen to me." He waited until the only sound was a horse stamping and the creak of saddle leather. "There's to be no killing unless they resist. Anyone lays hands on a woman or wean, I'll hang you with myself. So don't put me to it." He glanced at Wat. "Half with us, Wat, and the others will follow Sir Thomas."

As Wat shouted to the men, dividing them into two troops, Randolph stepped his horse close and said in a low voice, "We might should see they don't flee and warn the castle."

"No point in that. The smoke will be warning anyway." He raked Randolph up and down with a look. "You know you have to burn the whole town after you have anything worth taking. You can do that, can you?"

Randolph's eyes narrowed. "I'll obey the King's commands."

James thought about making the point that Randolph would also follow his as he was in command, but it wasn't worth arguing. Not as long as the man did what needed to be done. "Good. Anything they can carry, they can take if we don't want it. It's the priory will have riches for the treasury." James wheeled his horse. "Form up on me!"

A bell clanged and clanged, the sound drifting from the priory. James clapped his heels to the horse's flanks, and it took off with an arm-numbing jerk at an open gallop. He led through the deserted street and then past green fields, pounding down the brown dirt road. They must reach the gatehouse before the monks had time to bar their gates. His starred pennant snapped in the wind as they rode. Black-robed friars threw down scythes and dashed toward the walls of the enclosure as they passed. Wat fell in beside him. Behind James, "Scotland!" his men shouted raggedly and "Douglas! Douglas!"

A tonsured, black-robed porter had the wooden gate pushed half-closed. A friar, robe flapping around his shanks as he ran, darted through. Fergus was off his horse and back-handed the porter, knocking him out of the way. He pushed the gate fully open, and they swept through. A moon-faced monk watched from the steps of the chapter and turned to flee through the door. It slammed behind him. A dove cooed from the top of the gatehouse roof. Like a clutch of black quail, a dozen monks huddled together in a far corner of the courtyard.

"Fergus, take fifty men. Fire the buildings outwith the walls," James ordered. "Barn, granaries, as long as it's not sacred. Then fire the fields. Spare any horses. We'll use them." James fastened a cold, hard look on the monks. "Where is the abbot? Either bring him before me, or I'll send my men for him."

Fergus shouted for a file to join him and didn't wait for further orders.

"My lord, look," one of the men called, pointing to the west. Smoke boiled up, thick and gray, and spread in a streaming river across the sky. Thinner ribbons twisted around it from nearby.

A tall man, hawk-nosed, his shaven pate surrounded by thin, gray hair stepped through the door to face James. He folded his hands into the wide sleeves of his finely woven black robe and inclined his head slightly. "Sirrah, you called for me, I am told." He gave James an assessing look. "Excommunicants are not allowed on church grounds."

James bared his teeth in a smile. "We won't be staying long, priest. Since, unlike we Scots, you have treasure in heaven, you have no need for what you've stolen from us. So I'll have it. Coin, jewels, plate. You give it over freely, or we'll tear the place apart searching. Your choice."

The man was trembling with anger, his face pale and gaze boring into James's face. "How dare you! This sacrilege. How dare you!"

James went cold with rage, his heart thumping hard enough to tear from his chest. He reached a hand out and grabbed the man's robe in his fist, lifting the priest from his feet. Gave the man a savage shake. "You'll live through this day. Be grateful." James tossed him onto the ground.

The abbot lay there, still shaking with anger and glaring up at James.

"My people—ones I loved—driven to their deaths. A priest of my barony nailed to a church door. The church goods taken, our own Rude of Saint Margaret stolen, every abbey in Scotland despoiled. Pah." James bent to spit on the ground next to the man's head. He shifted so that his mount sidled, snorting. "Hypocrite. Moneys, plates, chalices, ewers... I'll have it all. Give it up, or my men will do what they must to find it."

The abbot tore his gaze from James's face to stare at the smoke rising from all directions. His Adam's apple bobbed as he swallowed, lines graven deep about his mouth. "You'd burn Lanercost Abbey. It's beauty..." His head shook with tremors. "You'll spare the priory?"

"Wat, you help the good abbot with gathering *our* goods. Use the packhorses that they're so kindly giving us and join me. I'll be awaiting the King." James's lip curled in a sneer. "Remember the name Douglas, Abbot. You'll hear it again."

James wheeled his horse around and trotted out of the gate. He looked up as the rolling clouds of smoke joined overhead. A cow lowed as one of his men slit its throat and jumped back from the splatter of blood. Fergus shouted as he jumped from the hayloft of a barn as flames broke through the wooden roof and leapt into the sky. Sparks flew like fire-flies, landed in a haystack. It smoked and then was flames crackled in it, too.

Allane thrust a torch into the fire and threw it, overhand, into a field of yellow-green barley. Another followed. He turned and saw James. "My lord. The curst field will nae catch."

Even from this distance, screams and shouting carried from the town. A mob of townspeople had gathered in the bend of the river. Above the roofs, flames burst through, playing hide and seek in the roiling smoke.

"Get more men. Trample it."

James sat ahorse as around him, the valley became a smoking ruin. His men laughed and cursed as they galloped back and forth across a field, flattening the grain. Another field caught and sent up thick gray smoke. Iain galloped up chasing a bawling cow and hacked its head half off with a brutal swing of his sword. The air stank of ash and burning and blood.

Hacking from the smoke, Wat rode up beside him. "Ten sacks of anything worth sending to the lord treasurer. Gold plate, silver ewers, gold candlesticks, a few bags of coin."

James laughed. "The King will have done better at Laner-cost. Half the treasure in Scotland ended up there."

The burning barn collapsed with a deafening crash. Sparks gusted on the wind, whirling like sparkling pinwheels.

James's horse danced and snorted. "Time to go. Blow retiral."

Wat shouted to one of the men, and his horn blew. It was growing as dark as sunset with smoke covering the noonday sun as they rode toward the town, Richert bringing up the rear with the packhorses of looted treasure. James hacked as he rode and leaned to spit the taste of bitter ash from his mouth. Thomas Randolph led his column out of the burning town, his banner streaming overhead. The King's force rode into view over a distant rise, and James shouted a command to ride.

CHAPTER 26

That night they made a rough camp in the defile of the Tibalt Burn, cooked oak bannocks over small campfires, and slept in their armor wrapped in their cloaks.

A rock dug into James's back. He pulled his cloak closer around him and rolled over with a grunt. In the darkness, someone snored and grunted, another hacked, and the footsteps of one of the sentries whispered through the grass. A warm night wind that carried a stink of fire rustled the branches. The moon, old and tarnished, hung high in the sky.

James rolled onto his other side and then gave up with a long breath that he kept from being a sigh. What good were sighs or groans? What was lost was lost. He got up, sure there was still some wine in the cask the King had liberated from Lanercost Abbey, Malmsey, red and fruity, meant for the abbot's table. A few more drinks might let him snatch an hour's rest before the early summer sunrise.

He poured himself a cup and settled cross-legged by the dying campfire, a red ember peering out. A sharp rap on the back of his head made him jerk. "Robbie," he grunted.

"Did you leave any for me?"

"Check for yourself." He shouldn't take his foul mood out on Boyd. God knew...

The tun of wine gurgled as Boyd emptied it into a wooden cup. "The King has the right of it. You're as sour as a fishwife lately." Boyd folded himself into a slouch on the other side of the campfire, and the silence stretched out. An owl hooted from a tree. "You're not like yourself."

"It's been..." James turned the crude cup in his hands. "It's been a hard year."

"When has it not been a hard year since most of us can remember?" He took a drink and his eyes gleamed, looking feral in the moonlight. "What happened?"

James didn't want to talk about it. He most definitely did not want to say the terrible words, but Boyd sat waiting. Finally, James said, "Alycie..." To his horror, his voice broke. It felt as though a rock lodged in his throat, blocking his voice, his very breath. He gulped down some wine to wash the damned rock away. He forced his voice to be hard. "Alycie died. Whilst they were in hiding."

"Sometimes, I'm not sure if I'm lucky to have never cared deeply or cursed," Boyd said softly. "You seemed happy, and I envied you, seeing how you were the little that I saw you together. Laughing and all. Though..."

James looked up and considered how strange that the stars held their course, unchanged. They should have fallen like rain. When it hurt so much, just to look at them and be alone.

Sounding amused, Boyd said, "The King says I should marry. Too many of us haven't, and we must." He snorted. "When has there been time, but Master David brought his goodniece back from France."

A grim laugh came out, and James wasn't sure where it came from. "Yes. I know."

"I suppose that he's right. With the English mostly out of the land, we need to build... something. But..."

"But you're damned if you know how, you mean?"

Boyd took a drink and seemed to think it over. "Something like that. When have we done anything but war since either of us was a lad? And Jesu knows, I'm older than you. An old man, near enough."

"Not that old." He thought about it. "How old are you, anyway?"

"I was nineteen when we lost the Battle of Dunbar. Fourteen years since we've been fighting this war. If that doesn't make me old, what would?"

"I was with my father at Berwick then. Before he sent me to France. I was ten." James counted, a little surprised because it had been a long time since he'd thought of how old he was. "Twenty-two now, but I feel—older."

Boyd snorted a laugh. "Do you? Well, with some luck, you may live to be old." He leaned back on an elbow and saluted James with his cup. "Not that I'm so old I may not yet enjoy that wife Robert says I must have. I have a mind to ask for her hand. Caitrina. A nice name. She is..." His teeth gleamed as he grinned. "Oh, she is a fierce one."

Boyd got up and took both their cups to refill. Already there was a rime of gray dawn at the edge of the sky. "No point in trying to sleep. Wonder if they'll make any fight of it at Hawtewysill."

"Probably not. Well... if they got reinforcements from Thirlwall Castle, they might. But most of the forces from Thirlwall are with Edward of Caernarfon in Berwick, so..." He shrugged. "Probably not."

Boyd grunted assent and fell silent. In the quiet camp, someone groaned in their sleep. A nightingale trilled and whistled. "Jamie..." Boyd said in a hesitant voice. "How did it happen?"

James swallowed so that his voice would hold firm. "The wonder is that more didn't die. Hiding in caves. The cold. Not enough food." His voice wobbled, and he took a breath. "She sickened. Just... sickened."

Boyd threw a stick into the dying embers of the fire. "Only two hours to the town. Do you know what he plans?"

James grasped the change in topic gladly. Talking about Alycie just was like peeling the scab from a wound nearly mortal. "Just that they'll be the devil to pay if we don't keep our men in check."

"The King or the devil... I think I'd take the devil's bad side."

A rumble of voice across the camp made James look up. Against the gray light of dawn, he saw the King. "He might send us there if we're careless." He stood up, stretched his back and kicked dirt over the ash of the campfire. He picked up his sword belt and unsheathed the weapon, turned it in his hand. He tossed it from his right hand to his left and tried a cut. "Time to rouse the men."

The men muttered curses and crude jokes as they mounted in the faint light. Wisps of fog drifted through the sweet morning air. The King called his commanders to his side as they rode in ranks, hooves drumming on the stone of the old Roman road as it twisted through the hills. A spire poked into view, and a church bell tolled the Angelus. The morning sun gleamed the roof, and the narrow burn was a silver ribbon.

"Look," one of their outriders shouted.

A line of horses cleared the hill. "Fools," James muttered. Those were no knights nor even men-at-arms, but they had helms and weapons in their hands. There were twenty or so, burghers most likely thinking they could defend their town.

"James, have your men take care of those," the King said brusquely. "We'll secure the town."

177

"Front three files to me," James snapped out. He clapped his spurs to the horse's flanks. "A Douglas!"

The burgers sawed at their reins, mounts rearing and sidling. By the time James reached them, many had already thrown down their weapons and scrambled from their horses. "Yield," James shouted. A big-shoulders man swung a falchion, and James rocked back. He ducked and hacked backhand and slashed to bone and gut. The man slid sideways, foot caught in his stirrup. The horse pounded away, leaving a glistening trail of crimson.

"We yield," a gray-haired man was shouting. He raised empty hands over his head. "Please. We're not fighters."

James gave the man a hard look. "Be sensible, and no harm will come to you." He turned his skittering mount in a tight circle. "You men, gather the mounts, their weapons. Escort our guests back to town. Gelleys, with me." He flicked his reins and cantered to catch up with the King's party.

Ahead he heard a din as he rode past a stone sheep pin. A cow lowed inside a wooden barn. The cobblestone street that wound up a grassy hill lined with stone houses with thatch roofs. At the summit stood the large church, which they'd seen from a distance.

Men and women were being rousted from their homes with some shouts of the men-at-arms. A bairn wailed at the top of its lungs as its mother whirled to scream at the man who shoved her into the street. One of the men was thrown struggling onto the cobblestones. When he pulled a knife from his belt, Philp kicked the weapon from his hand and skewered him with a hard thrust to the gut. He jerked his sword free. The man scrambled crab-wise back, blood leaking down. A woman screamed, "Murderers!" and pulled at his arm as he crumpled.

"James, you see to things here and keep tight control," the King said. He motioned to his men to follow as he turned his mount. "That church belongs to the See of Aberdeen and owes their tithes."

"Hear you," James shouted. "Anyone who raises a hand against us will die."

The defeated burghers were beginning to straggle into sight.

"Gather those people together outwith the town," James said to Wat. He raised his voice to be heard over the murmur of voices and weeping of the knot of townspeople. "Search the houses. Make sure none are hiding. And make a good job of searching for valuables."

An ululating scream so high and piercing it cut the air and raised the hair on the back of James's neck. He pointed to the open door of the house. There was another long scream that must have ripped someone's throat.

"If that's what I think..." James threw himself from his saddle and sprinted through the open door. Within, a low fire burned on an open hearth, and a wooden table was over-turned, a chair tossed aside. James saw only the man's back as he humped, and white legs spread beneath him. There was a broken whimper. James pulled his sword, reversed it and hammered down with the hilt on the man's dark head. The rapist flattened with a grunt.

"God damn me," Wat said behind him. "The King will have our heads on a pike."

James gave the fallen man a vicious kick in the side to roll him over and expelled a long breath of relief to see that it wasn't one of his. "Drag him outside."

He looked down at the woman who had curled herself into a ball on the floor, shoulders heaving. He rubbed a hand over his face. He'd send one of the townswomen to bring her out, but there was business to take care of first.

Wat grabbed the miscreant's feet and backed his way out. The man's head thudded hard on the doorstep, and blood

179

dribbled from where the blow had split his scalp open. James sheathed his sword, shook his head, sighed again and followed. He climbed into the saddle feeling unreasonably weary. This was somehow much less satisfying than it should have been.

Wat had already tied the man's hands behind his back, though he still lay limp and slack. James nodded brusquely, and their gazes locked for a grim moment. "Bring a rope." He looked around for a good spot for the job. There were trees between the houses, oaks mostly with branches too low to the ground. He turned his horse and beside the largest of the houses, one with three stories that must belong to a wealthy burgher, he spotted a tall pine, thick and hoary, the lowest branch higher than a man could reach sitting astride. "There."

The man groaned and shook his head. Gelleys and Wat pulled him to his feet. He jerked, looked around eyes rolling, showing the whites. "It was play! Just a little play... our right. We took the town."

Philp ran up with a chair and rope. At James's nod, the other man uncoiled the rope and threw it over the lowest branch of the pine. A sparrow flew out with a flash of black and white wings, scolding with an angry *cree cree cree*. The rope's end was knotted around the tree. The man began to toss and lunge. He was dragged as he kicked and tried to dig his feet into the stones. Under the dangling rope, Wat jerked the man around to face James, where he sat in icy silence.

James let the moment run out as a breathless silence fell over the town. "You disobeyed the commands of your lawful lords and commanders. You broke the law of God and of Scotland. In the name of Lord Robert, King of Scots, I sentence you to death."

The man's mouth worked as wordless croaks came out. He was hoisted onto the chair. "Mercy," he pleaded.

Philp jerked the chair free. The man swung once. Wat grabbed his body and pulled, lifting his own legs to give his full weight.

It was done.

James backed his horse up a step and wheeled to face his men. He looked from one to another, pale faces, open-mouthed. "The next man who commits rape will have the lash before he is hanged. Now search the houses. Seize any money, jewels or plate. Wat, find a woman to care for that lass, and get her with the others. Then fire the town."

CHAPTER 27

Standing in the broom beside the Tweedside road, King Robert narrowed his eyes at his nephew. "See you move them well away."

The sun was already low to the west, and the beeches cast long, dark shadows.

Randolph scowled at James but nodded to his uncle in grudging submission. "Yes, sire."

James could see him biting back an argument at being sent ahead with their hostages and the gold they'd taken in tribute for leaving at least part of Durham and the Tyme unburnt.

"I'll not chance losing what we went for while I'm taking Berwick. You hurry them as far to the east as you can before you make a cold camp."

Randolph pulled a small grimace that the King ignored as the man swung into the saddle and shouted for the half of their men who would ride with him to mount. Half a dozen finely dress lads, heirs of burghers who would be held until a ransom was paid, bunched together on their horses. A couple glared, but most kept their eyes down from the fearsome

Scots. James's mouth twitched. The fact was they'd be well treated. King Robert did not take revenge on children, however much his own family had suffered. Besides, they were worth gold only alive.

They watched together as the troop of five hundred clattered their way around the hill. James prodded a back tooth with his tongue as he turned his attention to the silver river that flowed nearby, splashing over gray outcroppings. "We need most of the men near enough to come on our call when we open the gate. But not so close, they'll raise a alarm."

The Bruce raised a sardonic eyebrow. "Thank you, Jamie. I'd never have thought of that."

"Pardon, Your Grace." James shrugged. "I was wondering if we dare take them closer. We only have ten ladders. So... How many with us?"

"It's been a very long while since I was in Berwick." The King was staring in the direction of the town that had once been Scotland's greatest port—until the English raped it. He gave his head a sharp shake. "Yes. They will wait here out of sight whilst we open the gates. This is close enough to hear a horn in the quiet of the night."

"We'll have to hold it until they reach us..." He blew out a breath. There was no point in trying to tell the King not to risk himself. "Wat." He motioned his sergeant over. "Send two men with horns close to town. I want to be sure you're on your way when we need you. Keep your horses and swords to hand."

In the shade of the beeches, the men remaining with them stood, tending their horses, scratching, checking their bags for bannocks left from their last camp, and talking. When the King called to them, the talk died, and they gathered around.

"Fifty men," the King said. "Ones who can move quietly and kill with their dirks. Who'll step up?"

Fergus was the first to step forward.

James snorted. Fergus always wanted to be first in a fight. "You come on the run when we need you instead. Big ox."

Instead, Philp was the first, and the King counted until they had fifty. "Off with your armor," he said as he stripped off his mail hauberk. "Only the men who are raising the ladders should have pikes."

James dropped his hauberk and re-buckled his sword belt around his bare waist. There was no wood ash for they'd built no fires, so he thrust his chin towards the edge of the river. He strode to the river's edge and knelt in the shallows to slather mud across his chest. The King squatted next to him and smeared mud across his own face, and they daubed themselves accompanied by the grunts and splashing of their men.

James bit the inside of his lip as he smeared mud across his cheeks. "They've three hundred men. It will be a hard fight."

"Don't fash yourself, Jamie. It's hardly my first."

"Does that really mean you must always risk yourself?"

The Bruce snorted and stood up. "We can follow the road. That will make it easier going in our bare feet. By the time we walk to the castle, it will be full dark."

James suppressed a sigh as the King took one of the pikes and slung a coiled rope ladder over his shoulder. He'd stay at the King's back. It was all he could do.

So he strode at the King's back as they walked single file through the murky night. A sea wind raised goosebumps across his arms, and beech branches rattled beside the road. Every sound had his hand on his hilt. They made their way beside the river, where it rounded the hill and the hugely looming cliff where Berwick Castle stood rose before them. Watchfires lit each corner tower. Otherwise, it was a monstrous mass of black against a purple night sky.

The Bruce paused, and James strained to make out the

town at the base of the cliff. Nothing moved. The spars of a single ship bobbed at a pier past the darkened warehouses and homes.

"Let's go." The King strode up the steep, rocky hillside, veering off the road.

James grunted when he caught his bare foot in a gash of broken ground. The tourney grounds. It went up to the east wall between two of the towers. Below, the tide washed on the rocks like a sleepy lullaby. He could only hope it had put the guards to sleep enough for them to make it up the ladders. It was hard to fight halfway up a ladder. Or to guard a King's back.

In front of him, the King jumped down into the dry ditch that circled Berwick. James followed and scrambled up the far edge to stand on the narrow strip against the castle's rough wall. "Spread out," he said softly to the men who followed. They knew their business though, so that was his only order.

There were scrapes and a few soft clangs as the King and Philp fastened the ladder onto their pikes. James drew his dirk and gripped it between his teeth, the metal cold and bitter in his mouth. You can't draw a sword while you're climbing.

There were a few clatters as the pikes were placed on the ground. James strained his eyes and ears. Somewhere there must be guards patrolling the ramparts, but there was no sound of marching feet. The great castle could hold off a siege for many months. Perhaps it had made them complacent.

He brushed by the King to put his foot on the first rung and began to climb. There was a faint snort but no other argument. He climbed the rough wooden boards of the ladder. Scanning both ways to see that the parapet was clear, he vaulted his legs over the crenelated wall onto the parapet-walk.

A dog barked in the yard below. It began to howl. Someone shouted, "Attackers!"

The King was half-over the edge of the wall. Gelleys vaulted into view. Footsteps pounded from both directions. Below, the dog barked and growled as it ran back and forth.

"'Ware the wall!"

"Down," James shouted, drawing his sword. "We're discovered." A guard rushed James, steel catching the faint light of a watchfire. The blade slid across the flesh of James's chest as he sidestepped, a slash of fire. He sucked in a breath as he smashed his sword into the side of the guard's head. The blow was hard enough to smash in the side of the man's helmet. The man fell back, blood dripping down his neck. James drew a killing backstroke across his gut and sent him off the edge of the parapet with a kick.

The King grabbed James by the arm and threw him towards the ladder. "Go!"

He could feel blood dripping down his belly and legs. The slash hurt like the very devil, but it didn't feel as though it were very deep. He scrambled over the wall and down the ladder. He jumped the last few feet and went to his knees. If he could bandage it before he bled out, he'd live. A horn was blowing. He wasn't sure if it was theirs or the English, but it would bring their men.

The King was hoisting James's arm over a shoulder. "Run!"

Gelleys was on his other side. Between the two of them, he half-ran and was dragged, feet knocking on hard stones.

There was a hammer of hooves on the road. Wat shouted, "The gates coming down."

The King hoisted him into the saddle. "Ride!"

James thrust his bare feet into the stirrups and clapped

them to the horse's flank. He pressed a hand to the slash where blood sluggishly leaked.

"Can you stay ahorse?" the King called to him.

A bark of laughter tore into his chest. God that hurt. "No choice. I'll make it.

ames scraped the razor across his chin, shaving away half of his short beard. "Everyone knows I wear a beard, Wat. I won't be recognized." Nearby the River Tweet rustled its way past bare oaks mixed with dark pines that scraped the sky.

His sergeant scowled at him. "Too many have seen you in battle. Or know you from negotiations. It's an insane risk, my lord."

James kept his face straight, although his lips twitched. How many years had they been having this selfsame argument? He shaved the other side of his chin before he answered. "I have to see Roxburgh. Look more closely at its defenses if we are to take it. And we must have it. Before summer."

He bent over the basin and splashed water on his face. He wiped his face dry on a strip of rough cloth. How odd it felt to have the skin around his mouth free of the beard he had worn for years. He ran his hand thoughtfully over his face. Perhaps he'd remain clean-shaven.

Wat shook his head. "You've never grown a whit less

stubborn. Not since the first day I served you."

James picked up his ivory comb from the rock he was using as a table and paused. "Did you think that I would?"

"I keep hoping. So does my lord intend to tell me his plan? You've not brought horses to sell."

"No, I fear I've used that trick one too many times. The commander there is Guillemin de Fiennes from Guyenne. I believe I can still make shift to be French if I put my mind to it. A tradesman with word from his home in Boulogne." James ran the comb through his hair and smoothed the front of his woolen tunic.

Wat widened his eyes. "Do you have any word from Boulogne?"

"No. But Fiennes doesn't need to know that." James grinned. When Wat slapped his forehead with his palm, they both laughed. James threw his arm around Wat's shoulder. "Now, don't be an old henwife. I'll take a good look at the place even if I don't talk to Fiennes. Then I shall make us a plan."

"If you don't get yourself captured," Wat muttered. He sighed heavily as they walked to the four horses hobbled within the thick stand of hawthorns.

James shoved aside the bare branches and picked up a large pack. "I've cleared our stores of lace and silk. Most of it did come from France at some point."

"Before we took it from the English, you mean."

"Well... Yes. I mind most of this came from that visit last summer to Hartlepool. No point in letting it burn." James strapped the pack into place on the back of the placid sumpter horse. "I'll be back by nightfall tomorrow. Meet me here."

"God speed," Wat grumbled as James swung into the saddle.

"Don't fash yourself so much. It's not the first time I've

climbed into the leopard's mouth." James took the sumpter horse's lead and ducked under a low hanging branch as his horses sloshed through the icy slush on the ground.

He turned onto the road, slick, frozen under a skin of snowy slush. The road began to rise and beyond the massive towers of Roxburgh Castle brooded above the tops of the trees. He'd never been inside this castle. He had no reason as a squire serving Bishop Lamberton and no opportunity since with it tightly in enemy hands.

The trees ended, and before him rose the bare cliff, topped by the light stone of the huge keep. No fools the English. There would be no cover near the castle. It had a certain majesty where it crowned the narrow promontory. He smiled grimly. The cliff was not tall, but the rise sheer and massive, taking up all the summit. The only way to it was a narrow pasture glittering with a coating of ice. A cow lowed as he passed and then raised its head to gaze beyond him.

A half-grown lad in homespun carrying a stave drove a couple of shaggy, red-hided cattle before him. One of them stopped, shaking its head. The boy shouted, "Hoi. Go on with you." He flicked it on the flank with his staff, and the cow lumbered on.

The bridge over the frozen moat was down, but two mail-clad guardsmen, pikes in their hands, stood in the shadow of the barbican. James dismounted and strolled toward them. He nodded. "Sirs, I am Jacque de Guyenne, a merchant. Might I have entry into this beautiful château-fort?"

"Risky traveling alone," one of the guards, older, grizzled and scarred, said.

"Indeed, monsieur. We were attacked near the forest and my guard slain. I hope to hire another but the risk..." He shrugged. "...it may be no one will be willing to take such, and what am I to do?"

A younger guard put in, "What you selling then, Frenchie?"

The older man grunted. "Nothing you can afford, I'd wager."

"Fine lace and silks I carried with me from Guyenne. But with the war, this has been a lean year."

"Won't sell nothing here in the gate. Might as well go in. Don't think you're no danger of attacking the place."

"Merci." James nodded and tugged on his horse's reins to lead them through the shadowy passage. Watery beams of light through the murder holes lit the way.

Inside the walls of the wide outer bailey yard, everything was castle business and noise. Above on the battlements, a crossbow-bearing guardsman paced. A hound met James, curiously sniffing at his heels. Across the way, the wide doors of the forge were flung open and within a smith bent, hammering over his anvil. A wain was being unloaded and horses unharnessed, the men grumbling and gossiping. A servant in homespun, cloak flapping in the light wind, bent under the weight of a barrel as he carried it toward the inner gate. Another lugged blades wrapped in a cloth to a large wooden building James guessed was the armory.

A light snow began to fall as James led his horse toward the doors of the long wooden stable against the far outer wall. As he neared it, another guard rounded the corner of the embattlement overhead, striding into view. It seemed few guards for so large a place, but its strength was in its twenty-foot-high walls thicker than a man was tall. Even the wall barring the way to the inner bailey was tall as a man.

A rangy man stood in the wide doorway of the stable shouting orders as a stable boy led an animal into the stable. Another ragged boy staggered by the door carrying a head-high pile of hay.

"Bonjour, Maître d'écurie, have you room for my horses?"

"And who might you be?" he said. "We don't have hay for every horse in Scotland."

"Merely a humble merchant. I stay one night unless the commander of your château-fort invites me to stay longer. But such goods as I carry do not take long to show."

The man grunted. "I don't know. Don't like the chance of our own mounts going short what with the Black Douglas and King Hob ambushing supply trains and all."

"Ah, Maître, of course, your stable is your concern. Now mine is that my packs are so full, I must be rid of some of what I carry." James handed the man his reins with a wry smile and unfastened the pack. He took out a folded piece of heavy yellow silk. "Perhaps you would aid me with accepting this piece?"

The man took the cloth and ran a thumb over its smooth surface. "It might do for a tunic. To help you out, I'll take it off your hands. I guess you could stable those animals of yours in one of the stalls. There's one in the back corner big enough for both. Better keep well away from the destriers. They don't take kindly to strangers." He thrust the reins back into James's hands as he turned on his heel.

"Maître d'écurie, if you happen to know someone looking for work, I need to hire a new guard. The former one I fear may have met a sad fate at the hands of les Ecossais."

The man paused and frowned at James. "And where might that have been?"

"Not so very far. A day's ride—where the road goes along... I think it is the River Tweed? Is that the correct name?"

"Nothing unusual these days, but you'd best tell that story to Sir Guillemin."

"I will be pleased to. Perhaps he will know of someone I can hire." James led the horses into the barn's warmth, rich with the smell of horse sweat and hay and the shit one of the stable boys was shoveling up as James walked past. In the far back corner, he unsaddled his mount and took the pack from the sumpter horse. He'd care for them later but found a bucket of water and hay. A slap to his horse's flank, and he shouldered the heavy pack and strode out into the watery sunlight.

"Most like you'll find Sir Guillemin in the great hall," the stable master called to him as he passed.

James smiled and nodded his thanks. The thick plank gate to the inner bailey stood open, so James strolled through behind a servant bent under the weight of faggots strapped to his back. They passed a man lazily sweeping snow from the cobbles as they passed through the smaller yard to the door of the keep where a single guard stood watch. A servant cursed when a squawking chicken he carried pecked at his hand. The servant opened the door and entered, but James paused.

"Is Sir Guillemin within?" James asked.

"That he is."

James looked up. Four stories, a good-sized keep. "I'll find him then." He stomped the wet snow from his boots before he went in. The fire on the wide hearth gave off a welcome warmth, and a rough-coated hound stretched out in front of it at the feet of a man reading a parchment and a black-robed friar waiting. Torches flickered in sconces along the white-washed walls interspersed with painted shields. A pair of servants were lifting the top of a long trestle table from its legs. Another was shoving the rushes on the floor into a pile whilst one gathered an armload to carry out.

"Damn me. Cleaning the whole hall. Waste of sweat," one of them said as he hoisted up the table.

The other grunted. "His Lordship wants his fine feast come Shrove Tuesday. Not but what I don't want my share."

James approached heavy muscled, grizzled man with the

parchment and the friar at his side. "Boujour." James gave a slight bow. "Sir Guillemin de Fiennes?"

The man looked up, dark eyes looking distracted. "What?"

"Your pardon, sir. I'm Jacque de Guyenne. A merchant." He let the pack onto the floor. "I beg the courtesy of the castle for the night. Also, the stable master suggested I mention that I and my guard were attacked..." He shrugged. "Oh, about a day's ride away. My guard, he did not escape."

Sir Guillemin thrust the letter at the friar. "You see what I'm up against. Write the answer to Lord Clifford that I'll hold out until the English army arrives. But if the King's army does not come this time, we will lose the castle." He waved the friar away and gave James a raking look. "There is nothing I can do about your guard. You should give thanks to the Good God that you escaped."

"I do. Though if there is someone here who might be hired for a guard for my return to Guyenne, that would be most wondrous. And if the knights of the castle might want to look over my goods..." He smiled amiably. "... I would give thanks even more, my lord."

"I'd give much to be returning there myself." He looked around the hall and spotted one of the servants. "Bring a flagon of wine and cups. Now show me these goods you've brought and tell me when was the last time you were home? Hearing of home will make you welcome to stay for our Shrove Tuesday feast." His mouth gave a sour twist. "Not like we would have at home, but I've managed to put back a tun of good wine. Not the vinegar they drink here."

James picked up his pack. "I fear two days is longer than I can stay, but I'm pleased to talk about home." As he followed the knight to the high-backed lord's chair on the dais, he swallowed down a satisfied smile.

CHAPTER 29

*T*he sky was deep purple, strewn with stars, and a thin crescent of the moon hovered at the top of the trees. Men muttered in the winter chill. Armor was donned, rope ladders sorted, and dirks sharpened. James looked around for Walter and saw the lad still kneeling over his armor. "Hurry," James said. "We haven't all night." Syme came trotting out of the darkness carrying one of the ladders he took such pride in making. "I want ten for the attackers. Do we have that many?"

"More than that," Syme said. "Do you want to take all of them?"

"No. But see that they're well wrapped, so they don't rattle."

James sat on the edge of a boulder and stripped off his leather shoes. "Where are my boots?" he barked at Walter. "No, not the mail for climbing. The leather." Walter helped him to don the hauberk over his head and knelt to shove the boots onto his feet. It was tempting to make the lad stay behind, but he'd pleaded until James finally gave in. "You stay well behind me, lad. You're not a knight yet, and don't forget it."

"Do you want your sword or just your dirk? And your helm?"

"No helm. Dirks for tonight's work, my black cloak, and I'll carry one of the pikes. And blacken your face and your hands." He raised his voice over the camp's clamor. "All of you who are going with me, wear your darkest cloak. Use the ash to blacken your faces and hands and bring only your dirks."

He tested the point of his dirk on this thumb and sucked away a drop of blood. He'd never led a riskier attack for if they were spotted it would be too late to retreat. If they were spotted... He expelled a long breath. No point in thinking of that. It would be what it would be. He knelt and scooped up ash and smeared it until only his eyes gleamed in the faint light.

James stuck his dirk in his belt and motioned Wat over. "If the attack goes against us, get the rest of the men away. Do not, and I mean this most direly, do not try to come to our aid if we're captured."

Wat sucked a whistling breath through his teeth and opened his mouth to object.

"I don't want to hear it. You have your orders." He fastened his cape and pulled the hood up over his head. "Let's go," he called and strode through the trees for the road, ice sheathed leaves crunching under his feet. Behind his men hurried after him, icy bracken crunching underfoot. Bare branches scraped overhead with a sound of rattling bones. James wondered whether this was the last night they would see... whether he was, at last, leading his men to disaster. Syme fell in behind him, and the rest of the men followed, silent in their own thoughts.

In the dark, James didn't see the end of the trees until he stepped into the open. "On hands and knees," he whispered to Sym. "Pass the word back. Follow in twos and threes and spread out when we reach the moat."

James dropped onto the hard-rimed ice. He tucked the pike under one arm and draped his cloak over it, letting it drag a behind--awkward as Hades. He began to creep up the slope, angling into the meadow away from the road. The cold burned his fingers. He crawled. The hard ground scraped his palms and his knees until they were on fire. The head of the pike smacked his chin; he sucked in a breath and kept crawling.

When the ground slanted downward under his hands, he dared a glance ahead—the ice surface of the moat reflected the thin sickle of the moon. From inside the castle, James heard laughter and what sounded like drunken singing.

"What's that?" a loud voice said overhead.

James froze in place, his heart trying to hammer its way out of his chest.

Another voice brayed a laugh. "Crofter Duncansone and that boy of his must be making a merry Shrove Tuesday. Too drunk to take in their cattle."

"God damn." The voice became fainter. "Wish I was."

"If you hadn't pissed off the sergeant..." and the men were too far to hear. James strained his ears and let out a breath he hadn't known he was holding.

Now would the ice over the moat hold their weight? The best he'd been able to do was toss a heavy stone to test it as he'd left at first light. It seemed thick and Jesu God, but it felt cold enough. He rested the weight of his hands on it. His body shook with the chill as he crept forward, now his knees. Another creep forward and another. He climbed onto the narrow ridge of earth between the moat and the wall and leaned his back against the cold stone. As he untangled the pike from his cloak, Syme knelt, untied from around his shoulders the bag that held the ladder, and held up the hooks. James's fingers were so numb it took three tries to wriggle the point of the pike into the hole as Fergus worked a pike's tip into the other. Fergus's eyes gleamed as they exchanged a glance. James nodded, and together they lifted it. He let the pike lean against the wall. That always made catching the hook easier. It clattered once. James jerked. He nodded. Syme grinned before he clamped his dirk between his teeth and scrambled up. James followed close at his heels and could feel the warmth of Fergus, right behind.

Syme swung a leg over and grunted and whispered, "Hell mend it."

As James threw his arm over through the crenel, a guard raised his sword over his head. James froze with nowhere to dodge. The sword started down. Syme thrust, throwing his arm around the guard's neck to grab his mouth. Blood gushed as James managed to jerk back. Syme held on as the guard jerked. Philp ran up behind.

A rush of dark silhouettes spilled over the battlements. "Hell mend them," James muttered as he threw his leg over the gore-slimed stone. "Go. Go. Clear the walls, then follow to the gate." He pointed in the direction he'd heard the other guards walk. Fergus hoisted himself over the edge. "Syme, Philp, Fergus, with me." He paused until Gelleys and Walter hove themselves over. "You two with me. Hoist up the ladder. We'll need it."

Fergus worked the hooks loose and pulled the ladder up. James heard grunting and the sounds of a scuffle past the far corner tower. Even drunk, soon the keep would hear. "Hurry."

He dashed along the parapet to the narrow stairs, took

them three at a time, and ran to the inner wall. They'd have to manage without pikes this time. The sounds of a lute and voices raised in a bawdy song spilled over the inner wall.

"I can do it," Fergus grunted. He grasped the two hooks and strained overhead. "Curse it. Can't reach." Syme knelt and got onto his hands and knees. Fergus stepped onto his back and reached high overhead. The metal scraped on the stone. James was already shoving past him as Fergus jumped down. He scrambled up the ladder and swung a leg over. He dropped, knees bent, onto the ground.

The door of the keep was thrown open and spilled a path of light across the bailey and the sound of fiddles and pipes, laughing, calling, chattering. A man stumbled drunkenly out, unlacing his hose. Piss splashed onto the cobblestones. James eased his dirk out of his belt. A rumble of laughter boomed into the night. The man didn't look at James, turned back into the keep, and the door banged shut. James expelled a long breath, stuck the blade of his dirk between his teeth, and felt for the heavy bars that fastened the gate. He lifted the first and eased it to the ground. The second followed. He pushed the gate open.

"Sir James..." Walter yelped.

James cut him off with a hard hand across his mouth. "Quiet." He jerked the lad through the gate and held his dirk in one has as he shoved the lad against the wall. "You stay behind me." His men rushed through the gate in a dark wave. "Half on one side and half on the other," he commanded. "Through the door and you take that side to clear it. I'm through first."

The wave of men parted, half to the near side of the door. James waved the others away, and they dashed for the other side. He took a breath and burst through the door.

Dozens of brightly dressed men, wine goblets in hand,

199

eddied around the crowded hall. The bones of a boar picked clean and broken bread scattered the side tables. A few men sprawled on benches. One lay amidst the rushes on the floor, mouth open, snoring. Atop one of the tables, a squire stood spinning in a jig. A gray-haired knight at a side table had fallen forward, face in a puddle of spilt wine. The room reeked of the smell of sweating men, wine, roasted meat and wood smoke.

"God in heaven!" one of the English shouted. "Scots!"

A din of confusion and shouting broke out. The black-robed priest dropped a goblet of wine on the floor. A figure dashed through the door, shouting for a guard. One of the English knights leapt onto a table that overturned with a crash. He flung himself forward as the table went to use its momentum. James dropped to a knee and brought his dirk up with a grunt. It ripped through the satin and the gut beneath. James rolled to the side away from the gush of blood.

A foot kicked at his head and James slashed the back of the leg, jumped to his feet, and hammered his hilt on a bare head as another man went down.

Sir Guillemin bellowed, "Out! To the East Tower. Now!" He bulled into Gelleys with a shoulder. Gelleys flew backward with a yell. Sir Guillemin pounded for the door, jumped heavily over a body, and slashed at a reaching hand.

An arm encircled James's neck, a blade at his cheek. He slammed his elbow deep into a belly and brought his heel down hard on a softly shod foot. "Get him," James grunted as he slashed at his attacker's face. The man stumbled back. James plunged his dagger down into his throat and ripped it free. He kicked aside the gurgling body.

Gelleys was picking himself up off the floor, shaking his head like a stunned calf. Fergus bawled, "Come back here, you Sassenach scum," as he ran out the door. A dozen of James's men followed in his wake. A cold wind cut through the fug of the great hall.

The priest knelt next to the fireplace, hands raised, whimpering, *"Misericordia... Misericordia..."* Firelight gleamed on his sweaty face. Walter sat on the chest of a knight, his dirk at the man's throat. "I took him prisoner," the lad crowed proudly. Philp was kicking a man into submission as the man crouched, arms over his head. The drunken knight crashed to the floor and looked blearily around.

"So you did. Well done." James's mouth twitched. "Philp, enough. Get the prisoners bound. Walter, you help him." He strode to a stone basin beside the keep door and plunged his hands and dirk in, splashing them until the water was died red. He flicked the water off. "After that's done, Philp, take half a dozen men and go for Wat. We'll want all the men here." He strode out.

"Don't, you fool," one of his men yelled as he ran.

James looked up in time to see, silhouetted against the sliver of moon, one of the English atop the battlement climbing a merlon. He jumped. A scream echoed.

"Here," Fergus called, standing in front of a corner tower. He kicked the door with a resounding crack and kicked it again. He backed up a few steps and ran at it, bounced off with a yelp of pain.

"Never mind." James frowned up at the height of the tower. "They've picked a tight hidey-hole. Fergus, take a dozen men and make sure they don't decide they want a fight." He looked around at his men gathering, their breaths smoking in the icy air. "The rest of you search every corner. Make sure we haven't missed a single enemy."

Fergus stomped and rubbed his hands together. "Rotten way to spend a feast day."

James snorted a short laugh. "I'm thirsty. Think I'll try out that wine."

"What about us, my lord?" Fergus called to his back.

"I'll send out a flagon, but you'd best not get drunk. Call me when our men arrive." Inside the great hall, he slammed the door behind him. A knight knelt, hands bound, heaving into the rushes. Gelleys had one of the bodies by the arms, pulling it as he backed toward the door. Walter knelt behind the priest as he bound the man's hands. "Make sure those are tight," James said.

Gelleys slammed the door behind him and grunted as he grabbed the hands of another body to drag out into the cold.

The priest stared at him, his mouth working before he managed to stutter, "What... what will you do with us?"

James scowled, tempted to frighten the man into pissing himself. Instead, he said, "I don't kill priest, at least not unless they trying to kill me first." The room stank of blood and shit. All except the table on the dais was knocked over, food trampled into the rushes and wine puddling with splashes of blood. James strode across the long hall and sprang onto the dais. He sniffed the half-full flagon. The wine had a scent of grapes and cherries and violets. He picked up a silver goblet, tossed the dregs onto the floor, and filled it.

A deep drink, and he sighed. It warmed his belly and spread through his body like a caress. He drained the cup. "Walter, fill a flagon and take it out to the men. After tonight they deserve to have their bellies warmed. See if there's any food left fit to eat." He nudged a broken loaf with his foot and then threw himself down in the lord's chair, refilled his flagon, slid down in the chair and sprawled out his legs.

A fire crackled on the hearth. It felt good to be warm, and the wine was sweet. He drained the goblet again and let it drop from his hand beside him in the chair. He closed his eyes. They would call him when the men arrived. So much to do...

Alycie's arms were soft around his waist as she leaned into his chest.

"They told me you had died." He breathed in her scent of grass and lavender, but an icy river of horror washed through his veins. "How could I not know you were alive?"

"Wheesht, all is well," she whispered.

"It isn't." He wound his fingers into her hair. "How could I have thought that you dead?"

"My sweet lord..." Her voice was a rustling of wind.

Walter said, "My lord?"

James jerked his eyes open, heart trying to hammer its way out of his chest. He sat straight up, and the goblet clattered to the floor. "What?"

"I found rounds of cheese and bread and apples still in the kitchen." Walter sat a platter piled with food on the table. "You never ate. I thought you must be hungry. I took roast chicken and wine to the men on guard."

James rubbed the back of his neck and took a deep breath. He wasn't sure why dreaming that she was alive always left him with such a feeling of horror.

One of the prisoners, the knight, hands tied but asleep by the fire snorted in his sleep. The friar had his back propped against the wall and watched James, face knotted in a scowl. "What of the dead? The men you killed? Will you deny them a Christian burial?"

James got picked up the goblet, strolled to the table, and filled it. He tore off a hunk of bread. "If you want to stand in the cold, I'll let you say words over them."

"King Edward is raising an army, you know. He will make you pay for your treason. And hell will welcome you all."

His mouth full, James took a swallow of the red wine to wash the bread down. "Why, I am sure Edward will try, priest." James cut a piece of cheese and popped it into his mouth. He chewed lazily. "I'm sure he will try."

The door opened. Wat stepped inside, slapping his hands together. "Jesu God, it's cold out there."

"Warm up by the fire. I'll get the men set. We have a right nest of asps trapped in the tower."

James slapped Wat's shoulder as he passed and strolled out, surprised to see that he'd slept long enough for golden fingers of dawn to have reached into the eastern sky. He jogged up the steps to the parapet. The eastern tower had a high slit window. He squinted into the dim interior. A face peered out at him and jerked back. "Where is Igram?" he called down. "I want him." He strode past the tower and looked up at the other side—another slit but this one higher. If anyone was near, he couldn't see them.

His tall, lanky archer hurried up the twisting steps to the battlement.

"My lord?"

James pointed to the other side of the tower. "Over there. I want you to watch. Anything moves inside, you take a shot at it. Put one of your men on this side as well, but that has the better line of sight."

"I'll need a brazier to keep my hands warm enough for an aim."

James looked up at the cold, clear winter sky. A few stars were still scattered across the deep blue of the western horizon. He shrugged. "Take what you need, but keep a close watch. If it moves, shoot it."

Igram gave one of his brisk nods and bent to shout down, "Niniane, come up here."

James reached the bailey yard and called to Fergus, "Take your men inside. We'll stay warm whilst we can and send Philp out to take over the guard. Where is Syme?" He spotted the blacksmith near the door as he pulled it open. "Syme, I want you."

"Sir?"

"Come. The King will reward you right well for bringing this news to him at Perth." James kept going toward the narrow stairs that led up to where the lord's chamber would be. "You may tell him yourself that we have taken the royal castle of Roxburgh, and I await his command. But I'll give you a letter to carry as well."

* * *

JAMES LEANED BACK against the wall of the keep and propped up a foot. He glowered at the tower.

Wat sat on the step, running a whetstone along the edge of his blade. "Bad luck they had food and water in there."

"Not luck. Sir Guillemin is no fool and headed for where they had stores. But Igram said he's had at least two hits. They'll give up soon."

A bow snapped, and an arrow clattered on stone. Above on the parapet, one of the archers cursed at his miss.

"They must be short of food by now anyway."

"Mayhap. No way to be sure."

"How long you think until the King sends word what we're to do with the place?"

James shrugged. "He'll order it slighted, but—a royal castle?" James reached for his own whetstone and sank down beside Wat. He whisked the stone along the gleaming edge of his sword. "I must have his command."

A white cloth waved in the window slit. Released, it drifted down to the parapet and caught on the edge. James grunted as he stood. "Hold," he called up to the archer and took the stairs two and three at a time.

205

The edge of a face appeared in the narrow opening. "A truce? Whilst we talk?"

James craned his neck back and stared into the slit. It was a younger face, thin and anxious, not Sir Guillemin. "Talk then."

"Is it the Black Douglas I speak to?" The voice wavered a bit.

Wat tromped across the cobblestones and stood, fist gripped on his waist. "Sir James, Lord of Douglas, Englishman. You'll give my lord his rank."

"Sir... Sir James, will you treat with me? For our surrender?"

"Where is Sir Guillemin? He's the one I would treat with."

"He is sore injured by one of your arrows. He said I could speak for him."

"Why should we treat with you?" Wat yelled. "We can just starve you out."

"Enough," James said to his sergeant, who seemed to have, for the moment, forgotten his place. He shouted up, "Toss your weapons from the windows. My archers will hold their fire."

"You'll just kill us. We've heard..."

"Fool. Make me starve you out, and you'll die. I promise you that."

A larger figure pushed the youngster away from the window slit. "I don't want to die locked in this tower. I'd like to see home..." A sword tumbled out the slit and clattered onto the parapet. "...before this wound finishes me."

"Toss out the rest of your weapons and then throw open the door." James started down the stairs and paused halfway. "Find Richert. Have him see to the knight's wound. I'll allow him a horse if he can ride, but only him."

One of his men pelted through the gate of the inner

bailey. "Sir James." He paused and gulped down a breath. "A party approaches. A large one."

"Who?"

"Too far to tell. They're flying banners, but we can't make them out."

James jumped the rest of the way down. "Wat, see to it. Igram, all your archers on the walls." He strode for the gate, broke into a run, and dashed up the stairs next to the gatehouse. He leaned over the merlon, straining to see. The watery winter sun flashed off a party of armored knights in the lead. A banner flapped listlessly over their heads. Something on gold, but not the lion of Scotland, he was sure. Behind the rows of pikes waved like a field of grain. The prisoners he'd released might have brought their enemies on them though it wasn't likely. But surely the King wouldn't have sent so many.

A cold wind whipped, and James made out the Bruce red saltire. Not the King then. His brother, Edward de Bruce. How could he have already taken Stirling Castle? Or had the King ordered the siege lifted already? But James was not so much a fool as to lower the drawbridge until he recognized the man. More than one had been deceived by a captured banner. He grinned as he recalled using that deception one fine spring day.

He turned when Richert said, "My lord, I've seen to the English knight." Richert bit his lip and shifted. "He won't live if he travels and most likely, even if he doesn't. The arrow took one of his eyes. He's already fevered."

James grimaced. An ugly way to die.

Hooves pounded on the road, and a herald below called up, "Hail the castle for the Earl of Carrick."

The big figure leading the distant party glittered from head to heel. Now James could pick out the red saltire on a golden shield that hung from the saddle. "Sir Edward is most welcome," James called down. "Lower the drawbridge." Why the devil was the Earl of Carrick here?

"What should we do with them?" Richert asked.

"I doubt we can get a ransom for his body even if we had time for nursing him. Give the knight a mount and toss them all out the postern gate. And be quick about it."

The lines of pikemen were breaking up; wagons rattled up the rutted road, shouting and clanging drifted up from the chaos. Frowning, James strolled down to the outer bailey.

Edward de Bruce was the first to appear through the shadows of the gateway, caracoled his dancing bay charger, and drew up. The silver sheen of his armor was filigreed with golden flowers. James shook his head. It was no wonder the women favored him.

"My lord earl, welcome." James gave the man a half-bow.

Sir Edward swung from the saddle, mail clattering. "Douglas. My squire carries a letter from my brother--commands for you. We've preparations to make for the summer's campaign."

"And your army—" James paused, trying to think how to diplomatically ask why they were here.

"My army will slight Roxburgh." Edward turned slowly, shaking his blond head. "I've always liked the place. It's a shame to destroy it." A dozen other knights and their squires were dismounting, calling for stable boys, cursing the cold. "The men will make camp outwith the walls. Too bad we'll have to soon join them."

James swallowed a sigh. "There is good wine and food aplenty in the great hall, Sir Edward, and a fire on the hearth. My men will care for your mounts." He took the sealed parchment that a lad in the Bruce colors held out to him. "Andro," he called over his shoulder. "Get men out here to see to these horses."

The heavy parchment bore the royal seal, the lion of Scotland with, the superscription: To James Lord of Douglas at Roxburgh Castle. James broke the seal with his thumb and smoothed out the folds of the letter. It was notably short.

Sir James,

The Earl of Carrick has lifted the siege of Stirling Castle on the word of Sir Philip de Mowbray that it shall be surrendered if relief does not reach it from Edward of England. Carry the fiery cross across Douglasdale and all your lands in Lothian. Join me in Perth within the month to prepare for battle.

Lord Robert, King of Scots

CHAPTER 30

*J*ames opened the thick plank door of the manor house the King's master at arms had obtained for him, begrimed, hungry, and weary. He was unbuckling his sword belt and telling the bowing steward to bring him food and drink when the master at arms of the King's household banged on the door and told him that a meeting of the Privy Council was being convened. The presence of the Lord Warden of the Marches was required. James scrubbed his face with his hands. "Surely it can wait until I have something in my belly."

The man blinked. "My lord wishes me to convey that message to the King?"

"By the Holy Rude, of course not," James snapped. "But I can hardly attend the Privy Council in my travel soil. Pray, tell the King I will be there forthwith."

"Yes, my lord," the Master at Arms said. "The King has taken a manor house hard by Saint John's Church. If it please you, I'll wait and show you the way."

"That would please me well." James stripped off his traveling cloak and tossed it across a table near the entry.

"My lord, you will not be dining then?" his steward asked with a nervous twist of his mouth.

"Later. It seems the Privy Council has need of me. Have a meal ready upon my return." James started for the wide stairs to the upper floor. "I'll see my chambers and wash. Have the servants bring me hot water—quickly now. See that my men are settled after they see to the horses. My sergeant is following with a wagon of supplies."

So a short time later, James strode into a small chamber, irritable and his belly grumbling, to find the King and five of the Privy Council awaiting him. The chamber was simply furnished. Rushes scented with lavender covered the floor, and a long, polished table took up most of the space. Shields and crossed weapons decorated all the walls except one where the lion banner of the King hung, eyes of rubies glittering in its snarling face.

Robbie Boyd stood by the banner, talking to Robert de Keith. Bernard de Linton bent over a stack of parchment sitting beside Gilbert de Hay.

Thomas Randolph rose from a place at the King's right hand and bowed deeply. "Lord Douglas, I heard of your great victory at Roxburgh Castle. What a triumph to take that impregnable fortress." Randolph sauntered to the flagon at the end of the table and filled a goblet. "It inspired me so that—I hied myself to Edinburgh Castle and took it." He raised his cup and bared his teeth in a distinctly triumphant grin.

Robbie Boyd's mouth twitched with a sardonic smile. James couldn't hold back a bark of laughter. He should have known that Randolph would find some way to best him. Apparently, he'd wronged the man, but the King had been wise not to kill him. "Congratulations, my lord earl. Well done. I'd like to hear the story of how you managed the feat." He realized now that he had been so angry with Randolph

211

when he captured him that he had forgotten how much he was like the King.

"Enough, the two of you. You've both done well, but I've no time for japes." More gray streaked the King's golden blond hair over his weather-worn face.

James took an empty place at the King's left hand. "I apologize if I kept you waiting, sirs."

The others took their places as they assured him they had only just come, and it struck James that Edward de Bruce was not here. "Sir Edward will not join us?"

"Sir Edward has completed slighting Roxburgh," put in Gilbert de Hay. "But, he is still carrying the fiery cross in Carrick."

"How many men did you raise, Jamie?" the King asked, mildly.

"More than a thousand. Every man of an age to fight in my lands, but Walter is still in his own lands raising men, so I don't count those."

"Robbie, your men from Kilmarnock?"

"Only five hundred, Your Grace."

"Neill is on his way, his men and mine make two thousand. Thomas, another two thousand from Moray." The King sighed. "They must be fed. That is the least of the costs though. They must all have pikes and helmets—leather tunics and mail gloves."

Aghast, James blurted, "That will be six thousand men at least. Do we even have enough iron in the country to make so many?"

"We will not make all of them." The King gave a short laugh. "Although the iron we raided from England will help. Some weapons we've brought from Ireland and some have been purchased in Norway. But we need more." The King looked to Linton. "How much will the treasury bear?"

"You know what there is, sire," Linton said with a twist of

his mouth. "More than there was short years ago thanks to the tribute for peace from the towns in England. Forty thousand gold marks in the treasury. And not a pence more. Nor a chance of borrowing."

"Do we have blacksmiths enough to make what we need before the English are over our border?" Robbie said. "Who can make that much armor so quickly, even leather?"

"The men who ride on my raids have armor. And some who only ride with me on occasion," James said. "That is perhaps five hundred of mine, but none have pikes."

Randolph shook his blond head, his mouth in a grim line. "Against mounted knights, pikes will be better."

"We can retreat, Your Grace," Gilbert de Hay said in his mild voice. "Let them relieve Stirling Castle and burn the land before them as we did the last time they invaded. We need not stand against them."

"Hay is right." The Keith stood up, his chair scraping harshly on the floor. "We need not, and I fear that we cannot. How many mounted knights will I be able to lead against their thousands? Their many thousands? Five hundred? Mayhap even not so many as that?"

"So your advice, the two of you, is to retreat." Robert de Bruce looked from one to the other, his eyes hard. "Burn our lands—yet again. As we have burnt out the English."

Gilbert de Hay leaned back in his chair, eyes on his hands before he raised his eyes to face the King's gaze. "I like no more than you do, Sire. But so I advise."

The marischal crossed his arms over his chest and stared at his feet as he nodded brusquely.

"The rest of you? What do you say?"

"I say stand," Randolph said. "As I have always said. We must show that we can stand against them on the field, or they'll never sue for peace with us."

James leaned his elbows on the table, steepled his clasped

hands, and pressed them hard into his forehead. "I remember Methven. A loss such as that would finish us." He met each of their eyes. "It would. But I remember Loudon Hill as well. There we stood against mounted knights with little more than our pikes. It was pikes that won the day."

There was a mumbling of reluctant agreement from the others.

"I say we stand."

"But how can we advise?" Robbie Boyd said. "Without knowing for a certainty that we can arm all our men. How many we will have. Or even how many the English will raise."

"Then we must keep our options open. We will arm our men for a fight. And we will train them." The King rose, and a brief smile lightened his face, his eyes gleaming with amusement. They all jumped to their feet. "I have a new idea for using our schiltron. If what I have in mind works, it will take months to prepare whilst the armor and weapons are prepared. And James, I need news from the south. I expect you to keep your people out." He nodded to them and made for the door. "James, I'd have a word with you. Walk with me."

James followed. The King led him down a corridor busy with scurrying servants, past a room where a cleric bent over a table adding up long columns of numbers, and into a small courtyard. A brick wall cut it off from the noisy street though the sound of wagons and passing soldiers drifted in. The grass was winter brown and the hoary oak bare limbed. The King grasped one of the limbs as he looked closely into James's face.

"My liege?" Obviously, something else was afoot than plans for battle.

"You heard what Keith said. How do you judge it?"

James shrugged a shoulder. "Much truth to it. We will not

have knights to match the English, and he's never fought as
we did at Loudon Hill--pikes against knights. Many would
think it can't be done."

"Wallace fought so at Falkirk."

James made an assenting sound in his throat. Wallace had
fought so and lost. All knew this.

"Because he was betrayed."

"You think..." James stared at the King, eyes narrowing in
thought.

"That he plans it? No. But faced with an English army
three times our sides. And it will be. And he will command
the chivalry, what there is of it. He must." The King looked
hard at James. "So I must guarantee his loyalty. Must tie him
to me. To us."

Frowning, James knew he was somehow missing the
point. "How?"

"He has a daughter of marriageable age. A tie of marriage,
of blood, would secure his loyalty. I know the Keith. He
would be loyal—is a Scot after all. But we must need see that
fear does not overwhelm that. He must have more reason
than an oath he could be forgiven for foreswearing."

James examined the dry blades of grass on the ground,
which was easier than looking at the King. He rubbed the
back of his neck. "You'd have me betrothed to her?" It made
sense. How could he deny it? And grieving forever was a
weakness, one he had no right to. His duty was to his line
and his name.

"Why delay? I'll speak to Master David. He's here with
Andrew de Moray's sweet widow, since her marriage to
Robbie Boyd."

But Robert de Keith was a cousin of sorts, and James
breathed with relief. "There may be an impediment."

"Nonsense. It's no close relation, is it? What degree? I'll
talk to the bishop, and he'll take care of that. Her dower will

215

be my gift." The King beamed in satisfaction. "I'll breathe more easily with your goodfather at our back in battle. And it's past time you married." He gave James a buffet on the shoulder as they walked back through the corridor.

"Have you mentioned this plan to him?" James said irritably. "Mayhap he'll mislike it."

"He'll be pleased to have the lass well settled. Of course, he will."

The marischal would not argue with the King making a match for his daughter. That was true. And James wondered why was he resisting? He was foolish. The King had the right of it. It was past time that he married and had an heir.

* * *

JAMES STOOD FIDGETING before the great arch of the doors of Saint John's Church. Beside him beamed King Robert de Bruce in a gold velvet tunic decorated with a crowned lion. Robbie Boyd was with them, lips twitching with thinly veiled amusement. Easy for him, James thought. He was unreasonably pleased with his bride—one he had chosen. He wished that Bishop Lamberton were here to bless the union, but instead, Bishop David of Moray stood before the church doors dressed in ecclesiastical splendor in gleaming white robes edged with gold.

Velvet was hot for even early spring, and sweat dripped down his ribs under his blue doublet, chausses, and fine-tooled boots. A blue half-cloak was draped over one shoulder, the broach a silver star. He shifted and worked spit into his dry mouth. Hurry and let this be done. Just get it over with, but it wouldn't be long now. The sound of flutes, trumpets, lutes, and drums drifted up the street. He caught sight of the King's page carrying a silver goblet overflowing with rosemary and ribbons of purple and gold as they rounded the corner. Walter and her brother led Elayne's white palfrey, their sleeves twined in rosemary. He could make out the sound of laughter and chatter of lords and ladies around her.

She was lovely, dressed all in purple samite, tight of bodice and long, flowing skirt, a slender circlet about her brow. Her long, dagged sleeves were lined with green satin, and her golden hair tumbled in loose curls over her shoulders. Her father walked slowly by her side and her mother a little way behind. The musicians strolled after her palfrey and then a milling peacock-bright crowd jostling like hens in a run.

James stared at his feet for a moment, the polished boots fascinating, and then lifted his head and squared his shoulders. He had imagined his wedding otherwise. It was what it was, he thought.

Robert de Keith was helping the lass from her palfrey and leading her to the door of the church. He gave James her stiff, cold hand. Perhaps a smile would help, James thought, but she kept her gaze fixed straight ahead as though it would burn through the very doors of the church. In truth, he had never considered her feelings on the matter, even at the short betrothal ceremony when she'd been stiff and cold. How would she not, he had thought. Now he wondered...

After a moment as the chatter died, the bishop said, "James, Lord of Douglas, and Elayne de Keith, do you come here freely without coercion to give yourselves in marriage?"

Elayne made a strangled sound that the bishop apparently chose to hear as a yes.

James frowned and gave his assent.

At the bishop's nod, James took a deep breath. "Elayne de Keith, I take you to my wedded wife, for fair or for foul, in sickness and in health, until death us depart, and thereto I plight you my troth."

217

The bishop smiled at her and prompted, "James de Douglas, I take you..."

As her silence stretched into long seconds, there was a faint shuffling from the crowd of onlookers. Someone coughed, and James felt a burn creep up his face.

"Lass," the bishop said firmly, "you must say the vows of your own will. Were you forced?" He flicked a glance toward her father.

James knew his face was flaming. Thanks be to Saint Bride, his back was to everyone except the bishop who gave him a piercing look. He slid his eyes toward the King and caught him glaring at Robert de Keith.

She gave a stiff nod of her head. "I... must." James heard her swallow.

The bishop gave her a sympathetic look and prompted her again. "James de Douglas..."

She made another strangled sound. "I take you to my wedded husband, for fair or for foul..." She paused, a stubborn jut to her jaw until, behind her, her father whispered her name. "...in sickness and in health, until death us depart, and thereto I plight you my troth."

There was a long expelled breath that James suspected came from the Keith. Perhaps he wasn't the only one humiliated this day. James took the gold ring set with a sapphire from where he'd tucked it into his belt and handed it to Moray. The bishop blessed it and gave it back. Elayne's hand was stiff, fingers tightly together as she glared at his chest. *Jesu.* He angrily pushed the ring onto her middle finger. His jaw was so tight he could barely grind out the words, "With this ring, I you wed and with your dowry I endow you."

James spun on his heel and gave the Keith a look that promised words later. But there would be no more humiliation this day. He managed a smile. "My lady wife." He put a firm hand on her upper arm and strode to her father. If she dragged her feet, no one would see under her long skirts. He sucked in a long, calming breath. She was just frightened. She'd get over it. He had to be gentle. Patient. And not be angry.

In a bright voice, he called, "Musicians, play something merry to guide us." The lutist struck a chord, and the other musicians followed in a tinkling melody. Everyone clapped and cheered.

The King grasped his shoulder and shook it a little. "Aye. Lead the way to the feast." He gave James a little shove ahead toward the door of his manor a short way from the church. "Lord Marischal," he boomed, "your daughter is a lovely bride."

Elayne's mother put an arm around her daughter's waist. "Silly goose. But all is well now."

James kept a tight hand on Elayne's elbow, keeping her at his side as the music pulled him through the street to the door of the manor house. "A wedding feast in the King's own manor," her mother chattered as they walked. "Why I'd never have believed such an honor." The King and the bishop followed, and her father. The rest of the crowd fell in behind, babbling, laughing, and making jokes about tonight's bedding.

A guard in the King's livery opened the door for them, and they entered to the merry strains of the musicians. The hall was not as big as that of a castle but prepared with royal elegance. Lanterns shimmered in silver sconces though light flowed in from the arched windows in the north wall. Rushes sweetened with lavender covered the floor. Long trestle tables draped in white cloths were set with gleaming silver goblets. Pages scurried carrying silver platters and flagons of wine.

"I don't want to," Elayne whispered and stopped in the doorway.

219

"We must," James said through gritted teeth. He tried to soften his voice. "Come, I'll pour you a goblet of wine. You must tell me what dish you prefer."

Her lips pressed together so hard that they turned quite white. Please don't make me drag you, he thought. He tightened his hand on her arm and guided her past all the nobles as they stood in their places and up to the dais for the two of them would have a place at the right hand of the King.

"Be seated, my friends," the Bruce said as he sat. On the other side of the King, Robbie Boyd took his place with his recent bride. When she smiled and laid a hand on his arm, Robbie looked smug. James shook his head and called the page to pour a goblet of a honeyed vernage wine for him to share with his new lady wife.

The King called for the tumblers as the pages brought out a course of great loaves of brown bread, mounds of rich cheese laced with tracery of blue, trenchers of beef stewed in a peppery sauce, and apples poached in honey.

Robert de Keith, now James's good-father he realized with a start, leaned forward to look past his lady wife and raised his voice a little to be heard to say, "When will your men arrive, Sir James?"

James opened his mouth, but before he could manage a reply, the King cut in, "Not now, man." He shook his head with a genial smile. "Talk of the war at a wedding feast? For shame."

"Your pardon, sire. I've not had a chance to talk with my new goodson, but you have the right of it. Such things should wait."

"Indeed," his wife said and patted Elayne's hand, where it lay pressed flat on the tabletop. "You are beautiful today, child. You make us proud."

She turned her head to look at her mother but said nothing. James coaxed her to try the vernage. "You'll feel better."

She shook her head. He sipped it. Too honeyed for his taste but surely to the taste of a lass. He took her hand and bent it within his own around the goblet. "Just a sip."

She gave him a look that seemed more cold anger than fear, but he would be patient. He would. He put an arm around her shoulder and lifted the goblet, his hand wrapped around hers, to her lips. She narrowed her eyes but swallowed a bit.

"You see." He smiled stiffly. "No poison in the cup, my lady."

"Sir James, is it your plan to keep a manor here in Perth?" His good-mother asked.

He gave her a non-committal reply. In truth, he'd give it little thought and paused over the problem as he cut off a slice of the cheese, rich but it would be easy on a nervous stomach. He offered Elayne offered a sliver. When she shook her head, he popped it in his own mouth. They'd make it through this feast, somehow.

Courses followed and a singer came in to sing. Perhaps the feast would never end. Eel in wine. Buttered herbs. Goose stuffed with parsley and eggs. Almond milk blancmange. Honey cakes and berry tarts.

James's stomach was in a tight knot. He pushed aside the sweetened wine and signaled for the page to pour him a goblet of strong red wine. He sipped and tried to smile at the people around him. Caitrina, Robbie's lady wife, was smilingly chaffing the King whilst Robbie looked on. She was comely though well past the flower of youth with a son long in English hands. There was little meekness in her mien, which probably meant she could handle Robbie Boyd right well. From time to time, Robbie offered her a choice morsel from the point of his knife, and James remembered his own duty. He looked desperately around, spied a swan dressed in its feathers, and cut Elayne a bit of the breast. She looked

221

down her delicate nose but took it between her lips, rather as though he had indeed given her poison.

The guests were getting noisy. A fool the King had hired was capering about with a wooden sword, chasing a large cat painted with a leopard's spots around the room. The animal yowled and made for the door as everyone laughed. Ross's sons were arguing over a horse race as their sister Isabel looked on. Maol of Lennox was loudly criticizing the singer who didn't compare to the ones in his own household.

The King raised an eyebrow at the fool. "What can you expect after years of war? Few good to be had." He called for more music, and amiably went back to pressing food and drink on his guests. So far, no one had noticed his bride's grim countenance, but perhaps brides were often fearful. It wasn't as though he'd been to many weddings.

When the last course was down to a few broken tarts, Elayne's mother leaned forward, "It's time, daughter." She looked past at Caitrina. "My lady, you'll help with the bedding?"

Caitrina smile and reached to catch Matilda de Bruce's hand. The King's youngest sister, not much like him with her slender build and red hair, sat next to her. "You'll help as well, Mathilda? A lass her own age will make a gayer bedding."

Mathilda giggled a bit giddily. "May I, my lord?" she asked her brother.

James didn't see the King's response as he watched Elayne's white-fingered clutch on the edge of the table. He patted her arm and would have spoken, but her glare silenced him. She wanted no comfort from him, of that he was sure. Instead, he picked up his goblet and drained it as the three women led Elayne, her back as straight and stiff as a sword, toward the stairs. Isabella of Ross jumped up from her place, clapping her hands and scurried, skirts swishing, to join them. They rushed out to the sound of raucous laughter and cheers.

"Don't look so serious, Jamie." The King poured himself another goblet of wine and leaned back, his face a little flushed from drink. "A lass is nervous her wedding night. You'll be gentle, and she'll take to it. They do, you know."

James couldn't stop the laugh that erupted. Robert de Bruce should know. Women loved him even better than they did his brother, Edward, and with his wife in an English dungeon, he'd never played the monk. Not that James blamed him. No one did. But if anyone knew if women took to it, the King did. He was receiving an odd half-smile from his liege lord, and James said, "Mayhap I have a bit of nerves myself, sire."

"You're hardly a blushing maid, Jamie."

"No, but a wife..." James decided the King's idea of more wine was a wise one and motioned to the page to fill his goblet. "...a wife is a different thing. If she mislikes me, life will not have much joy."

The King grasped the back of his neck and gave him a fond shake. "She won't. Now give them a few minutes, and we'll escort you up to do your duty."

At that, Robbie Boyd grinned and slammed the flat of his hand down on the table. "About time! Let's drag him up the stairs and throw him into bed to get himself an heir!"

Amidst the cheers, whistles and laughter, James gave a quiet sigh. His close friends shoved away from the tables and gathered around him, like hounds on a hart. Robbie had him by one arm whilst Sir Hugh Ross grasped the other. Walter tugged at James's belt and stripped it off as they dragged him toward their upstairs chamber.

"Jamie can practice with his pole weapon tonight," Gilbert de Hay said, laughing and all the men joined in as he was hustled through the doorway. Elayne lay like a white-faced corpse, unmoving in the red-draped bed, the coverlet pulled up to her chin.

The King joined in the laughter. "His lady wife will be more receptive than the English, thank Jesu." James shoved them back. Walter had his tunic unfastened and tugged it off, tossing that and the belt onto a chair next to the hearth fire.

James managed a grin. He grabbed the King's arm and urged him toward the door. "Out! The lot of you."

"*Lese-Majeste!*" the King said. He smacked the back of James's head good-naturedly. "Did you see my Lord of Douglas lay hands on his liege?"

But the King had allowed himself to be pushed outwith the chamber, and James shoved Walter after him.

Robbie snickered and pulled Gilbert de Hay into the hall. "Leave him to sheath his sword. The poor lad hasn't the stamina to jest with us and do his duty." He dropped his eyelid in James's direction.

James slammed the door shut on their japes and laughter and leaned his forehead against it. The cool wood felt good on his heated skin. It would be a fine thing to just lean here for the rest of his life. This was what a wedding was supposed to be, so it shouldn't seem like ashes in his mouth. And a man didn't weep, so the stinging in the back of his eyes was from being weary. That was all. Of course, it was.

He turned to his bride, who stared at him, her eyes narrowed and wary. She looked cold but not of her body. James ran a hand down his bare chest as he walked softly to the bed and sat next to her. He picked up the silver flagon on the table beside the bed and poured a cup. He took a sip—hippocras... Perhaps it would calm her. They could both use calming, so he held it out to her. "It's been a wearying day, Elayne."

She scooted up in the bed, clasping the bedcovers to her breast, and took the cup. Staring into it, her lips in a thin line, she shook her head. "I don't belong here." She lifted her eyes with a challenging gaze. "I don't!"

"You're here. We're married before God." He licked his lips, wondering how he could ease this for her, for both of them. They had a lifetime before them—if he wasn't killed betimes. "If it wasn't what either of us would have chosen, that doesn't matter now."

She thrust the goblet at him. "I don't want it."

He rubbed a hand over his beard and took the thing from her, drained it, and set it firmly onto the table. He stripped off his hose and took the top of the coverlet in his hand. For a moment, she clutched it harder, and then she let go and threw herself flat in the bed, staring up at the embroidered draperies. He stripped the coverlet down with a jerk. Her hands pressed palm down into the mattress, body rigid, breath coming fast.

She was comely. He couldn't deny it, even white-faced and furious. Long golden curls flowed down over her shoulders. Her breasts were small, only buds but pink and puckering as cool night air touched them. He knelt beside her, his cock half-hard, and laid his fingers on a white thigh, stroking the soft skin. She flinched a little and closed her eyes tight. "You burned it," she whispered. "Everything. You're a demon from hell." She jerked her eyes open and turned her head to look at him, a grim expression as though today had been a death instead of their wedding. "I hate you."

He felt his arousal wilting. "It is war," he said hoarsely. "That's all. I'm... sworn to my King, do what I must." Why was he defending himself to this child? She knew nothing. Living soft in the south whilst Scotland was raped and torn.

Her gaze was steady and hard. "Do it. I don't care."

He sat back on his heels, heat that felt like hatred washing through him. "You're beside yourself." He slid off the bed and jerked the coverlet back over her. "This can wait. We're wed whether I bed you this night or not. So says the church. Later... when you are... calmer."

He took a deep breath. If he took her now, he might do her some harm. He strode to a chair beside the little fire in the hearth that crackled so merrily and shoved the tunic and belt onto the floor. He sat and glared at the flagon.

The simple truth was he didn't want her. He wanted Alycie. He ached for Alycie as a wild thing that bayed for the moon. He wanted her now. He wanted it to be three years ago before he sent her to her death when he didn't know how empty he would be without her.

The bed covers rustled as his wife moved in the bed. He dredged up a smile. "Sleep, child. It will be better tomorrow." Elbows on his knees, he thrust his fingers deep into his hair and pulled. What had he done? Holy Saint Bride, what had he done?

He closed his eyes and took a long calming breath. Another. Exhaustion seeped through his limbs, heavy as lead. The fire was warm, its sounds comforting. He closed his eyes, welcoming darkness and quiet, but after a while, he dreamt distant echo of shouts and blows, war horns and men screaming their last breaths away and then a soft voice that called out his name.

CHAPTER 31

*J*ames saw the haze from the camp's fires when they were still north in Ochil Hills. Noise drifted across the rolling plateau like the wash of the sea on rocks and growing as he rode closer. By the time he turned his horse to ride beside the Black Devon River, shimmering in the spring sunshine, he could make out the shouts and clatter of a large camp. James called to Robbie Boyd and set his horse to a canter, and the camp spread before them across the valley.

Wisps of smoke meandered into the air from a thousand campfires. A horse line stretched across the far side of the camp. Row upon row of canvas lean-tos and tents crouched in the heather in front of a line of knights' pavilions. Teamsters unloaded wagons stacked with barrels and crates. Men sat shoving steel skullcap helms on and leather brigandines over their bodies. Camp followers knelt to wash close by the river and sashayed by the men. Blacksmiths hammered blades onto the long poles of pikes. A shepherd drove bleating sheep, and a farrier bent over a horse's hoof.

All of Scotland had answered the King's call to arms. The

blue Saltire of Scotland was on tabards and servants' tunics. It waved and fluttered from staves and was painted on hundreds of shields. He spotted the red saltire of the House of Bruce that be the Earl of Carrick, the blue and white checky banner for Walter the Steward, Angus Og's black and white banner.

There was the banner of Maol of Lennox and the Earl of Strathearn. He even spotted a banner with the wheat sheaths of Buchan that must be some minor relation of the disgraced family. Somewhere amidst them all, no doubt Wat had set up his own pavilion and starred pennant. But most of the shelters were of minor knights and freeholders, for all of Scotland had flocked to the Ochils. At last, they had a hope to stand against their enemy.

Over the largest of the pavilions flew the King's own banner. From the top of the tallest of the staves, it shimmered gold. The crowned lion of Scotland reared proudly, claws extended, ready to defend the land. Beyond the pavilions gathered a huge press of men.

"Never saw so many Scots all in one spot," Boyd said as they across the narrow wooden bridge.

"Even more than we had at the Battle of Methven." James's mouth twisted at the sour memory, and he lowered his voice. His men were close behind. "But are they enough?"

Boyd grunted a neutral sound. "You think the King will decide to retreat?"

James flicked a glance over his shoulder. Rumor would run like fire through a camp like this. "I don't know. I saw the last army they brought, and the message I had from Bishop Lamberton said this one will be even larger." He shook his head and shifted in the saddle. Apparently, the King meant to prepare for battle. Why if he didn't mean to fight it?

"What the..." Boyd stood in his stirrups. "What's happening?"

James frowned at the sound of shouts and battle cries. They had been riding past the hodge-podge of rough tents and lean-tos. As they approached the press of men, the sound grew louder. Beyond, the field had been kept clear. Robert de Bruce sat on a small gray mount in plain armor, a simple coronet on his head, war axe resting across his saddle in front of him, in the corner of the field. A square schiltron had formed in the middle, and as hundreds of men moved in a line, pikes wavering like wheat in a hard wind held pointed before them. The lines of the schiltron wavered. Half of it broke, and a gaping hole appeared in the middle.

The King roared, "Stop! You just died. All of you!" He trotted to where the schiltron had divided and used his war axe to point to the hole in their line. "Together. You must move together."

James raised an eyebrow at Boyd. He ordered his men to find Wat and their place in the camp and leaned forward to watch.

"What the devil is he doing?" Boyd muttered.

The King shouted for the schiltron to start again. The men muttered and cursed as they slogged across the torn and muddy field. From the look of it, they had been at it for hours. They began again. "Let me hear our battle cry," the Bruce shouted. A ragged cry of "Scotland! Scotland!" went up, but they didn't march half way before one of the men stumbled. His pike tripped the two men next to him, and the half the line turned into stumbling chaos.

James snorted a laugh, but the King stopped them again. "Enough. Stack the pikes for tomorrow," he commanded.

"Whoever heard of such a thing? Having men with pikes try to charge?" a man-at-arms, the red saltire of the Bruces on his leather armor, complained.

The King sat astride watching as the hundreds of men

stacked the long, bladed pole weapons into piles. James swung from his horse to approach the King. "Your Grace."

"Jamie, good. Your men are already here, so tomorrow you can begin training them. You saw it will not be easy. And young Walter's men with yours." The King climbed from the saddle. "Robbie. Your men shall train with mine."

Boyd dismounted and led his horse to walk with the two of them toward the horse lines, his face knotted in a deep frown that pulled at the scar on his cheek. "You mean to have them charge, sire?"

"It can be done. Of that, I am sure." The Bruce shook his head. "No. It must be done. We've done much these past years they said was impossible. This will be only one more."

James tried to calculate as they led their horses through the muck of mud and horse shit. "We have... What? Eight thousand, we thought when we met in Perth. Is it that many?"

"Robbie, would you take our horses to the grooms? James, a word..." The King handed his reins to Boyd, who tilted a brow at James as he took the King's, and after a moment's hesitation, James handed his own.

The Bruce looked him up and down with a steady, assessing stare. At last, he said, "What are you about, Jamie? I heard complaints from your goodfather of how you're treating his daughter?"

"He..." James looked at the sky as he tamped down a flare of temper. "He complained? What did he want me to do? She's a child, and I wasn't going to..." He glared at the King. "Sire, I'll do my duty to her. But not yet."

"Then, you need to talk to the Keith and tell him you're not slighting his daughter." The King put an amiable arm around James's shoulder and walked with him toward the pavilions. "He was long in the English court, and you know

230

what that is. Edward of Caernarfon was for years prefer-
ring... other company to that of his Queen. He fears..."

James shrugged off his arm. Stopped walking. "You're
jesting. You must know better."

The King stopped, too. "I know you well, James. But he
does not." The King gave him a straight look. "This is important to me. To all of us. Talk to him and see that *he* knows
better."

James laughed though it wasn't funny. "That's one thing I
never thought to be accused of."

"Not accused, but he needs to be assured for the sake of
his daughter. And I need his loyalty." He shoved James in the
direction of the Keith's banner. "His pavilion is there. See
to it."

James laughed and shook his head as he strode past
squires sharpening swords. Three knights rode past on their
palfrey. The scent of roasting beef drifted from a cookfire.
James stuck his head through the opening of the Keith's
simple canvas pavilion. "I think we need to talk," he said.

The man looked up from where he sat in a camp chair.
"Indeed." He frowned quizzically at James. "Aye, we do."

James leaned against the edge of the table, folded his arms
across his chest. "So..." He tried to think about how to ease
into the subject. "You think what? That I should have been
harsher with my lady wife?"

"Harsh? No. But she says to her mother she is not truly
your wife. And I have to ask why." But it was no question.

"Because she's little more than a child—and a sullen child
at that." James studied his goodfather's face. "You can't truly
think that I won't do my duty by her."

The Keith rose and stepped to the door of the pavilion to
look outside. "I've seen that enough—you think the rumors
of the English King aren't true? I assure you they are and the

Queen... Well, I don't want my daughter in such a position."
He turned to scowl at James. "I won't have it."

"Have you any reason to think such a thing?"

"That you didn't bed her is reason enough. I don't know
what kind of man you are. I thought I did, but now I don't."

"Robert, I assure you that I'm just giving her time. She
thinks... Damn, you know what she's heard of me in England.
She just needs time." James clung to his patience. "We have a
lifetime together. Or if I live through this battle the King
seems to mean to fight, we will have. In the eyes of the
Church and of God, she is my wife. The rest will come—soon
enough."

The Keith said, "It seems to me there is more to it than
that. You don't look, even at your wedding feast you did not
look like a man pleased with a young bride to bed."

"No, I wasn't pleased. She was the next thing to being
forced, and that leaves out that I have no taste for a child in
my bed. A woman, yes. But not a child."

"You can't say you would have had to force her. She was
reared better than that!"

"And hated me for it. And I would have hated myself. I
want a woman in my arms who is not terrified of my touch,
Robert."

"Then why did you agree to it?"

James hung onto his patience. "Because the King wanted
me to. He was right. I must wed, and she won't always be a
child. She won't always think I'm the fearful Black Douglas
who devours bairns in their beds."

His goodfather snorted a little through his nose. "No
doubt she had heard the stories they tell of you."

"Oh, she had. But she's my wife. I'll treat her as such."

"All right. Good." The Keith shifted, shook his head. "I
didn't mean insult. But no one would think it of King
Edward either. So like his father, you wouldn't believe,

except in the matter of Piers Gaveston. He doted on the man."

"I give you my word. I will court her and make her my bride. I'll work it out. I give you oath on holy Saint Bride." James twitched a smile, thankful to have the discussion done with though he meant every word. He'd make himself stop pining for what was lost. "So you have command of all of the chivalry? How many do you think?"

"Few enough." The Keith grabbed the topic of knights with obvious eagerness. "Five hundred mayhap, and you know our horses are never the weight of the English. We'll do well to have chargers for so many, certainly not destriers."

"I'd ride with you if I could. But the King has me training my men in this new idea of his. Tomorrow we start."

The Keith shook his head. "Pikes against knights. I am none too sure it can be done."

As James straightened and stepped into the doorway, he said, "We did it at Loudon Hill. The Flemish did at Courtrai. Forbye, I trust the King. If he decides it won't work, we'll retreat. And burn the land before them again." He nodded crisply. "We'll know soon. In the meantime, I'd best see to my men."

CHAPTER 32

*J*ames could not deny the heat. His tunic stuck to his chest like a limpet. Thick, wet air covered the practice field, and men grumbled when they were called out of their tents to form the hedgehog of a schiltron and march time after time across the field.

Allane's pike dipped and swung in an arc. It whacked Sande in the belly, and he went down with a shout, cursing. The man next to him grabbed Sande's pike to save himself. The man behind Sande stumbled over him and went face down in the dry, trampled heather. Then the entire schiltron was chaos with a giant hole in the middle that would have got them all killed in battle. Sande shoved himself free of the tangle, got up, and limped a few steps. Blood dripped down his cheek, where a spearhead had hit him. Allane looked at his pike as though it had betrayed him.

Sweat dripped down James's face and ran into this beard. He wiped the sleeve of his tunic across his forehead as he tromped across the broken dirt of the field. He jerked the twelve-foot pike from Allane's hands. "Are you planning to kill the English? Or is it Sande you are aiming for?" He spaced his hands well apart on the pike and braced it against his side. "Don't let it wave about! When we are moving, you must hold it against you and steady." He braced the butt end of the pike against the ground behind him. "When we stop and the chivalry charge, you brace it so."

Wat joined James and gave him a cup of water, but instead of drinking it, he dumped it over his head. It dripped down his hair and ran down the back of his neck. The May sun blazed down until he felt he was sizzling in a pot.

"They're better," Wat said. "Almost they move together now."

"Almost won't be good enough against English knights," James snapped. He sighed and took a deep breath. Yelling at Wat wouldn't help, and he was right. The men had improved. "Take them through it one more time. The King has called a council, and I'm late. When we're through, I need a report of how much armor we're still lacking." Arming so many thousands of men had been no easy matter. The smiths had been day and night putting metal cheeks down the last foot of the ash poles to strengthen them and fastening on the razor-sharp spearheads. At first, they'd trained with just the poles until James decided they needed the spearheads to teach them to take care. Sande was glaring at Allane now, and he might well thump him once they reached camp. He'd take more care in handling his pike. Of that, James was sure.

Wat shouted the men back into position to begin the march again as James turned and strode down the long incline toward camp. Walter waved to him, and James smiled. The lad was still officially his squire, but since his father died last autumn, he was also the Steward of Scotland. He'd soon have his spurs, and he'd earned them.

"Another two wagons of armor arrived," Walter said as he fell into step beside James.

"Helmets?" James asked.

"Mostly brigandines, but good heavy studded leather. I have some camp followers painting the Saltire on the front."

Robbie Boyd went into the King's pavilion ahead of them. The King's pavilion was large as a small castle's hall with ample room for their meetings, but it was furnished for war and nothing more. A curtain closed off a corner where the King slept.

In the main, it was filled by a dozen camp chairs, a trestle table spread with maps and parchments, a flagon of wine and silver cups, and a shaggy-haired hound lay snoring in the corner. Beside the entry, the King's armor hung from a stand, a suit of steel hauberk picked out with gold embell-ishments, a great helm topped with a snarling lion's face above a gold coronet and before it rested the King's favorite war axe. He really meant to do this. James turned away with a jerk. He had saved the King at the Battle of Methven. They'd fought for eight years against odds that no army would hold against. And now it all came down to a throw of the dice.

Edward de Bruce lounged in one of the camp chairs, legs sprawled, a cup of wine in his hand. The King leaned over a large map, and William de Lamberton in a simple black cassock stood at his side next to Bernard de Linton.

"My lord bishop." James grinned at the sight of him. "How did you sneak past my men?"

"I slipped out of England with some of my Benedictine brethren. Your scouts I saw didn't recognize me. I wanted to surprise you."

"By the Holy Rude, you're a welcome sight. I had worried at no word from you these past weeks."

"It was time to come home is all. There is no more I can accomplish there." The bishop tapped the spot were Berwick-upon-Tweed was marked on the map. "The English chivalry gathers there at the turn of the month and go to join their foot soldiers gathering at Wark-upon-Tweed. When you fight them, my place is with you."

"They shouldn't have slipped past your scouts, James," the King said. "Increase your patrols."

James nodded. The King was right, but it was impossible to cover the entire border, even with men on fast horses, constantly patrolling. Every man on patrol meant another not in his schiltron, as well. He frowned and opened his mouth to say so. He closed it. He would have to manage... somehow.

The rest of the Privy Council drifted in, Maol of Lennox, Robert de Keith, and Thomas Randolph. The King sank into his chair and waved them to their places. "How goes the training?"

James snorted. "Painfully."

Randolph let out a jerky laugh. "Indeed. Two of my men managed to break their legs today, tripping over their pikes." He leaned back and tapped a hand on the table. "But they improve. I begin to think we may do it. Only begin —you mind."

"Mine improve as well," James said. "They only trip over their pikes once or twice every time they charge. But we still don't have helmets and studded brigandines for all. Half still don't have gloves."

Linton cleared his throat at a look from the King. "I'm using every groat in the treasury, Your Grace. But it takes time."

"We're out of time." The King's face grew angry and tight as a fist. "I don't care what you have to do, but see that the rest of the armor is here--in the week. Squeeze them for it. Promise payment. Threaten them. I don't care. Just get the armor here. My smiths here can make the pikes, but we must have the armor and helmets and gloves."

"I'll leave first thing on the morrow." The chancellor

237

shook his head. "I'm not sure how, but I'll buy what you need."

"See to it," the Bruce said in a tone that brooked no argument. "Now, there are other tasks we must set to." He tossed onto the table a handful of caltrops, each one two nails twisted together, so no matter how they landed, a sharp point was upward. "Half our smiths in the camp must start working on these. We need thousands of them. And then... "He took a rolled map from a stack and spread it onto the table. "Here is Stirling Castle. And here..." He pointed to a long line. "...is the old Roman road where it turns for Stirling."

Sir Edward shrugged. "So, that's where we meet them."

"That is where we most definitely do not meet them, though we'll sow the way with caltrops. But we must make sure we give them good reason to come to us on our own ground. For that, we must give them a good display." He pointed to a mark on the map in the opposite direction of the castle. "To the east, the Carse of Balquiderock. Here in this triangle, the Bannock and Pelstream burns meet and join on their way eastward to the River Forth. But all of this is boggy and marshy along their course." He dragged his finger west. "The Torwood extending into the forest of the New Park. The English cannot take a great army through so dense a wood and my lord of Douglas..." His glance met James's with an amused gleam. "...might perchance harry them if they did so. So they must come to us here. Before the hill of the Borestone where we'll be on the slope." He bared his teeth in a wolfish smile. "And here is the corse, full of bogs they must cross to reach us. Here horses will founder badly. It's deadly for knights, rough crossing even for infantry."

"Will they take the bait though? They could simply make for the castle and relieve it," James said

"And put their back to us, so we hit them from the rear.

That they will most definitely not do, or if they do, they shall regret it."

There was a long silence as they studied the map.

Robbie Boyd traced a route through the corse. "There is a good wide stretch that's solid ground through here, sire. I know this ground. Aymer de Valence and Robert de Clifford know it, too. They fought here often enough against Wallace."

James grunted as it dawned exactly what the King had in mind. "You mean to dig pits. As we did at Loudon Hill."

"Exactly. We'll line the pits with stakes, which means the men must be put to cutting and sharpening those when they're not training. Edward, Robbie, you'll put your men to that. James, Thomas, your men must begin digging the pits. That we'll all have a hand in. My own men will dig those as well. Once the English are over the border, we'll cover the pits with branches and sod so they can't be spotted."

"Though the King is leading, you know if Aymer de Valence is truly in command, there is a great risk. And Robert de Clifford," said the bishop. "They've learned your tactics. Ralph de Monthemer as well. They will remember the humiliation of Loudon Hill."

The King leaned forward elbows on the table, hands clasped. "Knowing them and getting past them are two different things, my old friend. Very different things."

Bishop Lamberton shook his head as he ran a finger over the line of march on the map where the King planned his strategy. "It is a huge risk. They are massing, I can't even think how large an army. Edward has called for every levy in England. The de Clares, the de Bohuns are leading their levies. However much they mislike their King... losing Stirling is a bitter potion they intend *not* to swallow." He looked around at the men. "Believe me. King Edward means to crush us this time. For once. For all."

239

"If we must retreat, if with every levy in Scotland raised and my best knights beside me, if then we cannot defeat them—we never will. And if they do not crush us, if we evade them, they will be back again. And again. And again." The King stared fiercely past the walls of the pavilion to—who knew what. "How many times can our people suffer? Lands burned. Homes. Chased into the hills to starve in the cold. If we cannot stand against them now, when?"

A smile flickered across Thomas Randolph's face. This was a fight he had always called for since the day he returned to the King's side. He gave a small nod.

James's heart thudded. "We've won before against terrible odds." He licked his lips, tried to keep his voice cool. For Alycie. For poor lost Isabella and all the others who had died in this war, he must say it. "Perhaps not so bad as this, but nearly. I think—I believe we must fight."

For once, Sir Edward de Bruce agreed with him, thumping a hand down on the table. Ever cautious, Maol of Lennox shook his head. "Before any decision is made, we must see the army we stand against. And be sure our people are prepared. Can Linton find us the armor we must have? Can our people—so very many—form the schiltrons you want—and manage to charge?"

"I am prepared to stand and fight. To die if it comes to that. But... for our kingdom's sake, we will keep the choice open. Until the day." The King stood. "We have much to do. We'll meet again in three days. I want reports on how your men progress in their training. Stakes cut and sharpened. Pits dug." He glared at his chancellor. "And that armor delivered." He turned abruptly and made for the door.

Outside, another line of wagons creaked into the camp stacked high with barrels of ale and apples, barley and oats and hay, rolling past men returning from the practice fields, sweat-drenched and weary. The camp was a chaos of snorting horses and shouting men.

The hot, oppressive day weighed James down as he strode through the throng. There was a threat of rain in the air, and yet it did not come. When he reached his pavilion, he sent for Gelleys. The scout came at once. "You sent for me, my lord?"

"Our scouts are not doing their job," James said. "Bishop Lamberton and a group of friars walked right into the camp. It will be the English next."

"I've kept every man you've given me out, my lord. I could spread them more thinly."

"We can't afford that. We must know every lark that flies over the border." James frowned. "But every man I give you is another not in the schiltron. And my best men to scout are ones I need here." James frowned. He had no choice even though he couldn't spare the men. "Double the number of scouts. Choose the ones you know best. And they're to return only with news. Nothing—and I mean nothing—is to cross the march that I do not know of."

"As you command, Sir James."

"I'd ride out myself, but the King would have my head. I have too many duties here." When he had gone, James sat in his camp chair with a cup of ale brooding. Somehow, they had to win this battle, and he didn't see how.

CHAPTER 33

JUNE 23, 1314

*T*he camp had begun to stir. James cantered with Robert de Keith and their half-dozen men past cook fires where oak bannocks steamed over cookfires, for today was the Eve of the Feast of Saint John. They'd break their fast with bread and with water. Archers sat around a small fire bent over their fletching. Men rubbed the sleep from their eyes and stumbled to the latrine pits to piss, grumbling.

Sweat dripped down James's face as he flung himself off his lathered horse. Even early in the day, the summer heat was like being boiled in a pot. "Gelleys, see to the men," he said and tossed the scout his reins. He strode for the door of the King's pavilion, the Keith panting behind him. He shoved his way through the door, not waiting for ceremony. "Sire."

Robert de Bruce stopped his pacing and raised his eyebrows.

James swallowed. "Today." He licked his chapped, peeling lips. "The reports were true... except not as dire as they should have been."

Robert de Keith cleared his throat. "Ten divisions. Each

with more men than we could count. Two thousand each division was the best I could guess. We spotted the High Constable's banner. Aymer de Valence... Henry de Beaumont... Robert de Clifford... Ralph de Monthermer..."

"I saw Comyn of Badenoch's banner and other of the traitors," James spit out.

"Never mind them," the King said, impatiently. "Who leads the van?"

"Hereford and Gloucester."

"Gloucester?" He leaned a hand on the table. "You're sure, James?"

James blinked. He wouldn't say it if he weren't sure, and so the King should well know.

The King broke his stare. "To give command of the van to a lad, even with the high constable to guide him... He is only newly knighted. Edward must be crazed. So Pembroke is not in the van then."

"Some of our scouts picked up rumors that there were arguments. The Edward is furious with Aymer de Valence and refused him the van. They're all still at odds, and the King still angry over Piers de Gaveston's murder. It's said that they've come near to blows over who is to lead. But the King made young Hereford constable of the entire army, it's said."

"How many chivalry?"

"More of those than we could count as well." James narrowed his eyes as he considered. "They cover the hills like a flood. Four thousand?" He raised a questioning eyebrow at the Keith.

The Keith grunted. "Mayhap. So many that it doesn't matter that we couldn't count them. Pembroke leads those. Never have I seen so many knights. On barded destriers all. Miles of them. The shine of the armor could blind you."

The King's eyes gleamed as he sat down and leaned back. He smiled a little. "And they force the march, you say?"

"My spies are still watching. Some have slipped into their train. If the English make camp, they're to bring word with all speed. But whilst we watched..." James puzzled over the King's good cheer. "Yes, they were forcing their march. They rested during the few hours of dark. We watched them march past Falkirk. They'll reach the Bannockburn before noontide."

The King jumped to his feet. He strode to the doorway. "William! Have the trumpets blow assembly for the Privy Council."

James crossed his arms and examined his feet as the King paced. The pavilion was silent except for a rustle as the Keith shifted his feet in the rushes that cushioned the ground. Sir Edward's voice boomed, "What is ado?" as he stomped inside.

The King continued his pacing back and forth across the wide enclosure. "Wait for the others."

Were the English three times their numbers? Four? They had at least one hundred times the Scottish heavy chivalry. And none of the Scots rode the barded destriers that the English had by the thousand. *Holy Mary, Mother of God.*

Boyd muttered a greeting, and Maol of Lennox followed on his heels. Panting, Bernard de Linton stood aside for Bishop Lamberton and Bishop David de Moray. James caught the others eyeing him as they waited. They must know that he and the Keith had brought news. Rumors had run wild for days. The King made another progress back and forth across the pavilion. Angus Og strode in, his mail clanking, polished to a brilliant shine though his arms were bare except for gold armbands.

The King turned and faced them, his face grim. "It's the moment of decision, my friends. We have no more time. We retire now. This moment. Or we stand and fight."

There was a deathly silence in the pavilion.

The King paused as his eyes, hot and blazing, raked over them. "Make no mistake. If we fight and lose, we will die. And not just in battle. They'll hang any they take. But if we win... If we win, we win *all*. I'll call no man a coward who says to retire. The decision is yours. Do we run? Again? Or do we stand and fight?"

"I will not run!" Edward de Bruce said. His sun-browned face reddened. "Enough of that. We must stand."

James almost smiled. When had Sir Edward ever said else?

"Stand! We must," Thomas Randolph put in over the competing mutter of voices, the cleric nodding and speaking at the same time, Maol of Lennox saying something softly under his breath.

"There are many of them, but..." the Keith was saying a worried tone.

"Fight!" Angus said loudly.

"It's time," Boyd said. "We stand."

James caught Sir Edward's glance and nodded. For once, they agreed. "I don't fear to die. Whatever more we suffer than already we have, our country shall be free."

The King slowly nodded. "If we do lose, someone must be prepared to lead whatever retreat is..."

"Your Grace!" William de Irvine burst through the doorway. "There is someone here... He's come from the English, he says."

"What the..." The King's mouth made a thin line. He gave a curt nod. "Bring him in."

"Sir?" Irvine said over his shoulder.

A man shouldered his way past young Irvine, wearing a pale blue cloak and mail clinking as he walked. He was spare, with streaks of gray in his brown hair and beard. He strode to the King and dropped to one knee. "Your Grace."

The King tilted back his head as he stared, set-faced, at the man. "Alexander Seaton. It is many a year since you have graced your *homeland*."

"Sire." The man's Adam's apple bobbed as he swallowed. "Will you hear me?"

When the King slowly nodded, Seaton went on. "I rode from the English—rode hard ahead because, Sir King, if you mean to win Scotland, now is the time. Never have you seen so much dissension. They have a boy who knows nothing of war commanding the van. The rest are at each other's throats. The men are weary. Beginning to despair of their leaders."

The Bruce raised an eyebrow. "And you, Sir Alexander, would now stand with us?"

Seaton glanced over his shoulder, and his eyes looked a bit wild, James thought, as he looked at the men glaring at him. But he looked back up at the King. "If you'll have me."

A little smile quirked the King's mouth. "In time to save your lands from being forfeit." But he held out his hands to take the knight's oath.

The man muttered the words, and the King waved him impatiently away, obviously no patience today for ceremony. "Angus, a quarter of your men are not in the schiltrons, so I want them to guard the small folks. See that all the camp followers and all the supplies are moved onto that wooded hill. The tents and pavilions must come down. Set guards and see that they only attack at the sound of your horn."

Angus grunted assent and left with an almost-bow, stubborn, willful islander that he was.

The King blandly watched the man leave, lifted his war axe from in front of his armor and said, "Thomas. See that your men are in place, guarding our flank. The rest of you with me. We'll inspect the field." He walked into the bright sunshine that gleamed on his simple coronet, shouting for his horse.

Philp galloped between the tents. A squire shouted as he dodged out of the way. Philp shouted, "My lord, they're crossing the Bannockburn!"

"Wat," James called, turning in a circle as he searched for a sign of his sergeant amidst the running, shouting chaos and spotted him shoving his way through men scattering in every direction. "Form up the men. They're to stand ready!"

The King grabbed his reins out of Irvine's hands. "It will take them the rest of the day to cross. We have time to look over the field one last time."

Walter pelted up leading two horses, his tunic only half fastened and his hair wild.

Sweat dripped into James's beard, and he gave a wry laugh, swinging into the saddle as Walter mounted. "Fighting when it's freezing or melting. I'll never decide which is worse."

Robbie Boyd snorted. "Freezing. Last winter, I was sure I'd freeze off something more precious than toes. My lady wife would be right annoyed."

Thomas Randolph shook his head. He never joined in the banter, but he wasn't so very bad. At least, he knew how to fight.

Bishop Lamberton made the sign of the cross over them. "We'll celebrate mass in the morning. In the meantime, the blessings of God go with you. I'll see that the clerics go with Sir Angus and are out of the way."

The trumpets began their call to battle, wild, clamorous. Sergeants shouted to form their squares, men ran yelling curses and crude jokes, pikes clattered, barrels were thrown into wagons, fires sizzled under buckets of water.

"Earl Thomas," Bishop Moray said blandly, "I've given my men who follow you into battle my blessings already."

Irvine twisted his hands in alarm, almost reaching for the King but not willing to lay hands on him. "Your Grace, of a certainty, you should don your armor."

"Not yet," the King said. "They'll take hours to move into position, but we must be ready." He wheeled his horse in a tight circle. "With me, my lords. Lord Marischal, summon your cavalry to ride with us." He wheeled his light gray palfrey in a tight circle and trotted off.

Robert de Keith stood, cupped his hand around his mouth, and shouted, "Trumpets." *To horse, to horse*, the trumpets called in a blaring clarion.

James gave Irvine a sympathetic look but managed not to roll his eyes behind the King's back.

"Watch him," Irvine said.

James snorted, put his spurs to his horse's flank, and rode to catch up. He had spent half his life trying to shield Robert de Bruce's back. This was not a day he would stop.

James's standard unfurled above a square of pikemen. Behind them, a double line of archers formed. Beyond, near Saint Ninian's road Thomas Randolph's banner rose above men massed in a hedgehog of spears.

Knights buckled on their sword belts as they ran to horses held by their squires. Mounts snorted and hoof falls drummed as they rode to catch up with the King as he rode eastwards.

The King slowed his trot for the others to catch up with him as they rounded the shoulder of land above the Forth. Below them, the sun glittered on a river of steel, wave upon wave of it as the English army crossed the sluggish little water of the Bannockburn. "We need a closer look. We'll go to the New Park, and I'll have a last look at those pits." The Bruce wheeled his horse and plunged down into a hollow, crushing through dried, brittle broom and gorse. The day smelled of horse sweat and dust as they rode, and behind

248

them strung out three hundred of Keith's men on their coursers. On the edge of the open plain, James pulled up beside the Bruce.

James leaned forward over his horse's neck. The plain's splotches of purple-red heather and sun-browned gorse were divided by the brown streak of empty road. A trumpet sounded in the distance, a long, peace-shattering sound. Past the bend a mile away, the first of the English army surged into view. Hundreds of horses, cavalry heavy with the weight of their armor, horses barded in chain and draped with bright cloths, massed together into a riot of colors under a hundred banners. The flood of steel spread and spread, under a leopard banner as large as a sail. Beside it flapped the banner of Saint George and dozens more. Hundreds. Armor like waves in a spreading sea.

"Hold here," the King called to Robert de Keith. "I don't want to chance the men getting near the pits. We have hours whilst the main of their force arrives." He paced his horse slowly into the plain, bending over the horse's withers and watching the ground.

James rubbed his nose and glanced at Robbie Boyd, who shrugged. If the King said to hold, they would hold. James rubbed the back of his neck as the King walked his horse along a line next to the broom-covered pits.

Below in the distance, a fragment of the river of steel broke away. A dozen knights surged onto the plain, trotting towards them. The silvered steel of their mail flashed and silken plums streamed from their war helms. As a trumpet blared, James stood in his stirrups and called to the King, "Sire!"

"What device is that?" Boyd said. He nudged his horse a few steps forward, hands twitching anxiously around his reins. The King was almost halfway between them and the galloping English riders. "Bohun?"

"Hell!" James drew his sword, heart hammering. "The High Constable? It can't be." There was no way he could reach the King first. He kicked his spurs into this horse's flank and bent over its withers as it surged into an arm-jolting gallop.

The King had turned his horse and was riding casually at an angle towards the oncoming riders. The knight in the lead, bearing a blue shield scattered with lions shouted, "The Bruce! Himself! He's mine!" His blue and white tabard flapped in the wind. The point of his lance glittered, pointed straight at the King. "Back! Back!" He crouched low over his lance and hurtled towards Robert the Bruce.

The other English drew up, horses skittering.

Dear Jesu God, the King didn't even carry a shield. James brought the flat of his sword down on his horse's flank, desperate.

The Bruce continued at his slow trot, turned his course slightly to face the man thundering towards him. He balanced his war axe in his hand. James could hear nothing over the thunder of his heart and his own horse's hooves. Too far. It was too far.

Bohun reached him. The King shifted the second before impact, jerked his reins, and kicked his mount. It danced to the side. Reared. The lance plunged past the King's face. He stood in his stirrups. Raised his axe high and slammed it down on Bohun's helm.

Bohun's horse carried him past as he slid sideways from the saddle. He sprawled in the dirt, a foot caught in his stir-rup, the horse snorting and dancing.

There were ululating shouts behind James. "A Bruce! A Bruce!"

The rush of relief made James sway in the saddle. He pulled up from his headlong gallop. Keith's men galloped past him and surged around the King and the body that lay leaking a thread of blood onto the ground. James took a deep breath as a sudden flush of hot fury went through him. They'd nearly lost the King and with him, they would have lost the battle and the country.

His hands were shaking with rage as he slowed to a walk. James knew his voice shook, but he couldn't help that, as he said, "You might have died."

Boyd's face was white as whey. "Sire..." He shook his head, obviously speechless. Maol of Lennox's mouth hung open.

The King held up the shattered shaft of his axe. "I broke it." He smiled a little and shrugged. "Keith, call your men back here." He swung from the saddle and squatted next to the body. The top of the helm was crushed but the tabard was clean as though the man might rise in a moment. "Sir Henry de Bohun, I think." The King stood and mounted. "Nephew of the High Constable."

Keith shouted for his men to retire as they strung out towards the fleeing knights.

James glared at the King. "What I'd expect from Sir Edward," he said through gritted teeth.

The King threw back his head and laughed. To James, the laugh had a feverish sound. He blew out a puff of breath as his anger faded. The King lived.

"He saw nothing of the pits." The King turned his horse's head and trotted back the way they had come. "The branches and sod that cover them are drying in this heat, but they needn't last long."

From a distance upon the hillock, James heard a roar of cheers like breakers on the shore: the Scots yelling, "Scotland! Scotland!" A torrent of men rushed towards them around the shoulder of land.

"Get your men back in place," the King snapped. But his mouth twitched in a near smile as he said it. "Keith, on the hill with your men and watch for archers trying to flank us."

251

James shouted for Wat and Gelleys as they rode onto the hillock overlooking the camp. "What is the ado here? Move the men into place." As he spoke, he raised an eyebrow at Thomas Randolph nearing at a trot.

"Sire!" Randolph called. "There are shouts all over camp. You were in single combat?"

"Holy Rude, Thomas. You'd think it was the first time."

"You..." Randolph blinked at the King and looked speechless. "Sire, it's not fitting."

James watched grimly as below the vast main force of the English King rolled into sight, with no sign of the end of them. The mass of men and horses crowded beside the water of the Burn in an ever-swelling tangle. Surely there was no room for such a force. The space just would not hold them.

Inexorably they spread onto the carse, a boundless tide spreading over the bogs and tide pools. Even from here, James could see the horses foundering and struggling, hock deep in muck. Thousand upon thousand of glittering knights, England's chivalry, flooded into the waterlogged plain. James glanced at the King. "They're stopping? In the carse?"

Then he caught a motion beyond Randolph. Something nearer, through the trees. A flash of light and color. He walked his horse a little past Randolph, frowning. A banner? He turned back to them.

"Your Grace." James pointed. "Look. On the road at Saint Ninian's."

"What?" The King jerked around.

Through a space in the trees a mile away, James could see the leading edge of a mounted troop of knights and men-at-arms, a huge yellow banner fluttering over their heads. They passed the tower of Saint Ninian's Kirk. "Clifford," James said. "I'd know that banner in the bowels of hell itself." Like a mailed arm, an English host thrust along the low road. "Five hundred?"

"More," the Bruce said.

James worried his lip. "What... Where are they going? Do they intend to attack? So few even on the flank?"

"Either they will claim they have relieved the castle... or wait until battle to take us in the flank. Perhaps both. My lord of Moray," the King barked, "how many men are you letting flank us? A rose has fallen from your garland of renown. Go save it. I gave you Saint Ninian's Kirk to hold."

His face flushed red, Randolph turned his horse and whipped it to a gallop for his men, out of sight within the woods.

The line of English might was strung out in a triple line along the road. They stopped. A trumpet blew, and the hair on the back of James's neck prickled at the sound. "They've spotted Randolph's schiltron."

The hedgehog of a thousand bristling pikes crept into view. Fifty yards from the English, blocking the road, they stopped and braced their pikes, shoulder to shoulder, one line of pikes over the shoulder of the outer who knelt. Someone unfurled Moray's banner, and it waved in the above them.

"They'll be ridden down," Maol of Lennox muttered. "They haven't a chance. Not foot against cavalry."

"We have no choice but to see," the King said as trumpets blared.

"That's too many," James said. "They can't hold against so many." Each destrier was a thousand pounds of moving death. It couldn't be done. "Let me go to their aid."

"No. We can't take the chance of a surprise attack on our front. Remember Methven."

A trumpet blew again and like a rushing tide, the line of armored horsemen surged forward. It met the square of sharp steel, swirled around it, surrounded it. Dust rose in a cloud. James strained to see through the dusty fog. Horses reared. The cavalry was a seething mass. Sounds drifted up, faint with distance.

"Sire! Please!" James said. "If I go, they'll have to split their men."

The King's hands were in fists, white fingered, as he clutched hard at his reins. "All right. Go!"

James wheeled his horse and slapped its flank. "Wat! To their aid!" He galloped ahead of his men, halfway down the slope. As he went the sounds of battle turned into a cacophony of screaming horses. Shouts. Grunts. Clanking mail. Moans. James pulled up and raised his arm high over his head. "Hold!" he shouted. "Hold!"

Now he saw what he couldn't from a distance through the dust of battle, horses down, dead and dying piled around the schiltron. Bodies of men were caught in the tangle. The ground was a trampled, bloody bog. But the schiltron held with Moray's banner waving above it.

A man-at-arms backed his horse up and threw his sword in a furious arc into the mass of pikes. It flew past the helmeted heads, and James gave a snort of laughter.

Wat trotted up beside him. "Should we..."

"Hold. The glory is theirs. We'll not steal it."

Furiously riding at the steely thistle, a knight's blue draped destrier reared and shied away, refusing to impale itself, screaming terror.

A trumpet gave three long blasts. Commands were shouted. The cavalry scattered back to the road to reform into a ragged double line. The bristling schiltron, pikes red in the sunshine, froze into place. There were groans and cries. A pikeman raised his weapon and brought the point down in a vicious strike.

"Scotland! A Moray! A Moray!" James shouted grinning.

Behind him echoed thousands of cries and cheers. James leaned close to Wat to be heard over the chaos, "Give them a moment to cheer and then move the men back into place." He slid from the saddle and walked toward Randolph's schiltron. Randolph shoved his way through the line of men as they dropped to their knees. Pikes clattered to the ground. They scooped off helms and dropped them. Sweat dripped down their faces. An armored man crawled out from under a pile of the dead. Randolph paused to roll the man onto his back with a foot and spoke to a pikeman.

"Bravely done," James said. He couldn't stop grinning as he squelched through the bloody muck. "Bravely done, my lord earl." He offered Randolph his hand. Perhaps one day, they might even be friends if they both lived through the battle. The fighting today was barely a foretaste of what was to come.

Randolph grasped his hand for a moment. "I thought that you would join the fight."

"No. The glory was yours. You earned it." He looked at the billowing dust from the cavalry as they retired. "And tomorrow, there'll be enough to share."

CHAPTER 34

The King sat astride a warhorse in his battle armor, his tabard of cloth-of-gold, the lion of Scotland rearing, bejeweled, on its front. In caught the fading red rays of sunset.

It seemed strange to James that so large an army could be silent as they waited for the King to speak.

"In the morning we fight. At sunrise we hear mass and with banners flying we meet our enemy. A powerful enemy—one that would fill us with terror, in their numbers and their might and strength.

"But they mistake, for we have strengths they have not counted. First, that they despise us, spit on us, and attack us in our own land. But it is *our* land. Second, if we defeat them, we are steeped in spoils and in glory. But there is a third reason, the most important.

"We fight for our lives, for our children, our wives, our country's very freedom. They fight only because they hate and would destroy us. Well, I promise you this, if we stand with courage and valor, they will rue the day."

Men cheered, if grimly, and shouted.

"We cannot forget that if we are cowards, if we lose this battle, no worse fate can befall us than to fall into their hands. They have no mercy. As they killed Wallace and my own brother, Nigel, deaths more horrible than we can imagine, so they would kill us.

"There was a day, long past, when we lived in thralldom to the English and their might. No more! You demanded your freedom. Now we stand together, and we can win. What they do is evil, not blessed by God. They are moved only by a desire to conquer, by greed. We are moved by love of our homes and our people.

"We are not here for plunder nor prisoners nor riches. We are here to defend our homes and all that we love. Prepare yourselves for battle on the morrow. For our strength is in God!"

A snarling cheer, ferocious and angry, rose from the rank upon rank of men. Most had waited a lifetime to throw off, once and for all, the yoke of their conqueror.

The King inclined his head in dismissal and turned his horse's head to ride to his pavilion. James walked through the scattering men. He was conscious of the talk of the coming battle all around him. He felt the eyes that followed him as he wended his way through the crush.

The late summer dusk settled over the camp. The banners turned to black, the men passing shadows. Walter Stewart spoke to him from out of the murk, "No cookfires tonight."

"No. We must fast for the Mass anyway."

As they walked, around them the camp sank into an uneasy silence. The men were gathered into their own camps in battle array, Edward de Bruce in the van. James found Gelleys and Allane passing between them a skin of wine. They gave a guilty start when he clapped Gelleys on the shoulder. "I won't tell the priests if you don't," James said.

He heard the deep rumble of Fergus's laughter booming

through the dark. He followed it to where a dozen of his men sat on their haunches on the cold ground. He squatted in their midst. "You're to sleep in your armor."

"I was too far to hear," Philp said. "What did the King say?"

James gazed up at the midnight blue of the sky scattered with stars. How small their battles sometimes seemed in the dark of the night. "He said that tomorrow we win or we die." James put a smile in his voice. "And the Black Douglas is not going to die."

Fergus broke off half an oat bannock and handed it to him. "Dawn comes early on a midsummer day."

"Aye. So it does." James's stomach rumbled, and he couldn't remember the last time he'd eaten. He ruefully crammed the bannock in his mouth. Chewing, he found a dark spot under a scrawny little tree. He pulled off his helm, unbuckled his sword belt and laid them beside him as he settled against the rough trunk. He thought he should pray but no words came to him. He could die on the morrow, might well die on the morrow. But in the quiet of the night with stars above them and the familiar smell of sweat and iron and leather, it seemed not such a bad thing. Perhaps if he did, he would... No, he'd not think of that. It was his duty to live and to keep his men alive.

James took his sword from its sheath and tested the edge on his thumb. He sucked the blood from the cut off with a smile. He went to sleep, smiling.

He awoke to a hand shaking his shoulder in the dove-gray light of near dawn. Grunting, he shook his head and used the trunk of the tree to lever himself to his feet. Walter handed him a cup of stale water. He swished it around his teeth and spit on the ground. The morning breeze carried the scent of the distant sea. "Wat," James called, "why is my banner not flying? Where is Walter's banner?"

The camp was a murmur of low voices, the clatter of pikes, the creak of leather armor.

"The Mass is about to begin," Wat answered.

"Raise my banner," James said as he dropped to his knees. A rock gouged into in shin. Down the slope, like a phantom the Bishop raised his hands over his head. James strained to hear the words of the Mass, but the Bishop was too far. When the men around him muttered "Christe elèison," James added his voice. Christ have mercy indeed.

As he rose to his feet, William de Irvine trotted up and bent over his horse's withers to say, "The King sends word that Sir Edward's schiltron is in position and moving. You know what to do."

"I know." Irvine's face was a pale moon in the faint light. "Go with God."

"And you." The young man pulled his horse's head around and rode into the murk. It was too dark for James to tell if the other of the divisions were in position. They had to trust. Especially they had to trust that the marischal, his good-father, would lead the cavalry to break up the archers. If he failed them...

James shrugged. He had his own job to do. Dawn stained the faces around him with a faint golden light. He shoved his pot helm onto his head and buckled his sword belt. "Ready?"

Walter nodded.

"Hurry!" Wat was saying as he went from man to man. "Into position. Pikes at the ready."

"Gelleys." James put his hand on the man's shoulder. "Hie to Earl Thomas's position. Run back and let me know when they start to move forward."

He pushed Walter towards the schiltron. They would take up a position within the square, protected but with their own duties, to command and to fill any breach when men went down under the weight of charging destriers or the shattering of their own weapons. Even the knights, except for the cavalry with the marischal, would fight afoot.

"My lord," Gelleys called. "The earl has begun to charge." The man grabbed up his pike from where he had dropped it and jumped into position.

"Now," James said. "Stay together, men. Shoulder to shoulder."

At every step of the long march down the slope, James strained to hear the sound of battle. It was eerily quiet. He could smell the nervous sweat of his men. The crunch of a thousand footsteps in the dry bracken. Walter's fast breath. The flap of their pennants over their heads. So long a march...

To his left, a trumpet sounded one long blast. James lifted his visor and worked spit onto his dry tongue. "Kneel," he commanded and dropped to his knees one last time. All around him rose the murmur of a heartfelt prayer:

"*Pater Noster, qui es in caelis, sanctificetur nomen tuum. Adveniat regnum tuum. Fiat voluntas tua, sicut in caelo et in terra. Panem nostrum quotidianum da nobis hodie, et dimitte nobis debita nostra sicut et nos dimittimus debitoribus nostris. Et ne nos inducas in tentationem, sed libera nos a malo.* Amen."

Trumpets shrilled and called from the direction of the far scattered English army. *To arms, to arms, to arms, to arms,* they cried.

A shout bellowed from the left. "Scotland! Scotland!"

James cursed that he couldn't see beyond his own men. "Onward," James ordered. James couldn't see the battle beginning but he heard it. Trumpets. Hoofbeats from thousands of mounts that shook the ground under his feet. The skin-crawling screech of impaled horses. The crash of shattering pikes. And the war cries. "A Bruce! Scotland! Moray! Moray!"

Then his men began to shout, "A Douglas! A Douglas!"

"Keep moving," James shouted as knights, so close-packed

they couldn't turn, hurtled themselves onto their pikes. "On them!"

A horse reared, hooves slashing and was gutted, gushing a crimson fountain. There were grunts and curses as his men forced another step forward. Another draped all in blue rammed into Philp's pike. It shattered with a crash. He went down. The knight slashed right and left in great figure eights. James dashed forward, caught the blade on his shield and whacked at his helm. "Close up!" he shouted. The knight lifted his sword for another swing. He stopped. His sword slipped from his hands as he went to his knees and then flat on his face.

Walter put his foot in the middle of his back and jerked his blade free. The blood on his gauntlets glistened red. James thumped his shoulder and turned back to the battle. Another step. James darted between two of the pikemen who had spread apart. A knight, mounted but helmetless, hacked at his head. James dodged. He slashed the knight's leg open and dashed back. The man would bleed out without his help.

Allane's pike shattered. A knight wearing the blue and red of the earl of Pembroke drove his lance through the man's chest. James hacked at him. Another pike went through the neck of his horse. James slipped in the gore and slid sideways in ankle-deep muck. His sword spun out of his hand.

He grabbed his dirk from his belt and lurched to his feet. It was a chaos of fighting. The King's trumpet blew a triple call, the signal for the Keith to attack. An arrow landed in front of him and one bounced off his shield. He wondered if the marischal was faithful and then he was fighting again.

Men lurched between the pikes of the spreading schiltron. James grabbed up a fallen sword. He swung it, shouting, "A Douglas!" Some men he killed. He wounded some. Others went down under someone else's blade. Always there was another. And another.

He looked up and saw that the sun was high in the sky. How long had they fought? James was too tired to remember. His arm felt leaden as he raised it to swing. In front of him, Philp stumbled and went to one knee, holding himself up with his pike. James cursed. "Up," he grated. "You must get up."

The man raised his blood-splattered face to stare at James. "It's too many."

James swayed. "On your feet, damn you."

Philp pushed himself using his pike. He lurched back into the line of pikemen. James turned back to the raging chaos. His feet squelched in the torn, bloody dirt. Before him, a confusion of banners waved over the sea of struggling men; mounted knights hacked against the press of the pikes in a pandemonium of screams and shouts and blood and mire. He pressed on, stumbling, floundering, wading, and cursing. "On them!" he said, his throat raw from shouting.

He suddenly realized that there were no arrows raining on them. Hadn't been for some time. The Keith had stood true.

Some of the knights, tabards blackened and slime streaked, threw themselves from their saddles and hacked at the line of pikes with their lances. James slashed at the points. His men struggled to stay shoulder to shoulder against the press. One of the unhorsed knights was trampled underfoot by another knight, adding his screams to the cacophony.

Trumpets blew to his left. The King's. James lurched and thrust his sword into the ground to catch himself. Walter stumbled, and James grabbed his arm, righting him. He looked behind him past the hard-fought spaced they had bought, littered with bodies. "Look!" He turned Walter by his arm.

Down the hill, men shouted, "Scotland! Scotland!"

Banners flew over their heads as they ran. Their shouts added to the groans and screams all around.

"Who...?" Walter swallowed.

"The ghillies..." The ones on the hill. James tried to work spit into his mouth, his tongue dry as leather. "A few of Angus Og's men. Priests. Grooms."

Walter groaned. But there were screams and shouts on the other side of the hedge of pikes. The line of knights and horses seemed to shudder. It wavered. There were screams of "Flee!"

"On them!" James shouted through his raw throat.

English trumpets shrilled, again and again, *Retire! Retire!* cutting through the madness.

"They fail! They fail!" The shout rose all around James. He hacked at another blade, but the thick press of English buckled, and one of the knights slashed at his horse as he jerked its head around. But there was nowhere for him to go in the press of his own men

"On them!" James laughed, drunk with victory. "They fail!"

HISTORICAL NOTES

I have tried as much as possible to weave my fiction into the known facts of this immensely complex period of history. Much information has been lost to time and the destruction of wars. Often even the dates of some events such as the Battle of the Pass of Brander are unknown or in dispute.

The members of James Douglas's army to whom I refer to by name are fictional although I am careful to use names which records show were used during that time period in lowland Scotland. The Dickson family did exist, and Thomas Dickson died in the service of young James Douglas and Scotland during the first attack on Douglas Castle which was in *A Kingdom's Cost*. His son and daughter are fictional although his freestead was passed down through his family, so no doubt he had heirs. Nothing is known of the woman who James Douglas married; it was thought at one time that he hadn't married. However, in recent years evidence has come to light which indicates that he did.

None of the battles are fictional, and the techniques used in battle are as close as I can portray what they used. The ladder I describe in *Countenance of War* was invented by a

Scot and used in sneak attacks, including the one on Berwick Castle. When the English captured one after the unsuccessful attack on Berwick Castle, it was described with astonishment in the *Chronicle of Lanercost.*

My description of the Scottish policy of not attacking the English who didn't resist Scottish raids is not fiction; that was, in fact, the Scottish policy. Even the English *Chronicle of Lanercost* states that those who did not resist were left unharmed. It would have taken amazing control over an angry medieval army to achieve that.

This did not mean that the English of northern England didn't suffer under those raids. By the end of the period, much of the area was depopulated because of the loss of crops and herds. This combined with severe weather during the period meant a great deal of suffering whilst the King and nobles refused to make peace with the Scots and admit that it was an independent nation.

As for my historical references, some of the major ones are *The Brus* by John Barbour, *Chronicle of Lanercost* translated by Sir Herbert Maxwell, *Robert Bruce and the Community of the Realm of Scotland* by Geoffrey W. S. Barrow, *Robert the Bruce, King of Scots* by Ronald McNair Scott, *James the Good, The Black Douglas* by David R. Ross, and *The Scottish War of Independence* by Evan M. Barron.

LIST OF HISTORICAL CHARACTERS

•**Sir James Douglas, Lord of Douglas** – known as the Sir James the Good to the Scots and the Black Douglas to the English, Scottish soldier and knight, lieutenant and friend to King Robert de Bruce, Baron of Douglas, Lord Warden of the Marches of Scotland

•**William de Lamberton,** -- Bishop of St Andrews who campaigned for the cause of Scottish freedom under Andrew de Moray, William Wallace and Robert de Bruce

•**Robert de Bruce** – King of the Scots

•**David de Moray** – Bishop of Moray and supporter of Scottish freedom and of King Robert de Bruce

•**Sir Thomas Randolph** – Earl of Moray, nephew of King Robert de Bruce

•**Maol Choluim II** – Earl of Lennox and loyal follower of Robert de Bruce

•**Sir Niall Campbell** – brother-in-law of King Robert de Bruce and husband of Mary de Bruce

•**Sir Robert Boyd** – Scottish nobleman and loyal follower of King Robert de Bruce

•**Sir Robert de Keith** – Lord Marischal of Scotland

- **Sir Gilbert de la Haye** – a supporter of King Robert de Bruce, Baron of Errol and Lord High Constable of Scotland
- **Angus Óg MacDonald**, Lord of the Isles -- Scottish nobleman and supporter of King Robert de Bruce
- **Walter Stewart** – Hereditary High Stewart of Scotland
- **Bernard de Linton** – Chancellor of Scotland
- **Edward II of England** – King of England
- **Aymer de Valence** – Earl of Pembroke, one of the commanders of the English forces during the invasion of Scotland
- **Robert de Clifford** – Baron of Clifford, Lord of Skipton, English commander during the war with Scotland also first Lord Warden of the Marches of England.

GLOSSARY

In writing historical fiction, an author sometimes must choose between making language understandable and making it authentic. While I use modern English in this novel, the people of 14th century Scotland, of course, spoke mainly Scots, Gaelic and French. To give at least a feel of their language and because some concepts can only be expressed using terms we no longer use, there are Scottish and archaic English words in this work. Many are close to or even identical to current English although used in a medieval context. The following is a list of terms in which I explain some of the words and usages that might be unfamiliar. I hope you will find the list interesting and useful."

- •Aright: In a proper manner; correctly.
- •Aye: Yes.
- •Bailey: An enclosed courtyard within the walls of a castle.
- •Bairn: (*Scots*), Child.
- •Baldric: Leather belt worn over the right shoulder to the left hip for carrying a sword.
- •Banneret: A feudal knight ranking between a knight

bachelor and a baron, who was entitled to lead men into battle under his own standard.

•Bannock: (*Scots*), A flat, unleavened bread made of oatmeal or barley flour, generally cooked on a flat metal sheet.

•Barbican: A tower or other fortification on the approach to a castle or town, Especially one at a gate or drawbridge.

•Battlement: A parapet in which rectangular gaps occur at intervals to allow for firing arrows.

•Bedecked: To adorn or ornament in a showy fashion.

•Bend: A band passing from the upper dexter corner of an escutcheon to the lower sinister corner.

•Berlinn: Ship used in the medieval Highlands, Hebrides and Ireland having a single mast and from 18 to 40 oars.

•Betime: On occasion.

•Bracken: Weedy fern.

•Brae: (*Scots*), Hill or slope.

•Braeside: (*Scots*), Hillside.

•Barmy: Daft.

•Braw: (*Scots*), Fine or excellent.

•Brigandines: Body armor of leather lined with small steel plates riveted to the fabric.

•Brogans: Ankle-high work shoes.

•Buffet: A blow or cuff with or as if with the hand.

•Burgher: A citizen of a borough or town, especially one belonging to the middle class.

•Burn: (*Scots*), a name for watercourses from large streams to small rivers.

•Caltrop: A metal device with four projecting spikes so arranged that when three of the spikes are on the ground, the fourth points upward.

•Carillon: Music on chromatically tuned bells esp. in a bell tower.

•Cateran: Member of a Scottish Highland band of fighters.

•Ceilidh: A Scottish social gathering at which there is music, singing, dancing, and storytelling.

•Chancel: The space around the altar at the liturgical east end.

•Checky banner: In heraldry, having squares of alternating tinctures or furs.

•Chief: The upper section of a shield.

•Chivalry: As a military term, a group of mounted knights.

•Chivvied: Harassed.

•Cloying: To cause distaste or disgust by supplying with too much of something originally pleasant.

•Cot: Small building.

•Couched: To lower a lance to a horizontal position.

•Courser: A swift, strong horse, often used as a warhorse.

•Crenel: An open space or notch between two merlons in the battlement of a castle or city wall.

•Crook: Tool, such as a bishop's crosier or a shepherd's staff.

•Curtain wall: The defensive outer wall of a medieval castle.

•Curst: A past tense and a past participle of curse.

•Dagged: A series of decorative scallops along the edge of a garment such as a hanging sleeve.

•Defile: A narrow gorge or pass.

•Destrier: the heaviest class of warhorse.

•Din: A jumble of loud, usually discordant sounds.

•Dirk: A long, straight-bladed dagger.

•Dower: The part or interest of a deceased man's real estate allotted by law to his widow for her lifetime, often applied to property brought to the marriage by the bride.

•Draughty: Drafty.

271

•Empurple: To make or become purple.

•Erstwhile: In the past, at a former time, formerly.

•Ewer: A pitcher, especially a decorative one with a base, an oval body, and a flaring spout.

•Faggot: A bundle of sticks or twigs, esp. when bound together and used as fuel.

•Falchion: A short broadsword with a convex cutting edge and a sharp point.

•Farrier: One who shoes horses.

•Fash: Worry.

•Fetlock: A 'bump' and joint above and behind a horse's hoof.

•Forbye: Besides.

•Ford: A shallow crossing in a body of water, such as a river.

•Gambeson: Quilted and padded or stuffed leather or cloth garment worn under chain mail.

•Garron: A small, sturdy horse bred and used chiefly in Scotland and Ireland.

•Gilded: Cover with a thin layer of gold.

•Girth: Band around a horse's belly.

•Glen: A small, secluded valley.

•Gorse: A spiny yellow-flowered European shrub.

•Groat: An English silver coin worth fourpence.

•Hallo: A variant of Hello.

•Hart: A male deer.

•Hauberk: A long armor tunic made of chain mail.

•Haugh: (Scots) A low-lying meadow in a river valley.

•Hen: A term of address (often affectionate), used to women and girls.

•Hied: To go quickly; hasten.

•Hock: The joint at the tarsus of a horse or similar animal, pointing backward and corresponding to the human ankle.

•Holy Rude also Holy Rood: (*Scots*), The Holy Cross

•Hoyden: High-spirited; boisterous.

•Jape: Joke or quip.

•Jesu: Vocative form of Jesus.

•Ken: To know (a person or thing).

•Kirk: A church.

•Kirtle: A woman's dress typically worn over a chemise or smock.

•Laying: To engage energetically in an action.

•Loch: Lake or a narrow arm of the sea.

•Louring: Lowering.

•Lowed: The characteristic sound uttered by cattle; a moo.

•Malmsey: A sweet fortified Madeira wine

•Malting: A building where malt is made.

•Marischal: The hereditary custodian of the Royal Regalia of Scotland and the protector of the king's person.

•Maudlin: Effusively or tearfully sentimental.

•Mawkish: Excessively and objectionably sentimental.

•Mercies: Without any protection against; helpless before.

•Merk: (*Scots*), a coin worth 160 pence.

•Merlon: A solid portion between two crenels in a battlement or crenelated wall.

•Midges: A gnat-like fly found worldwide and frequently occurring in swarms near ponds and lakes, prevalent across Scotland.

•Mien: Bearing or manner, especially as it reveals an inner state of mind.

•Mount: Mountain or hill.

•Murk: An archaic variant of murky.

•Nae: No, Not.

•Nave: The central approach to a church's high altar, the main body of the church.

•Nock: To fit an arrow to a bowstring.

•Nook: Hidden or secluded spot.

•Outwith: (Scots) Outside, beyond.

•Palfrey: An ordinary saddle horse as opposed to a warhorse.

•Pap: Material lacking real value or substance.

•Parapet: A defensive wall, usually with a walk, above which the wall is chest to head high.

•Pate: Head or brain.

•Pell-mell: In a jumbled, confused manner, helter-skelter.

•Perfidy: The act or an instance of treachery.

•Pillion: Pad or cushion for an extra rider behind the saddle or riding on such a cushion.

•Piebald: Spotted or patched.

•Privily: Privately or secretly.

•Quintain: Object mounted on a post, used as a target in tilting exercises

•Retiral: The act of retiring or retreating.

•Rood: Crucifix.

•Runnels: A narrow channel.

•Saddlebow: The arched upper front part of a saddle.

•Saltire: An ordinary in the shape of a Saint Andrew's cross, when capitalized: the flag of Scotland. (a white saltire on a blue field)

•Samite: A heavy silk fabric, often interwoven with gold or silver.

•Sassenach: (Scots), An Englishman, derived from the Scots Gaelic Sasunnach meaning, originally, "Saxon."

•Schiltron: A formation of soldiers wielding outward-pointing pikes.

•Seneschal: A steward or major-domo

•Siller: (Scots), Silver.

•Sirrah: Mister; fellow. Used as a contemptuous form of address.

•Sleekit: (Scots), Unctuous, deceitful, crafty.

•Sumpter horse: Pack animal, such as a horse or mule.

•Surcoat: An outer tunic often worn over armor.

•Tail: A noble's following of guards.

•Thralldom: One, such as a slave or serf, who is held in bondage.

•Tiddler: A small fish such as a minnow

•Tisane: An herbal infusion drunk as a beverage or for its mildly medicinal effect.

•Tooing and froing: Coming and going.

•Trailed: To drag (the body, for example) wearily or heavily.

•Trebuchet: A medieval catapult-type siege engine for hurling heavy projectiles.

•Trencher: A wooden plate or platter for food.

•Trestle table: A table made up of two or three trestle supports over which a tabletop is placed.

•Trews: Close-fitting trousers, usually of tartan.

•Tun: Large cask for liquids, especially wine.

•Villein: A medieval peasant or tenant farmer

•Wain: Open farm wagon.

•Wattles: A fleshy, wrinkled, often brightly colored fold of skin hanging from the neck.

•Westering: To move westward.

•Wheedling: To use flattery or cajolery to achieve one's ends.

•Whey: The watery part of milk separated from the curd.

•Whilst: While.

•Whist: To be silent—often used as an interjection to urge silence.

•Wroth: Angry.

Made in the USA
Coppell, TX
05 August 2020